OUT OF NOWHERE

FELICIA DAVIN

ETYMON PRESS

ISBN-13: 978-0-9989957-4-8
Copyright © 2019 Felicia Davin
All rights reserved.

To everyone who took their time figuring it out

CONTENTS

1. Double — 1
2. Messing with Recognition — 13
3. The Reality Next Door — 25
4. Get in Trouble — 37
5. Practice — 55
6. Your Body Already Knows How — 69
7. A Joke or an Experiment — 75
8. Harebrained Scheme — 89
9. Upgrade — 99
10. The Void — 115
11. Fact-checked — 131
12. Rabbit — 147
13. Two Truths and a Lie — 159
14. Undisguised — 171
15. Solidarity — 179
16. Forty-two — 191
17. Innocent — 205
18. Confessions — 227
19. Do What I'm Told — 239
20. Knees, Elbows, Fingers, Twist — 255
21. There's Only One You — 265
22. I Know a Place — 277

Acknowledgments — 291
Also by Felicia Davin — 293
About the Author — 295

[1]
DOUBLE

Aidan dropped the notebook, the rustle of pages and the click of its metal spine against the lab bench resounding in the silence of the room. He'd had to turn on the overhead light to take photos. Even lit up, dread haunted the lab.

The notebook splayed open to a random page of observations with neat handwriting in blue ink. It was dated September 20, 2093—six days ago—and the first line said *Subject No. 1 resistant, still unable to access the Nowhere.*

Damn right he'd been resistant.

Aidan picked up the tablet he'd set aside, snapped a picture, and sent it. He'd already sent dozens of other photos like it, plus a written account of what had happened to him, to his contacts in the Runners' Union. The first news articles about the experiments Quint Services had performed on Laila and Aidan had already surfaced. It wasn't enough. Oswin Lewis Quint wasn't in prison yet.

Shoving aside his revulsion, Aidan lifted the page and flipped it. The scientist who'd written these notes was already serving time. Not for hurting him or Laila, but for fraud. A false charge. Whatever else you could say of Heath and her collaborator Winslow—cruel, greedy assholes, both of them—they'd done their own experiments.

Their careers were over. They'd never do this to anyone again. But Heath and Winslow were lackeys. None of it had touched Quint, that slimy piece of shit. Aidan snapped another picture and sent it. A fucking cover-up. He intended to uncover it.

As long as Quint was out there, unspeakably rich and powerful, no runners would ever be safe. He'd figure out some new impossible prison to hide them in, and then somebody else would get strapped down and starved.

The page in his hand ripped.

"Aidan? What are you doing in here? It's the middle of the night."

Caleb. Better him than anyone else who might have caught Aidan here. He unclenched his hand from the crumpled page but didn't turn around. "We're in space, it's always the middle of the night."

Caleb didn't laugh. "Aidan."

It was concern coloring Caleb's voice, but it felt like a rebuke. Aidan was supposed to be resting, not secretly gathering evidence. "I couldn't sleep," he said, which was true. It had been true for days.

"So you broke into Heath's lab to photograph her notes? What are you doing with those, anyway?" Caleb paused and Aidan heard him walk closer. Caleb yawned. "Is that my tablet?"

Of course it was Caleb's tablet. Aidan didn't have any personal possessions at Facility 17 because he'd arrived here by getting fucking *kidnapped*. It was Caleb's clothes hanging off his even-scrawnier-than-usual body. He was barefoot because neither of them had thought to grab his shoes out of the cell before blowing it the fuck up. Where else would he have gotten a tablet?

Instead of saying any of that, Aidan said, "I didn't break in. The door was unlocked."

It had been deprogrammed after Heath and Winslow had been escorted from the premises three days ago. No one at Facility 17 had had time to go through the labs yet—except Aidan. He had to record this stuff before it was all swept under the rug.

"Hey," Caleb said, and there was no way his hand could possibly be that hot even through the sleeve of Aidan's t-shirt. Aidan must have taken a chill in the lab. He hadn't noticed until now. "Look at me."

If Aidan did that, it would be his undoing. He could withstand Caleb's worried voice and even his careful touches, but not his expression. They'd been friends so long that Aidan knew it by heart without looking: the pleading eyes, the strained twist of his mouth.

Aidan didn't have time to fall apart. He had to put Quint in prison.

Caleb reached across the lab bench and flipped the notebook shut. "It's four in the morning. We should both be asleep."

Aidan stared down at Caleb's hand pinning the notebook closed. It was a nice hand, broad and long-fingered with clean, blunt-tipped nails. That was the problem. Caleb's hand was attached to a nice forearm, warm beige skin lightly furred with dark brown hair, and a nice bicep, and a nice shoulder, and an even nicer face.

Fuck. He hadn't meant to look. Now not only was he magnetized by Caleb's ridiculously, offensively blue eyes, but worse, Caleb could see him. Aidan was mostly bones and under-eye shadows. He'd last combed the nest of black hair on his head three or maybe four days ago, something he only thought about when Caleb was regarding him with his perfect eyebrows drawn together like that. Rage was the only thing keeping Aidan upright, and he couldn't feel it with that much concern beamed directly at his face.

His shoulders sagged.

Caleb caught him in a hug. His scent was a comfort: clean laundry and a hint of sweat, the only soft thing in the lab's dry, recycled air. He'd been asleep before he came here; his cheek was marred by a pillow crease and his hair mussed. Caleb was only a couple inches taller. He didn't used to seem so much bigger. Aidan couldn't dwell on that, not when Caleb was enveloping him in warmth, not when Caleb's touch was making it possible to forget the smoking wreck of his life.

Shit. He had fires to put out. Aidan pushed Caleb away, the air cool where they no longer touched. "I just have to finish this."

"I woke up and you were gone," Caleb said, obviously still troubled.

Since the rescue six days ago, Aidan had been convalescing in Caleb's bed, and Caleb had been using an extra mattress that took up most of the remaining floor space in his room. Inconvenient, but familiar. Aidan had spent his vagabond adulthood shuffling from one shared room—or couch, or floor—to another. He'd spent his childhood with Caleb. No doubt this temporary arrangement was more pleasant than whatever came next.

"I'll be done soon," Aidan said. He had no way of knowing that. He could photograph every last pen stroke in this laboratory and Quint still might get away.

"You never said what you were doing. Is it Union business?"

Caleb always carefully respected the secrecy of the Runners' Union. He wasn't a runner, but for the first few years, he'd helped Aidan talk people into joining.

"I'm exposing Quint." Might as well be truthful. Caleb had

caught him, and anyway, he wasn't working on behalf of the Union. This was personal. "Or trying, anyway. I've been sending evidence for days and it's still barely making the news."

"Can I help?"

"No, it's fine, go back to bed."

"You should come with me. To sleep, I mean, not—you know what I mean."

A dull flush crept up his neck. It must be the late hour making Caleb trip over his tongue. He usually treated their closeness as something unquestionably platonic, as though the possibility of sex had never occurred to him. Aidan should know, since he had to put in years' worth of work to keep his end of that bargain. The possibility occurred to him all the time.

"I worry about you," Caleb added unnecessarily. "You know this could wait for a more normal hour. You could sleep now and then come back to this."

"They'll clean this lab out and then what evidence will I have, besides my testimony and Laila's?"

"Emil and his team wouldn't do that, not if they knew what you were working on. They'd want to help you."

Aidan grimaced. Caleb might trust them, but they were strangers to him. No, worse than strangers: they were people who'd signed up to work for Quint. Aidan could only trust the Union. "I have help. And I'll sleep when I'm done."

Caleb searched him with a look, then bit his lip like he was biting back protests, and withdrew. By the time Aidan came to their room, Caleb was asleep. The brush of Aidan's fingertips against his own skin as he undressed was cold enough to make him shiver.

―――

THE BUZZ of the tablet woke Caleb. He reached over the edge

of his mattress, groping in the dark until his hand hit it. The screen lit up with a message from Deb—*answer my texts you jerk*, typical little-sister stuff. Caleb unlocked it.

She'd texted him *l'shanah tovah* on Monday, six days ago. Must have been Rosh Hashanah. Caleb had missed the holiday and Deb's message, as well as several subsequent messages, because he'd been busy rescuing Aidan.

Aidan, who was—thank fuck—currently asleep in his bed. Whatever he'd been doing in Heath's lab in the middle of the night, he'd finished.

Sorry, Caleb wrote back. He'd been saying that a lot for the past few months. Nobody had been happy with his decision to take a job with Quint Services, and Caleb couldn't tell his family he'd done it to spy on the company. They'd been even less thrilled with his transfer to space.

But he'd found Aidan, and now the two of them could go home.

Back down to the surface, back down to the city where he and Aidan had grown up, where Deb still lived. She was in college now, and his parents had retired to warmer climes, so *home* no longer meant the second-floor of the old brownstone where the three of them had been teenagers together. For a moment, he wished it did.

Happy new year to you too, he wrote to Deb. *Talk soon, I promise*.

Caleb didn't know what he was going to tell her. If Aidan's plan worked, the whole story would be in the news soon enough.

There was no need to keep a strict schedule since Emil's team had seized control of Facility 17, but Caleb was awake now so he might as well get up. He could check on Laila, who'd been in the cell with Aidan, and Lenny, who'd been wounded during the rescue. Both of them had been more receptive to care than Aidan.

Caleb kept the lights at ten percent while he got dressed, letting Aidan sleep.

He picked up his tablet again and went through the rest of his messages. It wasn't snooping. The damn thing belonged to him. No new photos. No record of new sent messages, either. Finding nothing made him feel worse for looking in the first place. Guilt and disappointment twisted in his stomach. He just wanted to help.

Being Aidan's best friend didn't come with a high enough security clearance for that, apparently. Neither did saving his extremely frustrating life.

Caleb carried the tablet with him to the brightly lit industrial kitchen, which was bustling as though nothing had changed. It smelled like coffee, and he could hear butter sizzling in a skillet. The routine was a comfort, especially since no one knew what to do now that Heath and Winslow were in prison. Caleb wasn't sure who was in charge, other than Emil. The other top scientist at Facility 17, a physicist named Solomon Lange, had disappeared in a lab accident before Caleb's arrival. Not died. Vanished into the Nowhere.

The team was still working on a plan to locate and, if possible, revive him. Discovering the secret prison cell where Aidan and Laila had been tortured had interrupted them, but now that they had a measure of control over the facility, Caleb was confident they'd solve that problem and any others that cropped up.

Emil, the team leader, an intimidatingly handsome guy of Indian descent, was seated at the long metal table in the room with a cup of tea and his own tablet in front of him. He smiled at Caleb. "Good morning."

Caleb smiled back and said good morning to all of them in

turn. He liked these people, but he wasn't one of them. Insinuating himself into social groups, at least superficially, was never hard. People were primed to like him because he was youthful, halfway fit, and blandly symmetrical. He made good on that advantage by smiling a lot and remembering names and personal details for small talk. It felt calculating to think about it in those terms, but he'd had to. Charming his way into a post at Quint Services' most secret research facility had been a lot of work.

Caleb hadn't needed to charm Emil's team into rescuing Aidan, which was a relief. They'd done it because it was the right thing to do.

He didn't see the violet-haired runner, Kit, who'd been instrumental in discovering the secret cell. Kit must not be a morning person.

Caleb grabbed a couple pieces of toast, sat, searched for Quint Services on the tablet, and sorted the results by most recent. It took several minutes to find any mention of the experiments, and the articles only implicated Heath and Winslow, not Quint himself. None of them were from major news sources. No wonder Aidan was disappointed. A story like that ought to be in the headlines. It ought to have spurred a massive criminal investigation.

Quint had to be burying the articles. That piece of shit.

"Do you think Quint will ever see consequences for what he did up here?" Caleb asked, setting the tablet down.

"Well, Kit vowed to destroy him," Emil said, as neutrally as if he was reporting the weather. He took a sip of tea. Caleb supposed it was bad form to be openly pessimistic about your boyfriend's chances of ruining a man with a net worth of 11 trillion dollars. It did seem like a long shot, even if said boyfriend could teleport.

"Are you asking because Aidan's been leaking sensitive information to the press?" Dax asked. The team's pale, redheaded physicist was methodically peeling the liner from their blueberry muffin, and they'd spoken without looking up from the task.

The question still gave Caleb pause. He wasn't here to snitch.

"I'm not mad," Dax clarified. "No one here cares. But I did notice."

"How?" Caleb asked. "It's barely made the news."

"I keep weird hours and I saw the lights on in Heath's lab in the middle of the night. Wasn't hard to put it together after that," Dax said. "It's good that he's trying, but he should be prepared for failure. Quint has a history of crushing journalists or outlets that report negative stuff about him."

"Yeah," Caleb said, dismayed. When Aidan had said *I'll sleep when I'm done*, he hadn't been talking about documenting evidence. He'd been talking about ruining Quint.

The conversation moved on, but Caleb didn't pay attention. He finished eating and put his plate in the dishwasher. Leaving after so little clean-up was definitely shirking, but no one called him on it.

The facility operated by having everyone who worked there take a hand in its maintenance. In his transfer interview, Caleb had claimed to be very handy, fabricating an anecdote about fixing a leaky faucet in his apartment. Any potentially leaky faucets in the facility would just have to keep dripping. There were bigger problems. If Aidan was awake when he got back to the room, Caleb would ask if he wanted breakfast. Then they'd discuss Quint.

He didn't know what he'd say. There were only so many variations on *please let me help you*, and none had worked so far. He came to the door of his own room too quickly. Kept walking.

The facility, carved inside of an asteroid, was far larger than it initially seemed and almost all on a single level. The kitchen and the greenhouse were clustered together at one end and there were labs and medical exam rooms at the other.

This hallway passed by a lab with caution tape on the door. There had once been windows permitting outsider to peer in, but an accident had shattered them and now there was brown paper blocking the view. Inside this space—Dr. Lange's former lab—was something the team had taken to calling *the breach*. Dr. Lange had designed a machine meant to open a door into the Nowhere, and in a way, he'd succeeded. The problem was that nobody could close it.

Caleb knew this space disturbed runners. He'd witnessed Kit's reaction to it. But he couldn't feel anything wrong with it. The papered-over windows and the caution tape on the door were enough to keep him out, though. He turned the corner.

He ran straight into himself.

It took him a full two minutes to realize that. At first he was only aware of having run into another person, one about the same size as him. How had that happened? He'd been thinking, sure, but his eyes had been open. It was as if the person had materialized right in front of him. A runner?

They both grunted and began to apologize and disentangle themselves, and that was when Caleb began to take stock of the guy. A white man, about the same build as him, dressed in grey and black, with brown hair and blue eyes and—*holy fucking shit*.

That was his face.

Backwards—no, not backwards, just not a mirror image—and with two days' scruff on his cheeks, but that was his mouth and those were his cheekbones. That was the angle of his nose and the surprised arch of his eyebrows. Caleb had an absurd moment of thinking *wow, handsome*, and then he blinked it away and said, "What the fuck."

Caleb was wearing blue scrubs and sneakers because habit was a powerful force. His double was dressed for some other purpose, way less friendly—boots, a utilitarian black jacket, black jeans, and a gun holstered around his thigh. Panic stabbed through Caleb's chest. He checked the man's face again. *I wouldn't shoot anyone*, he thought, as though he could will this other man's body like it was his own.

"Like what you see?"

This motherfucker even had his voice. It was as disconcerting as the gun. The double didn't reach for the gun, though. He put his hands on Caleb's shoulders as if to steady him—or to size him up. His grip was heavy but loose, almost lazy. Not a touch intended to force Caleb in any particular direction. Between two people who knew each other, it would have been affection; between two strangers, an advance. Between him and his double, Caleb had no idea.

The sound of his double's question echoed in his mind. Caleb would use that voice if he was flirting. But why would he flirt with himself? Sure, Caleb wanted people to like him, enjoyed making people giggle and blush, but he'd never been so overtly sexual with another man.

His double was smirking. Caleb had never looked that smug in his life. As for his own face, he wished he could muster an expression other than bewildered. "Who are you? Where did you come from?"

His double pulled him close and kissed Caleb on the mouth.

Stubble scraped Caleb's skin, a tongue plunged between his lips, and fingers threaded through his hair before he could collect any thoughts. Panic strobed through his brain, flashes of fear and arousal accelerating his pulse. When the kiss continued past its rude beginning, smoothing into something steadier, but still commanding, Caleb leaned into it.

No, that couldn't be right. He'd meant to back away.

The heat of the kiss melted his resolve and all his common

sense. His hands fisted in the thick material of his double's jacket.

Caleb had kissed a lot of people, none of whom had been men, or total strangers, or identical to him. This wasn't normal, and he should think carefully—and *that* was an arm around his back, tugging him closer. A very forceful arm. None of the people Caleb had kissed had ever been this aggressive. He'd never been pressed so close to another man.

He *liked* it.

It was the best explanation for why he hadn't squirmed away yet. The magnitude of the realization shook him. Had he really lived his whole life until now without knowing that? What did it mean?

Before he had time to consider it, something pinched the side of his neck and he passed out.

[2]
MESSING WITH RECOGNITION

A WEEK AND A HALF OF CAPTIVITY IN SPACE PLUS SIX DAYS of freedom still wasn't enough to accustom Aidan to the strangeness of life without sunrise and sunset. Caleb's room, carved deep into the asteroid, was windowless, and Aidan came awake in the darkness with no sense of where he was.

Caleb's mattress on the floor was unoccupied, its sheets neatly replaced. It must be morning, or at least one of the hours arbitrarily designated as morning by the Facility 17 schedule. Aidan reached for Caleb's tablet to check the time, but that was gone too. He lifted his head and squinted at the red numbers of the clock on the wall. 10:08. He'd slept for four hours.

Aidan flopped back to the pillow, rolled onto his side and then his stomach. He didn't want to be awake, or stuck in this facility, or dealing with any part of his life. Closing his eyes didn't lull him back to sleep. Despite his fatigue, restless energy chased through his veins. Before his captivity, back when he could still jump, this kind of feeling would have sent him to another continent. Now he was trapped.

He'd have to tell Caleb eventually. Stupid to dread it. Caleb would tell him everything would be alright and hug him again.

The memory of their middle-of-the-night hug in the lab froze his brain, and for a moment, no other thoughts would load. He'd needed that. It was so reassuring to be touched by someone who wasn't taking his vital signs or giving him an injection, so comforting to be touched with concern and tenderness. It was even better to be touched by Caleb. Too good. It made Aidan want things he couldn't have.

Aidan should stop thinking about the way Caleb smelled, the warm, slightly spicy scent of his skin overlaid with whatever was in his soap or his laundry detergent. Cedar, maybe. That faint clean scent emanated from the sheets—and the t-shirt and boxers Aidan was wearing—all of which belonged to Caleb. It was a different kind of embrace.

He's straight, Aidan reminded himself. And more importantly, their friendship had already put Caleb in danger more than once. The only safe thing to do was to diminish their contact. Aidan would put Quint in prison and then he'd disappear. It would hurt Caleb, but he'd live. He had plenty of other people in his life.

As for Aidan, all he had was the memory of touching Caleb and the sensation of lying in Caleb's bed with his pulse thrumming under his skin. The mattress provided a pleasant pressure against his dick, and he couldn't resist grinding down into it once. Fuck, that was good. He hissed out a breath. His captivity and its immediate aftermath had robbed him of desire. It only took one touch to remind him of what he'd missed. Desperation burned through him. He needed more.

It was risky—Caleb could walk in—but so was the rest of Aidan's life. And even if Caleb did come in, jerking off wasn't a crime. Jerking off to thoughts of your best friend, well... Caleb wasn't a mind-reader; he wouldn't *know*.

Aidan would know. And he'd feel guilty. But he could do that later. Right now, the allure of a few minutes of physical pleasure was overpowering. He rolled onto his back, put his knees up to tent the sheet over his body, and shoved his underwear to mid-thigh.

Fuck, what a jolt of relief to finally wrap his hand around his dick. He was hard already. In an instant his hand and shaft were sticky-slick from dripping liquid. Aidan kept his strokes slow despite the risk—or was it a thrill?

He pictured Caleb in the lab last night, with his big sad eyes and his worry-bitten lower lip. Aidan should have kissed that look off his face, should have sunk *his* teeth into the plump curve of Caleb's mouth. Caleb's breath would hitch from the shock of it. He'd make the same sound when Aidan grasped his dick. Caleb was cut, unlike him. He'd flush deep pink from root to tip, quivering with want, his balls drawn up tight and aching.

Aidan brushed his fingers under his own balls and his hips twitched. The idea of Caleb wanting him was powerfully intoxicating. His heart raced and his hand sped up to match.

Aidan would crush their cocks together in his grip—just thinking of the friction made him shiver—and grind until he'd stripped every last drop from both of them. Caleb would cry out and spill in his hand, and Aidan would kiss him again and drink in the sweet taste of his mouth. The thought undid him. He came with a burst of pleasure and a wordless gasp, come pulsing into his hand in hot spurts.

He lay there for a long time, breathless and sated and guilty, with the evidence cooling on his skin. The whirr of the ventilation was far too quiet to keep him from his wishes and regrets.

Then the door opened.

Oh, hell, Caleb's timing was something else. Granted, a few minutes earlier would have been worse. Aidan wiped his hand on his stomach and sat up, trying to project an air of innocence, something he'd never been good at. The ability to teleport away from the scene of the crime had ruined him for the skill. Caleb would see right through him.

Caleb stood in the doorway and assessed the room and Aidan, then strode in and sat right next to Aidan. "Still in bed?"

It was the lightest of teases, but it made Aidan's neck burn. "Late night," he said, which Caleb already knew. Aidan had to shut down this line of inquiry and direct the conversation elsewhere, but before he could, Caleb leaned in closer.

What the fuck was he doing? It was like a parody of what Aidan had been fantasizing about, and Aidan wanted to squirm out of reach. He didn't move.

"I'll bet," Caleb said, leering. Aidan had seen Caleb flirt with a lot of women, and he'd never seen a smile anywhere near that filthy.

The two of them teased each other all the time, but not like this, by unspoken agreement that it was too much.

Come to think of it, Caleb looked a little different. Scruffier. Caleb was hairier than Aidan, but not so hairy that a few hours would make a difference in his beard growth. Maybe Aidan hadn't been paying attention in the lab. He'd been too focused on collecting records.

"Yeah, the lab was really exciting," Aidan said dryly. Time to take back control of whatever was happening here. "What have you been doing this morning?"

Caleb seemed to read that cue, since he withdrew a degree or two and said, "Sorry, I know you were up late working."

Then he laid a hand on Aidan's leg.

Jesus.

In the split second when he'd moved, Aidan could have sworn his hand was trembling. He thought of the way his mom's hands had trembled in the last years of her life.

But Aidan was seeing things. Caleb wasn't sick, and now his hand was perfectly still, and very much on Aidan's thigh. Even with the sheets between them, it was an unusual intimacy, bordering on aggressive.

When Aidan fantasized about Caleb, he didn't behave like this. Doubt shadowed his mind. Maybe he didn't know his best friend as well as he thought.

Caleb let his gaze wander the room's stark grey walls, pausing to stare at the mattress on the floor and the black suitcase propped open against the back wall as if he'd never seen them before. Then he said, "It's been a weird morning. I went by that... rift, you know?"

"The breach?"

"Yeah, the breach. It freaked me out."

"I thought you couldn't feel it? Or is it just the idea that freaks you out?"

"Yeah, the idea of it. It must be really strange for you, since you're a runner."

Aidan's mouth dropped open, but no sound came out. He'd expected to be able to reveal this truth on his own terms. He picked at the hem of the sheet in his lap and said, "Not anymore."

"Oh, sorry again. I just can't stop fucking up this morning, can I?" Caleb let out a huff of laughter. He didn't do or say anything reassuring. The continued presence of his hand on Aidan's thigh was anything but.

Aidan's stomach dipped.

Caleb continued, "I'm gonna blame the breach. At least I didn't see that *thing*."

"Dr. Lange?"

Caleb was acting so strange. Aidan scrutinized him for signs of intoxication, but his pupils and his breathing gave nothing away.

"Yeah," Caleb said, leaning forward again. "Dr. Lange."

Leaning back felt like giving up ground, but Aidan did it

anyway. "Are you okay? Was there something weird in your breakfast? And can you not—" Aidan gestured at Caleb's hand.

Ironic to ask him to back off, considering what Aidan had been doing before he arrived, but Christ, this situation was bizarre.

Caleb laughed again. He removed his hand with a lingering slowness. Aidan almost suspected Caleb was deliberately fucking with him, but that would be uncharacteristically cruel.

"Sorry, man. I just can't stop thinking about the breach and Dr. Lange."

"It is all pretty strange. But it's not like you can feel the breach or see Dr. Lange. At least, not unless he knocked something over or threw something across a room."

"Yeah, I mean, it's just... Do you think he'll ever really be Dr. Lange again?"

"I hope so for his sake, but it's really not my problem. That's for Quint Services to solve. All I care about is getting out of here, and it's all you should care about, too. You don't owe them anything. You did what you came here to do."

"Which was?" Caleb smiled at him. It was the first normal thing he'd done since walking into the room.

"Oh, sure, make me say it. Fine. Saving my life."

Just like that, Caleb's hand was back. His eyes lit up. "Sounds like I'm pretty heroic. Have you thanked me properly?"

Aidan was too disturbed to enjoy what might otherwise have been a dream come true. Something was wrong. Caleb normally treated their friendship with more care. "Caleb. This isn't funny."

"I'm not laughing."

"You're straight. You're my best friend. You're my straight best friend."

"Are you sure about that? Because I'm not."

Holy shit. His heart leapt. It was the opening line to a truly embarrassing number of fantasies. But if Aidan opened this box, no matter what came out, he'd never be able to put it back inside. "Are you fucking with me because I told you that I don't need or want your help? I know I've been kind of an asshole, but I swear I have my reasons. This isn't necessary."

"I am definitely not fucking with you. I wish you'd let me in." Caleb waggled his eyebrows. "And I mean that in all kinds of ways."

"Fuck off," Aidan said, less heated and more exhausted. He pried Caleb's hand off his thigh. "I can't think about this right now. There's too much other stuff going on."

Even as he said it, he knew it was a lie. He'd be thinking about it with his right hand soon enough. But that was *all* he could do. The goal was to get Caleb out and away from all the dangers of Aidan's life.

Caleb held up his hands in surrender. "Alright. I'll drop it. Pretend it never happened. We can talk about... Quint Services. Or Dr. Lange. Or the rift. Breach, I mean."

This conversation was giving him whiplash, and he wanted it to be over. The only thing that stopped him from snapping at Caleb was a knock on the door and Laila calling, "Hey, can I come in?"

"Yes," Aidan called back, relieved. He shoved at Caleb's shoulder. "Let her in."

Caleb got out of bed and opened the door for her. Aidan didn't think of Caleb as being physically imposing or threatening, but he loomed over Laila. Short, thick, and unimpressed with Caleb's weird theatrics, she didn't give him an inch.

Laila pushed past him and strode to the bed. She'd been in the cell with Aidan, mistreated in all the same ways, so he knew how much that quick movement had cost her.

"I'll leave you two alone," Caleb said, and for maybe the first time ever, Aidan was glad when the door closed behind him.

"Move," Laila said, squeezing into bed next to him. The soft bulk of her upper arm pressed against his, comfortable and familiar. She laid her head on his shoulder, the limp ends of her pink hair brushing his neck and falling down his back.

Aidan had known Laila before they shared a cell, but he'd never seen her dressed down, with no makeup and with the black roots of her unbrushed hair showing. Then again, they hadn't been close. They were both infamous, a militant activist for runners' rights and a foiled bank robber who'd spent her teen years in prison. She'd stayed away from him for years, not wanting her bad reputation to taint his work with the Runners' Union, but he'd sought her out. They'd formed a professional sort of friendship.

Suffering together had changed that.

"What the hell did I interrupt?" Laila asked, her voice bleary with sleep. Unlike Aidan, she'd taken the advice about resting seriously, and he hadn't seen much of her outside of her bed. She'd probably just woken up.

"I wish I knew," Aidan said. "He was being weird."

"Yeah, he was. I could tell that much just from looking when he opened the door," she agreed. "But I bet you were, too."

"Wow, thanks."

"We spent a week in a cell together. I know everything about you," she said, her tone a reminder of what it felt like to be teased with affection instead of deliberately provoked and unsettled. "You were definitely being weird."

Laila didn't know what had happened with Caleb and Aidan wasn't in the mood to tell her, so he played up his exasperation and said, "Did you come in here just to be rude to me?"

"Yeah," she said, lifting her head to grin at him.

"You did not."

She slumped down and hugged her knees. The pair of sweatpants she was wearing, borrowed from someone much taller, was rolled several times at the cuffs, exposing her brown ankles. "I want to get out of here and I can't."

"I can't feel it either," he said. He didn't need to be any more specific with a fellow runner. She'd know he was talking about the Nowhere. "I jumped us out of the cell, but since then it's faded."

"It sucks," she said.

"It makes it hard for me to imagine the future," he confessed. "Who am I, if I'm not a runner?"

"Aidan," she said, answering his question and offering sympathy at the same time. She wrapped an arm around his shoulders. "It might come back in time. More rest, more food. We're both pretty fucked up right now. And if it doesn't, we'll figure it out."

He grimaced and she dropped her arm. He'd devoted his life to founding the Runners' Union. Without his ability, he couldn't help them. He wouldn't be good for anything.

"We got out," she reminded him. "We'll be okay."

"I don't trust anyone here." Even Caleb was acting strange.

"Chill. You're so paranoid."

"You wear wild, asymmetrical makeup every day of your life to trick facial recognition software."

"I wear it to look cool. Messing with recognition is a bonus." She nudged him with her elbow. "I'm serious, Aidan. Take a breath. I trust Kit and I trust his friends. They rescued us. Yes, they were working for Quint, but most of them didn't know what happened to us, and when they found out, they were horrified. They took action. They're decent. Nobody's out to get you. It's like you haven't realized yet that you got out."

"What does it matter that we got out of that cell if they

fucked us up for the rest of our lives? We're runners, Laila. They took that from us."

She shook her head. "It's shitty, but it's not what bothers me the most. Other people manage to live without access to the Nowhere. I imagine it sucks, but so would dying in a cell. It's the rest of it. Being a runner didn't save me from getting abducted. I keep wondering if it'll happen again."

"It won't," he said. He had to believe it. Oswin Lewis Quint wouldn't go unpunished.

"I know you're trying," she said gently. "But buying up news outlets is like swatting flies for Quint."

"There've been a few articles," he protested. "No results, though. I don't know how to get people to pay attention. A major corporation fucking *violated* two innocent people. Why isn't everyone pissed?"

"Innocent," Laila repeated ruefully. "It's been a while since anyone's described me like that."

"Me either. Shit. You think that's why no one cares? Because this happened to us?"

From Laila's apologetic expression, Aidan could tell she'd suspected that for a long time. She hadn't had the heart to tell him.

"Sorry, Aidan. Haven't you seen those campaign ads with the grainy security footage of me robbing Franklin Station Bank? All those 'the only thing that stops a runner is a bullet' asshole politicians love to use me to justify their bills. And you're not exactly a beloved public figure. Quint knew what he was doing when he picked us."

"But the principle—"

She patted his shoulder and he gave up on that argument. How fucking disheartening. The public was fine with torture as long as it was happening to people they didn't like.

"I hate it as much as you do, but the world's not fair. People like us don't get justice. Quint can bury journalists all day long. There's no criminal investigation yet because there won't ever be one."

"So let's get him another way," Aidan said. "Quint's just some guy. It's the money that gives him all that power. If you were going to rob him, how would you do it?"

She snorted. "I got caught last time, remember? Also, all my previous thefts were planned around my ability to fucking *teleport*. If I could access the Nowhere, I'd already have punched Quint in his stupid plastic face. And then I'd have jumped somewhere nobody could find me because—and I cannot emphasize this enough—I am not fucking going back to prison."

"Humor me," he said.

Laila met his eyes, and hers were wide. "Shit," she said. "I was just venting when I said that thing about punching Quint. You want our two sorry asses to rob a trillionaire."

"I heard we're a pair of hardened criminals. You're a bank robber. I'm a terrorist. We can do this."

Laila raised her eyebrows. Aidan's "terrorism" mostly consisted of jumping into places he shouldn't—the stage behind the president's podium, the board room of any organization that opposed runners' rights—and getting tackled. The media were always sure he planned to hurt someone, even though the most he'd done was point aggressively at the president's chest while yelling. Then the Secret Service had tackled him and he'd had to jump back to safety.

"The first step is to get access to the Nowhere again," Aidan said.

"Can we change the first step to be breakfast?" Laila asked. "I like to start small."

[3]

THE REALITY NEXT DOOR

Caleb woke up on a cot in one of the facility's exam rooms. He was on his back and there was something strapped to his thigh. Come to think of it, all of his clothes weighed on him, stiff and unfamiliar. Or maybe the weight lay in his limbs. He didn't remember falling asleep. He'd been drugged.

The door opened and in walked Dr. Jennifer Heath. Caleb jerked upright in alarm—she was supposed to be in prison so she couldn't experiment on anyone else—and she laid a hand on his shoulder. He wrenched out of the way.

"I gave you your treatment," she said, tucking the offending hand behind her back without commenting on his reaction. "I can't give you too many more, so we'll have to be careful. I know you're worried about jumping and getting stuck somewhere, but I'm worried about you getting the shakes. Anyway, I went ahead with today's, since I found you in here taking a little nap. God knows what you get up to on your missions, Caleb. I swear you look like you just fell out of somebody's bed. If we ever do encounter other sentient life forms, I'm sure you'll flirt them into submission."

Treatment? Missions? Caleb touched his arm, where she'd

pushed up the black sleeve of the jacket he was wearing and taped gauze over an injection site in his elbow. *Don't panic*, he thought, panicking. No matter his angle of approach, things looked bad. He'd woken up in his double's clothes—including the thigh holster, but excluding the gun it had contained—with an unscrupulous scientist who ought to be in prison, talking about how she'd injected him with some unknown substance.

His double had kissed him. And then knocked him out somehow. Caleb touched his neck. There was probably a needle prick there, but no bandage. Where had his double gone?

Or maybe the better question wasn't where he'd gone, but where he'd come from.

The Dr. Heath he knew *was* in prison. Caleb had met his own double, so maybe he was meeting hers. She certainly thought she'd met him before, based on all that talk about giving him some kind of treatment regimen. This version of Jennifer Heath was a researcher just like the other one, but Caleb's double wasn't a nurse. He was some kind of agent.

He'd taken Caleb's place and left Caleb here.

So much for not panicking. He had to get out of here and he didn't even know where *here* was. Caleb was rapidly coming to the unwanted conclusion that his double had jumped him to some other reality. His double must be a runner, in that case. But Caleb wasn't. He couldn't get back.

"Are you feeling alright?" Heath asked. "I know the treatment sometimes has unsettling side effects, but I've never seen you react to it." She smiled at him in a way that did nothing to settle his stomach or any other part of him. "You're our most successful runner."

She reached toward him.

He reacted without thinking and caught her by the wrist before she could touch him again. Shit. She was staring and now he had to talk his way out of this awkward moment. His double was a sleazy jerk, at least in their brief encounter, so he ran with that.

"Thanks, Jen, but I'm good. Maybe later." He offered her his oiliest, smuggest smile and then raked his gaze down her body for good measure. She'd better find this convincing. He didn't know what she'd do if she figured out he was a stranger, but if this facility was like the one he knew, it had secret prison cells.

"Ugh," she said, yanking her arm out of his grip. "Get out of here."

Caleb stood up and brushed past her before their conversation extended beyond his ability to fake it.

The hallway outside met his expectations exactly, dimly lit white flooring and grey walls in familiar dimensions. The floor plan must be identical. But the lab across the hall no longer had brown paper taped up over its broken windows. There were no windows at all. The room, situated at the center of the asteroid, was surrounded by thick walls and equipped with a door that would have been better suited to a bank vault.

The walls weren't enough to muffle the wailing.

The keening sound seized his whole body and he flinched like he'd been plunged into ice water. His half-formed plan to hole up and figure out how to get back home evaporated. Caleb swallowed. He'd been right about the cells. But who—or what—was on the other side?

The thought silenced everything. He lost his vision. Felt weightless, dizzy, like he might pass out.

He stayed conscious.

Caleb hadn't lost his sight. It was dark because he'd entered the Nowhere.

Shit. *You're our most successful runner*, that was what Heath's double had said. That injection she'd given him must be a reliable version of what Heath and Winslow had been trying to create, a serum containing dimensional prions that could grant anyone access to the Nowhere. His double was a runner, and now he was, too.

Caleb had been in the Nowhere before, always with Aidan. Every previous trip had turned him inside out with physical and psychological misery. The pain had been incomprehensible, like being crushed into a tiny airless space and stretched out on a rack at the same time. It was so seared into his memory that he hadn't recognized the Nowhere without it.

This must be what it felt like for Aidan. Painless. Free. His panic subsided. The Nowhere was silent and calm. No one could find him. He'd escaped.

There was only that instant of freedom from panic, the moment before it occurred to him that he didn't know how to get out. *No one could find him*, fuck.

He stepped back into the world an instant later. It should have been a relief, but he found himself in a darkened vault with panes of some transparent material—he wasn't fool enough to assume it was glass—separating him from the other half of the room. He'd jumped himself to the other side of the cell wall, but the mysterious wailing had stopped. Both halves of the room were stripped bare of furnishings. Not so much as a sign pinned to the walls. However, the half opposite Caleb contained something.

A set of medical scrubs.

Floating ten feet in the air.

Caleb squinted to make sure he'd seen things correctly. He had—but he'd missed the naked man lying on the floor, staring up at the clothes. He must have been the source of the sound, but he'd stopped when Caleb had appeared. The man began again, letting loose a wordless wail of agony. He gave no other sign of having seen Caleb.

The man was raggedly thin. His tight black curls were flattened on one side of his head and sticking out unevenly on the other. Dark stubble covered the brown skin of his face.

Caleb had never met Solomon Lange. The man had disappeared into the Nowhere before Caleb's arrival at Facility 17. But Lange was brilliant and famous. Caleb had packed a used paperback copy of *The Physics of the Nowhere* in his luggage, and while he hadn't read it yet, there was a professional black-and-white headshot of Lange on the back cover.

The man in the cell was distraught and unkempt, but Caleb recognized his sharp cheekbones. Sharper, now.

Lange could have a double. He probably did. But what were the chances of that double being here in this state? Lange's stint in the Nowhere had caused both his suffering and his strange new ability. Caleb would bet on it.

The bolt of the door clanked as someone on the other side slid it open. Shit, shit, shit. Panic pinched inside his chest and made it difficult to breathe. He had to hide and there was *nothing* in the room. He had to leave, but there was only one door.

He'd come here via the Nowhere, but it had been an accident. He couldn't reproduce it. He didn't even know if the injection he'd received was enough for more than one jump.

Aidan would have known what to do, Caleb thought, and just like that he was standing in his room again.

LAILA WOULDN'T TALK about robbing Quint until Aidan had agreed to get out of bed, take a shower, change clothes, and go to the kitchen with her. She'd thought she was driving a hard bargain. She'd underestimated how much he wanted to destroy Quint.

They had just reheated that morning's leftover pancakes

when Caleb materialized in the middle of the kitchen, ashen and white-eyed. Aidan jumped up from the table to go to him, but froze while his brain flipped through a gymnastics routine: *Caleb. Not Caleb. Caleb's not a runner. Caleb wasn't dressed like that last time I saw him.*

"Who are you?" Aidan finally asked. Laila was still seated at the long metal table and from the corner of his eye, he saw her face scrunch up in confusion. "If you're really Caleb, say something that proves you know me."

"You once got sent to the principal's office after raising your hand in Mr. Preston's history class and saying 'this country was founded on genocide and slavery and everything in our textbook is a lie.'"

Oh, thank fuck, it was him.

"As I recall, you got sent to the principal's office right after me," Aidan said. "For standing up and yelling 'you can't do that to him.' I was in the hallway at the time, so I can't confirm the part about you leaping out of your seat."

Caleb laughed. A hint of color returned to his face. Laila released the stiff set of her shoulders as the two of them talked, and Aidan could feel himself letting go of the fear that had pierced him.

Caleb sat down heavily on the bench and said, "And then when no one was looking, you jumped us out of the principal's office and we spent the rest of the afternoon lying around the park drinking bright blue slushies from the drugstore."

There was no further need for the story, but it was soothing to amass so much evidence of their shared past. And the next detail was too good to pass up. "You threatened to pour yours down the back of my shirt if I didn't shut up about how compulsory public education was meant to deaden our minds in order to further the evils of capitalism."

"And I'd do it again," Caleb said. "Alright, I'm me and

you're you. And this is Quint Services Facility 17, a secret research lab in an asteroid that was brought into lunar orbit decades ago and then forgotten? Until recently you were being tortured in a cell here?"

"Yeah. You wanna tell me how you walked out of your room an hour ago, changed into different clothes, and got into the Nowhere?" Aidan asked. Caleb was wearing a black jacket Aidan had never seen before. Earlier he'd been in blue scrubs. "Also, is that a thigh holster?"

"In my room an hour ago—oh God. What did I—*he* do?"

So there *were* two people who looked like Caleb. That was both disturbing, for its gigantic impact on Aidan's understanding of reality, and reassuring, because it meant the weird encounter he'd had earlier hadn't been with *his* Caleb. Paradoxically, the universe had been set to rights and turned upside down all at once.

Aidan slid his untouched plate of pancakes in front of Caleb, whose attention had suddenly fixed on the food. He wasn't making puppy eyes on purpose. Aidan knew from experience how hard it was to pay attention to anything other than that overpowering hunger right after a run. Caleb wouldn't.

"You were in the Nowhere. You need to eat. I'll talk."

Caleb dug in without making any polite protests. Aidan had been right, then. It was bittersweet to see his own lost ability manifest in Caleb. He didn't want to be jealous; he didn't seem to have a choice. His jaw clenched, unbidden.

Then again, if Caleb could become a runner, so could Aidan.

The break in their conversation gave him a moment to reflect on how to answer Caleb's question about what had happened with his double. Aidan decided to elide a detail or two. His own compromising position and what he'd been doing immediately prior. The other Caleb's hand on his thigh. Little things. "He didn't do anything. But now that I know it wasn't you, it makes more sense. You—he was being pretty cagey. Asking a lot of questions you should know the answer to. Especially interested in the breach. Why are you making that face? What happened to you?"

Caleb chewed his last bite, set his silverware on the empty plate, and swallowed. "He took me by surprise. Knocked me out. I woke up in his clothes with a creepy facsimile of Heath looming over me. She injected me with what I suspect was a serum containing dimensional prions, which is how I got back here." He paused and then rushed to add, "And I think I saw Solomon Lange."

"Wait, what?" Laila said. "Our Solomon Lange? The guy who was trapped in the Nowhere and maybe trying to kill Kit?"

"I guess I can't be sure it was *our* Solomon Lange. But yeah, that's who I mean."

"So everyone has a double," Aidan said. If there were two people who looked like Caleb, and two people who looked like Jennifer Heath, it stood to reason there were two people who looked like Oswin Lewis Quint. He could work with that.

"Not everyone," Caleb said. "Not based on what we know about runners. You're much less likely to have one. But most of us, yeah. Probably more than doubles. We just ran into the reality next door, so to speak. There are infinitely many."

"Have you actually read that copy of Lange's book I saw sticking out of your suitcase?" Laila asked.

"I've read the back cover very attentively."

"We should tell Kit and Emil about this," Laila said. She stood up without waiting for their input. "I'm going to get them."

In her absence, the atmosphere of the room shifted. They'd been sitting side by side on the bench, their elbows touching.

Aidan swung so they were face-to-face and inadvertently knocked his knees into Caleb's.

An accident. No reason to blush. Did they always sit that close together? Aidan glanced away and cleared his throat. "Sorry. You okay?"

"Are you asking because you bumped into me or because I was briefly abducted into an alternate reality where I was injected with something none of us understand?"

"Oh, fuck off. The latter." Caleb was treating it like a joke now, but Aidan had seen him right after he'd jumped. "I'm worried about you."

"Yeah? What's that like?"

"Caleb. Are you okay?"

Caleb smiled—bright-eyed, sanguine, nothing like his double—then gave an easy shrug and said, "Time will tell, I guess. As for right now, I know I ate all your food, but I'm still pretty hungry."

"Yeah, me too," Aidan retorted.

"Hey, you gave it to me!"

"You're welcome." Aidan got up and went to poke through one of the two giant fridges. Most of the contents were meticulously labelled as ingredients for future meals, meaning they were off-limits. He pulled out a block of cheddar and then searched the pantry until he found a couple of apples. By the time he'd sat back down to slice them, Laila had returned.

"Well, this is an unexpected development," Emil said. He and Kit joined Laila on the other side of the table. "Are you alright, Caleb?"

"I'm fine," Caleb said. "But keep in mind that every time any of you see me, you should make sure it's *me* and not somebody who looks like me."

"You two missed a charming anecdote," Laila said to Kit and

Emil. "I'm gonna collect so much blackmail material. Tell me some weird secrets for future use, Caleb."

Emil put a stop to that with a hand gesture. He said to Caleb, "You saw Lange. How was he?"

"He's in a prison cell," Caleb said. "It's located where his lab is located in this facility. He seemed disturbed. I don't think he knew I was there. He was naked, wailing like he was in pain. I think they'd provided him with clothes, but he'd taken them off. And they were, uh, floating. Almost as if he was controlling them telekinetically."

Emil's eyes widened at that. "Is that something other runners can do?"

"No," Aidan said. "None I've ever met, at least." And in founding the Runners' Union, he'd met a lot.

"So it's something that happened to Lange while he was trapped in the Nowhere."

Emil's usual calm slipped for just a second as he spoke, but he regained it quickly. Non-runners often found the mere concept of the Nowhere distressing. Caleb had, when they were teenagers discovering it.

"Or something that was done to him in that facility," Aidan said, and if it came out icy, he couldn't be held responsible for that. Emil had been part of his rescue. There was no reason to take it out on him personally. But still.

"Right," Emil said, dismayed. "Do you think that's likely?"

Aidan chewed his lip in thought, a bad habit he'd never been able to break, like so many others. "No," he said at last. "I think it was prolonged exposure to the Nowhere after he walked through the door. I can't say why that strikes me as more likely. The people on the other side obviously have more advanced technology than us, since they can make runners."

"A good point," Emil said. "I trust your intuition. If they could make telekinetics, they'd probably have a squad by now.

We haven't seen any evidence of that. They're keeping Lange in custody because they want to study him, I'd bet."

"Ugh."

"We have to get him out. He's our best shot at fixing the breach," Emil said.

"And he doesn't deserve to be held in a cell," Laila interrupted, her expression dark.

"Yes, that too. Do you three want to weigh in on how we should do this?"

Aidan hesitated. Emil had just said *I trust your intuition* and now was asking for his input. Emil seemed ready to accept him. Aidan wasn't sure he returned the sentiment, but he had to seize this opportunity. That other reality had a serum that could restore his ability. It also had a man identical to Oswin Lewis Quint. Aidan could do a lot of damage, if he had access to those things.

Laila held her hands up. "I'd go, but I can't get into the Nowhere right now. Neither can Aidan. The only runners here are Kit and Lenny, and Lenny recently got shot, so really it's just Kit."

Kit's mouth pulled to the side. "You want me to go alone to rescue the guy who almost killed me? You don't think he'll resist being dragged into the Nowhere? Or try to kill me again?"

"He didn't look like he was in a state to try to kill anyone," Caleb said. "But maybe the Nowhere will upset him, I don't know."

"It's the only way to get him back here," Emil said. He reached for Kit's hand, and to Aidan's surprise, Kit let him take it. "I wish I could send another runner with you."

"Caleb can do it," Aidan said, which made Caleb's brows jump. No wonder, since Aidan had been haranguing him for days about how foolish and dangerous taking a job with Quint Services had been. Now he was volunteering Caleb for further recklessness. Caleb was right to be surprised. But it was either sign Caleb up for one risk now, or let Quint loom over the rest of their lives.

It was a small risk. A manageable risk. He'd get Caleb in, get himself what he needed to ruin Quint, get it done, and get out of Caleb's life. Then they'd both be safe.

Aidan met his gaze. "You can do it. I'll teach you."

"Are you willing to do that? You don't have to," Emil said, directing all of his grave authority at Caleb.

Caleb's mouth was full, and he paused in crunching a slice of apple. "You really wanna teach me to run? How long will that take?"

"You've already done it twice," Aidan said, his gut twisting. He'd eaten hardly anything and still he had to slide the cutting board down the table. The sweet scent of the apples was making him sick. "And you've always been a quick study. Give us two days, we'll be ready."

[4]
GET IN TROUBLE

CALEB CAUGHT EMIL AS EVERYONE LEFT THE KITCHEN. "Hey, uh."

Concern crossed Emil's face. "You don't have to do this if you don't want to. It's not your job to go on dangerous missions."

"No, it's not that," Caleb said. Heat crept up his neck. Aidan and Laila had paused in the hallway, waiting for him. "I'll find you in a second," he told them, and addressed Emil again. "Can we go somewhere to talk?"

Emil nodded and together they walked to the greenhouse. After days in the enclosed, lifeless spaces of the rest of Facility 17, the expanse of the greenhouse was exhilarating. The invisible vastness of space rose above them, sunlight spilling into through the UV-filtered windows and rousing green, earthy aromas from the long, rectangular garden beds.

Unlike the rest of the team, Caleb hadn't dreamed of going to space. He'd only come here to find Aidan. So far, his experience of space had confirmed his desire to go back down to the surface.

Except here.

The greenhouse was the only place on this awful grey

asteroid worth seeing. In full sun, as they were now, the filtered light cast a red glow over everything, a match for the warmth of the air.

Emil smiled at him, understanding. "I like it here too. What was it you wanted to talk about?"

Emil walked to a bunch of basil plants and began to pluck their budding flowers. Caleb stood opposite him, imitating his behavior.

"I know we don't know each other that well, and this is really personal, but... you're gay, right?"

"Bisexual," Emil said gently. He moved down the bed and picked dead foliage off another plant. "But ask whatever you want. We might not have known each other long, but we've been through some things together."

"Oh. Um. Yeah. I guess I was just wondering how you knew."

"I knew because I developed a crush on a guy when I was a teenager," Emil said. "He was older than me, and probably straight, and I was hopelessly awkward. But the symptoms were obvious enough that even at fourteen, I got it."

Shit. Caleb crushed a basil flower between his fingers and let it drop into the soil. "So it was obvious. You knew for sure."

"It's not like that for everyone. And I know lots of bi people who took their time. I certainly got the societal message that it was normal and good for me to like women, which I do, and I think for a lot of bi guys, they stop there. No need to examine things."

"Yeah," Caleb said, because something in that sounded familiar. "And girls are just—I mean, they're everywhere, and it's so easy to get their attention, you don't even have to try. They're always offering themselves as dates or girlfriends or casual sex partners."

"You're funny."

"Wait, what?"

"You weren't joking?"

"No," Caleb said, surprised enough to turn toward Emil at last. "You know what I mean, right? You go to bars and they buy you drinks or pull you onto the dance floor and make you offers. Same thing at parties. You go to the grocery and women drop their phone numbers in your cart. You go out for coffee or to do your laundry or take a walk or get on the train and... there they are."

Emil was smiling with his lips pressed together, trying not to laugh. "I think your experience might be outside the norm."

"Women don't do that to you?" Caleb would've thought Emil—*Emil*, with his smooth brown skin, tousled black hair, strong jaw and incredible abs—turned down offers all the time. "But you're..."

Caleb gestured, then bit his lip, questioning how and why he was so sure that Emil was an exemplar of masculine beauty. It was the sort of thing he'd always known about men, but never thought much about. Everyone noticed that stuff. They had to. It was obvious.

"Vain?" Emil finished with a smile. When Caleb opened his mouth to protest, Emil waved him off. "The team reminds me all the time, and I can't say they're wrong. I *do* spend a lot of time in the gym. And sure, I get hit on. More often by men, though."

"Oh. Um. Do you think that happens because they can tell?"

"That I'm queer? Well, most of the instances were in gay bars, so yes, the men who hit on me knew they had a chance."

Caleb's double had thought the same thing. They'd been in the hallway, not a gay bar. Caleb frowned.

Emil came around so the table was no longer between them. He was very good at apportioning his attention: first a little bit of reassuring eye contact, then a little bit of poking at the plants so Caleb felt soothed instead of scrutinized.

It should have been working, but it wasn't. Maybe it was all the light in here making Caleb dizzy.

"Caleb, does this have anything to do with your doppelgänger?"

"Yes. Maybe. I don't know," Caleb said, unable to give voice to the real answer. *He kissed me and I liked it.* "I wasn't ever expecting to have this conversation. But some things have happened lately that... I don't know."

"He's not you," Emil said.

"It's hard to ignore what we have in common, though," Caleb said. "This sounds totally irrational, but I'm worried that injection might be changing me."

"In other ways than giving you access to the Nowhere?" Emil didn't manage to mask the skepticism in his tone.

"You don't think it's possible?"

"Who can say what's possible anymore? I recently put a lot of alien matter in my body and crossed into a different reality," Emil said. "But I don't feel like a different person. Not straighter or gayer, if that's what you're asking."

Having his unspoken question answered so plainly made Caleb blush. It was a silly idea, and he shouldn't have said anything. Caleb's double had kissed him *before* the injection. If Caleb had enjoyed that kiss, it was all him.

"I don't want you to think that *I* think there's anything wrong with being gay, or bi, or anything, because I don't," Caleb said hurriedly. "Aidan has been my best friend my whole life and I don't think there's anything wrong with him! Or you, or Chávez, or anyone else! I just—you understand why it might freak me out, to feel like some fundamental part of me was changed or is changing without my consent? And it's not the sexuality thing, really, but more like... what else might it be changing? Will I still be myself when it's done?"

Emil put a hand on his shoulder. "You know everyone here has been undergoing various treatments, similar to the one you received, for months. And I think we've all maintained our sense of self."

The treatments at Facility 17 had only produced one successful test. Lenny had learned to access the Nowhere. The other team members, Emil included, hadn't changed. Caleb had read the files. Emil had rescued Kit through a combination of wild risk-taking and luck, but his access to the Nowhere had been a one-time thing. He'd survived his walk through Lange's door. He wasn't a runner.

Caleb couldn't put all that into words. He was too distracted by the warm, heavy, *male* hand touching his shoulder. Why had he never noticed how he responded to men's touch before? It had to be new. Otherwise he would have known. He wouldn't have waited until he was twenty-six years old to have this revelation about himself.

Emil dropped his hand.

"Yeah," Caleb said, trying to remember what they'd been talking about. "Thanks for this."

"Sure," Emil said. "Any time. You don't have to figure it out right away, you know. Or ever. You can just be you. Do what feels good."

Caleb thought about the forceful kiss his doppelgänger had given him, the hot sweep of his tongue and the scrape of stubble beyond his soft lips. He turned away. Whatever was on his face, he didn't want Emil seeing it.

While Caleb was talking to Emil, Aidan took his leave of

Laila, slipping down the hall to Heath's lab. He didn't have any more evidence to record, but he guessed correctly that Dax might be working there now that the space was vacant. It wasn't Heath's notes spread out on the bench in front of them, but Lange's. Heath's notes were chillingly organized. Lange's were inscrutable, at least to Aidan. Based on the furrow in Dax's brow as they studied the minuscule handwriting tracking across one page, they weren't having an easy time of it.

Dax was standing at the lab bench, shifting their weight from foot to foot while they read, and they didn't react to Aidan's arrival.

"Hey."

Dax ran a hand through their already-messy short red hair, turning their curls to frizz. "Hey. What are you doing here?"

"I hear you're an all-purpose genius," Aidan said. "I need to get a message to someone on the surface, and I don't want any record of it."

Aidan had taken meticulous care when he'd been sending out photos, using encryption and covering his tracks, but all that information had been destined for the public. Calling an emergency Runners' Union meeting required even more rigor than usual.

To their credit, Dax didn't complain about being interrupted or ask any questions. They picked up a tablet and started tapping, while mumbling, "I'm a physicist. You just happened to get lucky that I know how to do this."

"Thanks."

"For the record, I'm helping because I know who you are and I like what you do," Dax said. "Not because you called me a genius. Who are we contacting?"

"I'll give you the number, but you can't keep any record of that, either."

The member he was contacting, Lisa Hendricks, was a

surgeon in Chicago and undoubtedly had public information available, but Aidan provided her private number. Like many of the union's members, no one in Lisa's life knew she could access the Nowhere, and Aidan wouldn't jeopardize that by contacting her publicly, even if his message was harmless.

Such secrecy was only an option for people whose abilities had manifested privately in their adolescence. More often than not, young runners made involuntary jumps and got caught. It was hard to become a surgeon, or hold down any job, if the rest of the world was too suspicious to house or hire you.

There was tension between members who lived openly as runners and those who didn't, and Aidan never knew how to manage it. But he liked and trusted Lisa, and he could rely on her to spread the word to their decentralized membership and get someone to pick him up.

"Actually, let's send this to one more person," Aidan said. It was always good to have backup. He provided Craig's number from memory.

He guarded the names and locations of his members with ferocity and entirely justified paranoia, never recording contact information digitally or on paper. It resided solely in his brain.

When he'd woken up in the cell in Facility 17, he'd been sure Quint was after his mental address book. He'd thought Quint's scientists were planning to starve him until he gave up his comrades. Then they'd brought in Laila, and his theory had fallen apart. Laila didn't have a list in her head.

Laila had been right. Quint had chosen them for their infamy. The public wouldn't miss them if word of their deaths got out. Aidan knew that now.

Dax had paused in their typing. "Okay. What's the message?"

"We're meeting at the usual place at 3:17am. Send Facility

17's coordinates for that time. Then say 'the canary can't breathe.'"

Dax's mouth quirked as they recorded that sentence, but they didn't ask. Union members had come up with a few lines like that, encrypted warnings and requests. They'd giggled about it while proposing codenames, but Aidan didn't feel like laughing now.

Dax sent the message and waited for confirmation, which came only a few minutes later. Aidan didn't make small talk, and neither did Dax.

"Thank you for this."

"Are you coming back?" Dax asked. "Or is this goodbye?"

"It's not goodbye. You won't even know I was gone," Aidan said. He had to come back here and train Caleb tomorrow so he could put the plan in motion. This meeting was the first step of many. "Neither will anyone else."

———

It wasn't Lisa who came to get Aidan, but another runner, a stage actor named Anna. Funny enough, Aidan had met her because she and Caleb had dated. She'd been his favorite of Caleb's rotating cast of girlfriends even before she'd joined the Union.

Anna popped into Caleb's room at 3:09am, eight minutes before the meeting time. Even in the darkness, her silver minidress shimmered. She was Canadian, of Ojibwe descent, but she'd been working in Inland New York for years. Aidan liked her—Caleb never seemed to take the end of any relationship too hard, maybe since women floated through his life like leaves in the wind, and Anna had been gentle with him—and if she wasn't moderately well-known, they might have been friends. Instead Aidan stayed out of her way in the city, not wanting to endanger her career by association. They only saw each other at Union meetings.

Aidan's chosen career had robbed him of so much. Regular friendships. A home.

The last real home he'd known had been with Caleb's family, the second floor of an old brownstone on a quiet, tree-lined street. It was no good to dwell on it. There'd never be anything like that again.

"Are you okay? What's going on?" Anna asked, squinting to find him. Aidan, with his vision already adjusted, could make out the dark slashes of eyeliner highlighting the angle of her eyes and her cheekbones. Her heels clicked against the floor when she took a step forward. "Sorry, I came right from the cast party. Lisa made it sound urgent."

"I'm okay," he said, getting out of bed. "Let's go."

"This place is so creepy. Aren't we basically on the Moon?" Anna asked. He'd declared himself fine, so now her curiosity was getting the better of her. "Everyone thinks I took a cab home, and instead I'm in *space*. I was magnificent tonight, by the way, not that you care."

"Shh," Aidan said. On the mattress on the floor, Caleb was stirring in his sleep.

"Oh my God, is that *Caleb*? We're in space and you're finally sleeping with Caleb?"

That was the opposite of being quiet. Besides, Caleb was clearly using a different bed. Aidan glared at her. She probably couldn't see it, but it was also possible she was ignoring it.

"I've missed you." Anna wrapped her arms around him and rocked from side to side in her excitement. She smelled like citrus perfume and champagne. Her hug transitioned instantly into travel, and after a passage through the Nowhere, they showed up in the unglamorous meeting location, a church basement in Omaha. In the middle of the low ceilings, dim lighting, and four long tables arranged in a square in the center of the room, Aidan's sweatpants and rumpled hair looked more at home than Anna's sleek updo. The scents of cigarettes and stale coffee were woven into the carpet and painted on the walls.

Anna let go of him, then kissed him on the cheek. "I want to hear everything."

"You will," Aidan said darkly. These meetings rarely lasted longer than a few minutes, especially when they were called with so little notice, but Aidan might need more time to explain himself. Everyone understood the necessity of meeting in the middle of the night so they didn't have to rent a room and record their location, but no one liked it, and he hated to keep people there.

Lisa was already present, her springy black curls covered by a silk bonnet and her infant daughter in her arms. She gave Aidan a tired smile. "I was up anyway."

The other union members were wearing whatever they'd slept in, if they were coming from nearby timezones, or whatever they'd worked in if they were coming from farther away, so Anna's silver dress stood out even more. No one stared. Meetings were always motley.

Still, this one lacked the small-talk chatter that preceded the others. The silence was apprehensive. They'd all been following his communications from Facility 17; they knew what he and Laila had been through at Quint's hands. The experiments. His powerlessness.

A few more people materialized, and when Aidan did a headcount, he came up with thirty-seven. The Runners' Union had a hundred and seventy-eight members, but they never all met in one place. Thirty-seven was an impressive showing. He wished it were a better occasion.

It would have been thirty-eight if he'd brought Laila, who

was a new but enthusiastic member. But she didn't need this warning.

"Let's get started."

Aidan's chosen career put him in the public eye all the time. Speaking to crowds didn't make him nervous. Still, he wasn't enthusiastic about announcing his own failures.

He took a breath. Fiddled with the hem of his t-shirt. He should've brought Caleb. Caleb wasn't technically a member and thus couldn't be present at meetings, but Aidan really wished he was here right now. If he were here, he would squeeze Aidan's shoulder and give him a reassuring smile. He'd point out that Aidan hadn't failed. Not yet.

"Everyone here is aware of my efforts to expose Oswin Lewis Quint and bring him to justice through the press. There's no shortage of evidence, but the articles that have surfaced so far haven't received the attention I expected."

"Every time one pops up, it disappears a few days later like it was never published. No redaction. Nothing. He's burying them," Lisa said.

Aidan nodded. She kept her eyes on him, willing him to go on.

"What will you do?" Craig asked. Thin and freckled, with sandy blond hair, Craig was one of the oldest members, both in age and in how long he'd been part of the union.

"I have a plan, but it's unorthodox. First, what I need you all to know," Aidan said, bracing himself for the shock, "is that we recently discovered that the Nowhere is not only a conduit to other places in our reality, but also to other realities, including one very similar to this one, where there are people who look nearly identical to people you may know."

"Doubles?" Lisa asked. "Does everyone have one?"

"Something like that, and no, as far as I can tell, we tend not to. The proposed explanation is that we're usually born from a union where one parent had crossed through the Nowhere accidentally. We have matter in our bodies from more than one reality.

"That's why so many of us grow up without one parent, or as orphans—one of our parents accidentally crossed through the Nowhere, and it damaged their body in some way. They didn't live long after that."

Most of the room gave solemn nods in response to that. Aidan had never known his father. He felt lucky to have known his mother for twelve years, even though her absence hurt that much more because of it. His whole life, she'd struggled with an illness no doctors could explain. Aidan stared down at his trembling hands, splaying his fingers and then closing them into a fist, wondering if he'd been the explanation all along.

He glanced around. He knew these people and their stories, and in this room, knowing one of his biological parents—getting to spend twelve years with her, no less—made him an outlier. Not only that, but Caleb's family had taken him in until he was eighteen. Aidan had suffered, but he knew what it was like to live with a loving family. Plenty of people in this room only had the Union. Aidan couldn't protect them from their pasts, but he could make sure Oswin Lewis Quint didn't threaten their futures.

Aidan said, "It's only people who aren't born runners who have doubles."

"What do you mean, *born* runners?" Craig asked. "What other kind are there?"

"They seem to be able to give people access to the Nowhere," Aidan said. "I don't know how it works, but they recently did it to my friend Caleb. A lot of you know him."

People nodded.

"This doesn't answer the question of what we're gonna do about it," Anna said. "So you know a way to get your ability back, maybe. That still leaves us the problem of Quint Services."

"Yes," Aidan said. "It does. I don't want this to be official union business. It will be dangerous, and I can't pretend it's not personal. But I hope some of you will be willing to help anyway."

"Of course," Anna said, her dress shimmering in the fluorescent light as she sat up straighter. "Whatever you need."

"I'm going to find Quint's double and get him to confess to Quint's crimes," Aidan said.

Instead of the volley of questions he'd expected, there was a beat of silence.

Trying to pretend he wasn't daunted, Aidan continued, "I don't think they use the same currency as us, so I can't pay him in money, but I bet they still value the same rare elements. Gold. Platinum. I'll figure out some kind of compensation, and hopefully Quint's double will want it. If he agrees, it will only be the work of a moment to switch him out with the real Quint before the police arrest him, provided I have enough runners helping me."

"What if he's already rich and doesn't want what you're offering?" Craig asked. "If he's Quint's double, won't he be a trillionaire, too?"

"So far my experience suggests that people resemble their double, but their personalities diverge," Aidan said, shoving away thoughts of Caleb's double touching his thigh. "I'm hoping that either Quint's double will be motivated by a reward, or, possibly, that he'll be moved to help me when he hears what Quint has done."

"You think people will pay attention to Quint—or someone who looks like him—confessing, even though the articles haven't produced a criminal investigation?" Lisa asked.

"They will if you do it with enough drama," Anna said. "You need a platform of some kind."

"Yes. I'm hoping we can all use our connections to find one. And I'll need logistical support, since I can't access the Nowhere myself. Like I said, I don't want this to be official Union business, but I wanted everyone to be aware of my plans. Participating is optional."

"I'm in," Anna said, and several other people nodded and murmured their agreement. "Quint hurt you and Laila. I don't want him to get away with it."

THE WHISPERING WOKE CALEB UP, but by the time he was awake enough to process language, Aidan and whoever he'd been talking to had vanished.

If Aidan wasn't getting up in the middle of the night to rifle through Heath's papers, he was disappearing for Runners' Union meetings. Caleb's recommendation that he rest had gone unheard.

Caleb closed his eyes, hoping for sleep, but none came. The secrecy surrounding the Union meetings was necessary, he knew that. And even though he'd helped Aidan found the organization, he wasn't a runner and couldn't attend.

Except he could have taken Aidan to this one. It would have been good practice. He could've waited outside the room and not listened to the meeting.

When Aidan came back, Caleb caught a whiff of cigarette smoke and some kind of perfume. It was too dark to see the runner who'd delivered him, but after a moment of squinting, Caleb could make out Aidan's outline. He stood rooted to the floor like he'd been caught.

"Union meeting?" Caleb asked. He already knew the

answer. It wasn't his intention to act like a parent waiting up for a delinquent kid, so he kept his tone friendly.

"Security check first," Aidan said, half-apologetically. "Tell me something only the real you would know."

Caleb tried not to bristle. They'd agreed to this policy, and it was logical, even though Caleb had been in bed the whole time. Aidan was the one who'd run off in the middle of the night.

He might as well take the opportunity to tell an embarrassing story.

"Fine. Some time in eighth grade, we went to a bodega—not ours, but one in another neighborhood—and shoplifted as many Zings as we could stuff into our pockets. It was your idea. It's a miracle we didn't get caught, laughing like we were. Afterward, back in my room, I said 'I don't even really like these, they're too spicy' and you thought I was daring you to eat all of them. You ate like twelve in a row and ended up rolling on the bedroom floor moaning in pain. I've never seen *anyone* turn that red."

Aidan gave a rueful laugh. "Yeah. Turns out I don't really like them, either."

"I bet," Caleb said. "You believe it's me now? Willing to answer my question?"

"Yes, I was at an emergency Union meeting." He paused for a long time, still standing at the foot of Caleb's mattress, obviously wrestling with how much to reveal. Finally, he said, "I have a plan. But it's dangerous."

God, he was a stubborn idiot. Caleb threw off the sheet and went to him. Shaking his shoulders would be overkill, but that didn't stop Caleb from wanting to. "Aidan. Do you think me lying my way up here to bust you out of that cell was *safe*?"

Caleb couldn't make out his expression, but he heard Aidan swallow. He waited for a response, but none came.

Giving in and grasping Aidan's shoulders came so naturally it was a relief. "I can help you, Aidan. Let me help you. I know it's dangerous. Why are you willing to let everybody in the Union take risks, but not me? I used to think it was because I wasn't a runner, but that doesn't apply anymore. Do you not trust me?"

"No. It's not that."

Aidan sounded miserable. Caleb would've thought he was afraid, except Aidan lived for reckless risk-taking. Even before he could access the Nowhere, he'd always had a penchant for sneaking into forbidden places and pissing off bigger kids. Caleb had seen Aidan leap out of tall trees and skateboard down flights of stairs without blinking. Caleb was the reluctant, fearful one. Not Aidan.

Caleb slid his hands down, intending to let go. Instead, his hands came to rest on Aidan's upper arms. His skin was smooth and surprisingly cool to the touch.

"I do trust you. Of course I trust you," Aidan said.

"So whatever it is you want to do, let's do it together," Caleb said. He let his hands travel farther down, his fingers pausing at the insides of Aidan's wrists. His pulse beat light and fast, possibly a lingering symptom of dehydration. Caleb set aside the flicker of worry that lit in him. He couldn't cajole Aidan into taking better care of himself right now, not if he wanted Aidan to accept other kinds of help.

Caleb brushed the pad of his thumb over the knuckles of Aidan's left hand, the round knobs of bone under chapped skin, and thought about how every articulation of the skeleton was its own little miracle. Every branching vein. Every fingerprint whorl. Caleb had a double, but there was only one Aidan. What would it be like to kiss him?

Caleb dropped his grip and stepped back so abruptly that his heel caught on the mattress.

It had been a long time since either of them had spoken, but as soon as Caleb moved, they both felt a need to fill the silence.

"Sorry, I—"

"Yeah, okay, let's do it," Aidan said, speaking quickly. "I figure if you have a double, then Quint must have a double, right? So let's find him and see if we can convince him to confess in Quint's place. That'll get the public's attention. I just need you to help me retrieve him and then I'll do the rest. Should be simple."

Not a single one of Aidan's suggestions—starting with their childhood climb up the school fire escape and continuing right up to this present moment—had ever been simple. This one certainly wasn't.

And yet Caleb said, "Sure."

"And then, you know, when this is over, things'll go back to how they were."

Caleb had no idea why Aidan sounded so grim about that, but he felt like the rope he'd been tugging on had suddenly gone slack, so winning and falling on his ass were one simultaneous action. He wasn't used to persuading Aidan.

Then he felt the inexorable pull of a smile. He knew what he had to say next. Aidan had said it before their ill-fated shoplifting and countless other misadventures. "Get in trouble with me?"

Aidan's soft laugh was a mercy. "Yeah. Just this once."

[5]
PRACTICE

When Aidan woke up the next morning, he wondered if the space-distending breach in Lange's lab could also make human relationships go haywire. The idea wasn't any weirder than anything else that had happened around here lately—secret experiments, people getting trapped in the Nowhere—and it was more plausible than Caleb wanting to kiss him.

They had known each other for almost two decades, during which Caleb had dated forty-two people, one hundred percent of whom had been women. He'd had plenty of time and opportunity to explore other options. Had the whim taken him to kiss a man, he could've had any man he wanted. Aidan, a perpetual grouchy mess, currently pasty and underfed, wasn't going to be anyone's sexual awakening. Whatever had passed between them in that long strange silence last night, it wasn't Caleb embarking on a journey of self-discovery out of nowhere. That shit only happened in Aidan's more shameful dreams.

Still, it was hard to stop thinking about Caleb's hands.

Aidan might have done more with his own hand if Caleb hadn't been lying awake a few feet from him. He shouldn't have indulged that urge in the first place. Now the guilt he felt was sticky with desire. He'd never be clean of it.

He got up and took a shower anyway. A cold one.

He crossed paths with Caleb on his way out of the bathroom. Even knowing exactly where Caleb had been for the past ten minutes, when he returned to the room, Aidan said, "Security check."

Caleb had dressed in the bathroom. He must've been in a hurry, since as he turned to hang up his towel, his t-shirt clung, half-transparent, to the skin between his shoulder blades.

Stop looking, Aidan thought, and didn't. Caleb showed no sign of noticing Aidan's stare once they were face to face again.

Caleb said, "You first jumped when we were twelve or thirteen years old. I woke up in the middle of the night and you were standing next to my bed in your pajamas, with no coat or shoes. I could tell from the streetlight outside my window that it was snowing. I hadn't heard the door open or the floorboards creak. You were just there."

He was picking embarrassing stories on purpose, damn him.

"You were terrified and I thought it was the coolest thing that had ever happened. I remember getting excited, asking if you could take me with you, and saying that if you could, we'd never get in trouble again. Neither of us had any idea what a runner was. I got out of bed to touch you, and then you were gone. That was when I realized maybe the whole thing was a little scarier and more complicated than a lifetime get-out-of-jail-free card."

That was accurate, although Caleb had excised all the mortifying details of the memory, like the damp spot in Aidan's boxers. Maybe he hadn't noticed. And it wasn't true that *neither* of them had any idea what a runner was. By that age, Aidan had heard enough to form a frightening mental image of unstoppable, inhuman criminals. It had only been six months since the Orbit Guard had caught Laila robbing Franklin Station Bank, and the question of how to sentence her had still been in the news.

"Guess you're you, then," Aidan said. "Let's get to work. Access to the Nowhere isn't worth anything unless you can use it reliably. That means instantly, whenever you need it, and with accuracy. You don't want to land in the wrong place."

Like most runners, Aidan had discovered the Nowhere in early adolescence. At first he'd only disappeared into the Nowhere for a moment or two, reappearing exactly where he had been. As Caleb had described, his first jump had been from his own room into Caleb's, a distance of two blocks. There'd been a number of accidents after that. It had taken him a couple of months to get the hang of it. Two long, terrifying months.

Caleb had witnessed the aftermath of a lot of Aidan's unintentional runs. No wonder he'd gone round-eyed. "How do I stop myself from landing in the wrong place?"

"You've done alright so far. You found your way back here. We'll practice with something small, just in this room, from right in front of the door to that spot near the back wall. I'll go with you so you don't end up stranded somewhere alone."

"Are you sure this is a good idea? You should be resting—"

"You're gonna do all the work," Aidan said. He stood up. "I'm just cargo. It'll be fine."

Caleb positioned himself in front of the door and stared at the other side of the room with determination. Aidan walked right up to him. Caleb jerked back, startled. That was strange. Caleb knew how running worked—you had to hold on tight to anything or anyone you planned to take with you. Maybe Aidan wasn't the only one wondering if something had changed between them last night.

"Oh. Right," Caleb said, glancing down at Aidan. Tentatively, he put his hands on Aidan's shoulders. Even through two layers of clothing, his hands were hot. He must be nervous about jumping.

"You did it before," Aidan said. "You can do it again."

"Yeah," he said, with a distracted laugh.

"Caleb. You have to hold on better than that."

"Do you think—uh, do you think becoming a runner made you feel different? As a person?"

"No." Although the pattern of Aidan's adolescent accidents had revealed more about his attachment to Caleb than he'd wanted to share, those feelings had always been there. It was only natural, really. A lonely young gay kid developing a hopeless crush on the only person who was nice to him. A person who just happened to be extraordinarily beautiful. It wasn't his fault, it didn't mean anything, and it wasn't going anywhere, so the only sensible thing to do about the crush was to keep a lid on it. And when that failed, Aidan kept his distance. He'd been managing one or the other for years. Caleb hadn't noticed.

Nothing had happened last night. Aidan was imagining things. Caleb was just nervous about using his new ability.

"What are you waiting for?" Aidan asked. He put his arms around Caleb's waist, since Caleb hadn't moved. A moment later, Caleb's hands drifted from his shoulders and came to settle on his back as Caleb returned the embrace. It wasn't tight enough, as if he were afraid that Aidan was too fragile after what he'd endured. Aidan cinched his grip to make up for it. He wasn't afraid for himself. The strange case of Dr. Lange aside, people couldn't get stranded in the Nowhere. If Caleb did let go when he jumped, Aidan would most likely not move at all. But he didn't want Caleb to end up alone.

"Uh, some instructions?"

What instructions? Stepping into the Nowhere was just something you did. You wanted it. It happened. You didn't move your body to do it. You barely even moved your mind. You just *felt* it. Aidan had never needed anyone to explain it to him, and he wasn't sure how to convey it to Caleb. "You can feel it, right? The Nowhere?"

"I think so?" Caleb shifted his weight from one foot to the other. They were so close that Aidan could feel every little adjustment he made.

"Focus on what you feel. It's all around you. You don't have to move to get into the Nowhere, but sometimes it helps to think about moving."

"Okay." Caleb's ribs expanded against his as he took a deep breath. They stood in silence for a moment. Nothing happened.

"You know, the first times, I didn't go anywhere. Just blinked into the Nowhere and back out. That's all you have to do. Forget about the other side of the room."

"Right." Another breath. Another few moments of waiting in silence. Nothing changed.

Maybe whatever "treatment" Caleb had received had only been enough for one jump. But what use would that be? And his double had jumped here and back, so that couldn't be right. "It's okay," Aidan said. "Take your time. My schedule's clear."

Caleb didn't laugh. "Do you think I could... try it by myself?" His gaze was directed at the ceiling as he spoke. Was he blushing?

"You think it will make a difference? I'm worried about you stranding yourself alone."

"I know. But I'll be careful. And besides, so far I haven't gone anywhere, so there's not that much risk, right?"

Aidan frowned. "Okay."

Caleb's arms dropped to his sides instantly. Aidan was a

little slower to let go, but as soon as he'd stepped back, Caleb vanished. Aidan hadn't even had time to see if he really was blushing.

He blinked back into reality a second later in the same spot. He gasped for air and then sat right down on the floor like a puppet whose strings had been cut. He crossed his legs and patted his face and then the floor and then his face again. "Holy shit."

His cheeks were bright pink.

It made Aidan remember the exhilaration and embarrassment of his first jump into Caleb's bedroom all those years ago. Maybe there was some emotional component to jumping after all. Caleb had no reason to be embarrassed. He'd known Aidan his whole life. They'd seen each other in all kinds of conditions —healthy and sick, clothed and naked—so having a little trouble mastering a new skill hardly seemed remarkable.

"Okay," Aidan said, pushing those thoughts aside. "Security check. Tell me something only the real Caleb would know."

Caleb took a steadying breath. "When Deborah's first boyfriend cheated on her and I tracked him down and punched him, you and Deb were both fucking pissed at me—her because it was none of my business, and you because you thought Deb should throw her own punches. So you spent the next few weeks teaching my little sister to fight."

Aidan smiled. Deb was as stormy as Caleb was sunny, and she'd been a good student of this particular subject. Did Deb know Caleb was up here? She must. Aidan could imagine her reaction that news, and it wouldn't be a happy one.

"A couple years later when we were off at college and Deb called me to say she'd decked a guy at a party, you sent her a card that said 'congratulations.' You've never sent anybody else a card in your entire life."

"I was proud of her," Aidan said. "I'm proud of you too. You jumped. Now do it again."

———

An afternoon of practice left Caleb physically drained, mentally prepared, and emotionally adrift. Aidan wanted this ability so badly, and Caleb would like nothing better than to give it to him. The sudden reversal in their positions explained why things were so weird between them. It had nothing to do with how many times they'd touched.

All that really mattered was completing this mission. Not just rescuing Lange, but finding Quint's double and enacting Aidan's plan. Caleb held that in his thoughts as Kit showed up in the kitchen, his face grim as he shouldered a backpack—its utilitarian black design was in contrast to the eye-searing pink-and-green checkered pattern of his t-shirt, which made Caleb suspect that the pack belonged to Emil. Kit couldn't be blamed for his reservations about this mission. He glanced between the two of them and addressed Caleb. "You ready?"

Kit and Aidan hadn't been actively hostile since Kit discovered Aidan in the cell. Still, that didn't make them friends. Kit might not have meant his question as a deliberate insult—salt in the wound of not being able to access the Nowhere—but Aidan probably took it that way.

Caleb wished he could fix it. But if he said something, Kit might overhear and point out that Aidan had no business accompanying them in the first place, and that would make everything worse.

So Caleb nodded at Kit, grabbed Aidan, and jumped.

Caleb brought himself and Aidan inside the cell but on the opposite side of the glass wall from Lange. He let go of Aidan quickly, giving them both some space. The cell was exactly as it had been, stripped bare of anything movable, with Lange lying on the floor in the center and staring up at his clothes, which were jerking back and forth in the air several feet above him. He was silent.

Kit appeared on Lange's side of the glass an instant later, and as soon as his feet touched the ground, red lights flashed and an alarm began to sound. Kit moved fast, crouching down to grab Lange and disappearing in one fluid motion.

Mission accomplished. They were supposed to see Kit and Lange safely home now, but instead Caleb grabbed Aidan and jumped him into the other Caleb's room. A short jump, but necessary for escaping the cell.

This was the plan they hadn't told Emil and Kit about, the one Caleb had talked his way into. He still wasn't clear on all the details, but Aidan had said to come here and Caleb was trying his damnedest to be useful.

He breathed a sigh of relief when his double wasn't in the room. That was one of the hardest parts of their plan accomplished, then; he wasn't sure either of them could have taken out his double. Aidan had been right that all attention would be on Lange's empty cell.

The room was as bare as the one Caleb had just moved into in Facility 17. He'd been planning to put up some art if his stay lasted, but his double apparently had no need for comfort or aesthetic pleasure. The bed was made. There was a tablet on the desk and a paper book with worn corners, face-down and splayed open to the last page read. It was *A Tale of Two Cities*, and Caleb couldn't resist picking it up and leafing through it to the first sentence, just to see if it was the same. He couldn't say why it mattered to him that his double had some sign of a personality outside his creepy job, but it did.

Outside the door, the whole facility was still blaring its warning. Through the tiny slit where the door wasn't quite flush with the floor, the light of the alarm bathed the tile red with every other blink. This was their moment.

Aidan was rifling through other Caleb's closet and desk drawers. The bottom one was locked, so he huffed and left it alone. He slapped a stack of cash on the desk and then touched the cover of the book. "Other you has fancy taste in literature, looks like," he said, smiling to himself. Then he picked up the tablet and handed it to Caleb.

"Search for Quint," Aidan instructed. The tablet was similar to the ones Caleb had used at home—an inert, rectangular slab of plastic and metal—but subtly different in design and branding. "I bet you can get other Caleb's tech to work."

Caleb held it up to his face and the machine scanned him and came alive, color rippling down its screen. "Can you find a person named Oswin Lewis Quint?" Caleb asked, feeling foolish.

"Did you mean Oswin 'Oz' Lewis, resident of Des Moines, Iowa?"

"Uh," Caleb said. "Does he run a corporation called Quint Services?"

"No such corporation exists."

Caleb couldn't tell if that was a bad sign or a good one. Aidan was watching him, nodding eagerly, encouraging him to pursue the matter.

"What else do you know about Oz Lewis?"

"Thirty-eight years old, white, male, five feet nine inches tall, unemployed, lives at 3209 Raynard Road, Apartment 1E," it answered. "Dental and medical records also available."

"Jesus," Aidan said. Their world had a lot of surveillance. This one had more. "Those details are about right, though. See what else you can find out."

"No thanks, I don't need medical records," Caleb said to the tablet. "Are there any photos?"

Oswin Lewis Quint had never had such a bad haircut, or such a shabby old t-shirt, and he must wear concealer in his fancy photoshoots, but that was his thin, long nose and those were his straight, symmetrical eyebrows. They'd found his double.

"Well then," Aidan said. "Let's go find him and have a chat."

"Can we discuss a few details first? That man's not Quint. I'm not okay with coercing him into anything."

"Of course not," Aidan said. He stuffed the stolen cash into a pocket and gestured for Caleb to keep the tablet. "All we need is for him to pretend to be Quint in public a few times. It'll be easy and he'll get rich. We'll get justice. What could go wrong?"

"So many things," Caleb said. He'd made Aidan agree to work with him and now his role in this scheme threatened to overwhelm him. "First of all, I don't know how to jump to a place I've never been. I jumped here, but this place is just like Facility 17, so I had that to hold onto. I don't know shit about Iowa."

Aidan patted his pocket. "This will pay for transportation if we end up far from the destination."

"It won't save us from dying in the void of space if I miss," Caleb said.

"You won't. We're not going to need the cash, either."

Caleb didn't believe that for a second.

"Your sense of where things are is different now. There's this map-sense that comes with being able to get into the Nowhere. That's how I think of it, anyway. All you need is a little bit of information about where to find something. Sometimes it's an address, sometimes it's coordinates, sometimes it's just a feeling. That's it. You can get there."

"I don't have any feelings about Des Moines."

Aidan tapped the tablet, which was still displaying a photo of unlucky Oz Lewis. "He lives there. Find him for me."

It was terrifying and a little bit intoxicating how strongly Aidan believed in him. Caleb wanted to make the jump, but as he grabbed Aidan, his body provided a sudden, violent inventory of aching joints and sore muscles.

They ended up in the hallway outside Lange's empty prison cell. He'd meant to jump them to Des Moines, but he'd failed. The world went grey for a moment, and he stumbled against Aidan, who caught him.

"You're okay," Aidan said. "Breathe. Can you walk? Let's take a walk."

Caleb couldn't organize his thoughts into sentences. It was too much effort to put one foot in front of the other. He felt weighed down and electrified at the same time, too tired to move and yet panicked.

Aidan guided him down the hallway for a few steps, and then Caleb came back to himself enough to say, "We can't stay here."

"Shh," Aidan said. "You're in no state to jump."

"Where are we going?"

"Let's just slip into one of the exam rooms," Aidan said. "You can take a second. Do you need food?"

Caleb was as hungry as if he hadn't eaten in days, but he didn't want Aidan sneaking off alone into other parts of the facility. Aidan couldn't run. If they got separated, Aidan would be trapped here. So Caleb said nothing.

The exam room was unlocked and Caleb dropped into a chair, letting his head loll back against the wall. Aidan sorted through all of the gauze and tissues and latex glove dispensers on the counter, then pulled open all the drawers. Occasionally he stopped to pick up an object and examine it. Caleb was too wrecked to put together what he was doing. There wasn't any food in the room. This was pointless.

Caleb's stomach growled. Aidan paused, reached into his pocket, and tossed Caleb a protein bar. Why put on such a show of searching the room if he'd had that the whole time? Caleb unwrapped the bar and took a bite.

Aidan began to go through the cabinets. He wasn't looking for food.

"The injection," Caleb said, after swallowing the last of the bar. He was still desperately hungry, but he could string a few thoughts together now. With the sudden clarity of anger, he added, "That's why you brought me in here. So you could steal it."

Even now that they were supposedly working together, Aidan was keeping things from him. That stung.

If Aidan became a runner again, he wouldn't need Caleb at all.

The cabinet clicked shut. "I'm trying to get us out of here," Aidan said, keeping his voice low and his words clipped.

Because Caleb had failed. He wasn't reliable. He'd fucked up and forced Aidan to resort to other methods.

"Hey."

When Caleb looked up, Aidan was standing right in front of him, his search abandoned.

"You did great, okay? Three jumps in a day is a lot for anyone. I shouldn't have put you on the spot like that. This is my fault, not yours."

These words, and the concern pinching Aidan's dark brows together, salved Caleb's despair and frustration. None of that made him any less hungry, exhausted, or trapped, but at least he could draw a line linking the physical crash and the emotional one. "Okay. What's your back-up plan?"

"Like you said, finding the injection. Heath's double gave it to you in here, right? There must be more somewhere."

"I don't think that's a good idea," Caleb said. "Heath's double said something about how she couldn't give me too many more. It must have cumulative side effects."

"It's a better idea than getting caught," Aidan said, then froze at the sound of the door sliding open behind him.

[6]
YOUR BODY ALREADY KNOWS HOW

Before Aidan could turn around to see who was at the door, Caleb grabbed him by the hips and pulled him in between his spread thighs. One of Caleb's hands wrapped around the back of his neck and jerked him down into a kiss, and the other slid under his shirt to touch the bare skin of his belly, and Aidan's brain seized up and ceased functioning. It was pure animal instinct that he parted his lips for Caleb's tongue, that his hands rose from where they hung at his sides and found their way to cupping Caleb's face and threading into his hair, that his body adjusted from an awkward bend at the waist into the more comfortable position of lifting one knee into Caleb's lap. None of those were decisions. He reacted.

Biting Caleb's bottom lip might have been a decision. It was premeditated, since Aidan had been longing to do it for years. Aidan had mostly learned to ignore the urge it sparked when Caleb chewed his lip in thought. Mostly. When Caleb's mouth was pressed up against his, and his sweet, plump bottom lip was right there, the impulse was more powerful than any worries or doubts.

Aidan wanted to move his other leg so he could straddle

Caleb's lap, but before he could, a woman said, "I knew you were kinky, Feldman, but really, leave my exam rooms out of your hookups."

Aidan nearly choked. That was the voice of one of his torturers. This version of Jennifer Heath didn't seem to recognize him, though. She thought he was one of the other Caleb's "hookups," which raised some questions about other Caleb's typical behavior.

Caleb broke the kiss and stared over Aidan's shoulder, twisting his kiss-bitten lips into a smirk. "You worried about the rules, Doctor?"

Aidan was half-sitting on top of him and still found the change in Caleb startling. The shift in his posture had been too subtle—or Aidan had been too distracted to notice while it was happening—but this new pose radiated lazy arrogance. Caleb didn't sit like that, legs spread and back slouched, his chin tipped up in defiance. He didn't sound like that, either, although Aidan was hard-pressed to identify what, exactly, was different about Caleb's voice. It was a hundred tiny changes all at once, where no individual difference was obvious, but the whole was more than the sum of its parts. Despite having been to all of Caleb's high school and college plays like a dutiful friend, Aidan had never seen this kind of performance.

Too late, it occurred to Aidan that the kiss, no matter how good, had been theater. He should have known from the beginning, of course. Caleb wouldn't have suddenly shucked off a lifetime of heterosexuality like that. It had been a distraction, a plausible reason for the two of them to be alone together in the room. Aidan had been too caught up in the moment to suss that out, but it soured him on the whole experience. He'd been a prop.

A glance down at Caleb's lap showed that maybe it wasn't all faked. Or maybe the bulge in his jeans was just a bodily reaction that couldn't be controlled or relied upon in any meaningful way. This wasn't the right time to think about these things, not when Heath was behind him.

They had to jump or talk their way out, and Caleb had been in bad shape when they'd walked in.

Heath's first scolding for Caleb had been exasperated and almost affectionate, but she didn't like being challenged. "I should have you written up, Feldman. You weren't given that ability so you could parade your random assortment of sex partners through my workspace."

"And you weren't given experimental subjects so you could fuck them, but that hasn't stopped you."

Caleb lifted an eyebrow and kept staring. It was a bold move. They couldn't be sure Heath's double had behaved in the same way, or that this facility was anything like the one they knew.

Judging from Caleb's smile, Heath must have reacted in the way he wanted.

With the hand that wasn't still possessively clutching Aidan's hip, Caleb gestured for her to turn and walk away. "You have your secrets, and I have mine. Let's keep it that way." Then he waved a tiny, cheerful goodbye and wiggled his fingers to shoo her out of the room.

Heath made an affronted sound. "You're an asshole, Feldman."

Caleb made another shooing gesture, his smirk unmoved, and then Aidan heard footsteps and the door closing. It had worked. Holy shit.

Caleb stood up, forcing Aidan to step back, and just like that they were no longer touching. Caleb was himself again, wrecked with exhaustion and uncertainty, smiling apologetically. "Sorry about all that. I had to think fast."

Aidan marveled at him. "Who *are* you?"

Caleb grimaced, even though Aidan had meant that as praise. He'd never seen someone transform like that. And after all these years, it amazed him that there was anything left about Caleb that he didn't know. Today was full of surprises.

"I don't recall anything half that convincing when you were on stage," Aidan continued, trying to make up for whatever he'd said wrong. A second later, when Caleb's mouth twisted further, he realized that this was also an insulting thing to say.

Caleb took a breath and squared his shoulders and said lightly, "Maybe I needed to find the right role."

"Yeah, but how did you know what to do? Didn't seem like you spent a lot of time with your double." *Aidan* knew the other Caleb was a flirt. But Caleb's only interaction with him had been getting knocked unconscious—or so he claimed.

"A lucky guess," Caleb said. "These people, our doubles… I thought maybe we might have more in common than just our looks."

Aidan studied Caleb, wondering if one of the things he had in common with his double was an attraction to men. But he didn't ask, and now that Caleb wasn't acting, Aidan could see the fatigue in his movements. He was standing, but he looked ready to sit back down. Shit. Aidan had more important things to worry about than whether Caleb would ever kiss him again.

Aidan said, "How are you?"

"I'm okay," Caleb said. "Still want to go to Des Moines?"

"Yeah." Aidan stepped forward, ready for the jump, and Caleb jerked back.

He flushed scarlet. "God," he swore. "I didn't mean to—I'm not—ugh."

Maybe that kiss hadn't been so meaningless after all. But Aidan couldn't think about that. It had to be meaningless. His own wants didn't matter. He had goals to achieve, and Caleb biting his lip like that—self-conscious, apologetic, charming—was an obstacle to every last one of them.

For the first time in a long time, thinking of his purpose didn't help. Caleb looking so rattled and unsure was a rare pleasure, and the fact that *kissing Aidan* had flustered him made it all the more delicious. Aidan couldn't resist bringing it up.

"Feel funny about touching me after that... *performance?*" he teased.

Caleb rubbed a hand over his face. "God, I don't know. I'm sorry. I've been freaking out about some things and that just... made it worse."

Teasing Caleb wasn't any fun if he was going to react with genuine uncertainty.

"I don't mean to be weird about touching you," Caleb said. "I'm sorry. Let's forget about this, okay?"

Rationally, Aidan knew he should agree. He could list all the reasons. If the technology existed to pluck that kiss out of his memory, it would be perfectly logical to have it excised. But he didn't want to.

Which made it awkward that Caleb, apparently, *did* want to forget.

Caleb stepped forward and extended his arms, allowing Aidan to move closer. It was a stiff embrace. Aidan shouldn't have enjoyed it. And yet his stupid, treacherous body perked up at Caleb's touch. He was always so warm and solid. Aidan didn't want to admit how much surreptitious enjoyment he'd gotten from holding onto Caleb in the Nowhere over the course of his life. Now that they'd kissed, it was harder to pretend that this was all business.

It would be over in a second. Caleb tightened his grip and Aidan took a breath in preparation for the jump.

Nothing happened.

Caleb blinked in surprise. His face was pale and drawn

from the exertion of the previous jumps, but he'd acted like he could make one more, and Aidan hadn't wanted to contradict him on that. Jumping was as mental as it was physical. Most of the time, if you believed you could do it, you could.

Caleb shifted, steadied himself, and tried again to no avail.

"You can do this," Aidan said, low and serious into Caleb's ear. He had to stretch upward a little to get there, which brought them closer together, which he was not thinking about. "Whatever you're freaking out about, put it aside. All that matters right now is getting into the Nowhere. It'll feel good, I promise. It's peaceful there. Dark and quiet. There's nothing. Your problems will all seem small and far away."

"Ha," Caleb said.

"You can do this," Aidan insisted again. "And trust me about the Nowhere. It's great for running away from everything. I've been doing it my whole life."

"You make it sound so easy," Caleb said. "But this isn't the kind of thing you can run from, and I don't think my problem is a lack of wanting to get there."

"That's the only problem there is," Aidan said. "You have to want it more than you want anything else. You have to focus. You're tired, I know, but you can use that. Think about how relieved you'll feel when we get the fuck out of here."

Aidan dropped until his heels were on the floor and offered Caleb a tilted smile.

Caleb tried to return it, then closed his eyes.

Aidan pressed a palm flat over Caleb's heart, which was beating faster than standing in this empty room warranted. "It's easy," he murmured. "It's just your body doing something your body already knows how to do, like breathing. You know how to do this. Stop thinking about it. Let it happen."

And then they were gone.

[7]
A JOKE OR AN EXPERIMENT

THE RIPE SCENT OF FLOWERS, UNDERLAID WITH CUT GRASS and muddy puddles, struck Caleb as they exited the Nowhere. The air was humid and thick with birdsong. A park.

He dropped to the ground, not caring how wet it was, and then snapped his head back up. He was so relieved not to have killed both of them that he hadn't checked where they'd landed. "Is this Des Moines?"

With some reluctance, Aidan turned his attention away from Caleb and toward the tablet he'd stolen from Caleb's double. The dappled sunlight of the park painted vivid reddish purple shadows on his bare forearms as he tapped at the screen. With his black hair and pale skin stark against the rich autumn color, Aidan might have been cut out of some other image and collaged against the background. Staring up at him made the whole thing even more dreamlike.

It had been a long time since either of them had been outside.

Caleb was glad to be spared the sight of himself. His brain felt like sludge. He could lie down on the squishy, lumpy ground and fall asleep right now, and it probably showed.

Aidan was nodding at the screen. "We're not far. Nice work."

"I was supposed to land us at his door."

"Close enough. Let's find you something to eat before you pass out."

Aidan didn't ask him what he wanted, which was just as well because Caleb wouldn't have known what to say. Caleb grasped Aidan's extended hand and stood up. His vision only blacked out for a second, and he stayed upright. Not bad. His jeans were muddy, but that was his own damn fault.

The walk dragged on for ages, at least in his mind. Concrete sidewalks, manicured lawns, brick buildings, blue skies, and finally a dim, wood-paneled basement. They could be in the real Des Moines, for all he knew. The plastic-covered menu in his hands was printed in English and the prices of the diner fare were listed in dollars.

A server with her hair coming loose from a plastic clip and a black apron around her waist approached their booth. Caleb ordered a burger and fries, too tired to examine the menu beyond that. It was only after the server left that Caleb realized she'd said *good morning*. They'd changed time zones; the sun had been such a shock that he hadn't thought about whether it was morning or evening. This place must have just opened for the day, since none of the other tables were occupied.

She probably thought he had a hangover. Close enough to the truth.

While the server was gone, Aidan discreetly shuffled through the cash he'd stolen, linen paper tinged with familiar green. Caleb hoped it was the right currency for wherever they were.

"We're good for it," Aidan said, shoving the cash out of sight.

"You're sure? There's a chance this is the wrong Des Moines."

"I'm sure," Aidan said, tilting his head at something behind Caleb.

The server came back to pour coffee for both of them. Aidan must have ordered it. Caleb was only absorbing fifty percent of what was happening around him. The coffee was bitter but welcome. When the server left, Caleb twisted in his seat, the cracked vinyl scratching against his jeans.

A collection of framed photos and posters covered the wood paneling, some catching the glare from the bar's haphazardly hung red and yellow lights. Aidan was studying the largest, most central poster, one of a young woman smiling and standing behind a podium with a microphone. She was wearing a short-sleeved blue dress, a garment intended for an upscale office rather than a gala. Her black hair was pinned back neatly. The photo was bordered in white and had the air of a historic image, something that might once have accompanied a news article. The caption read *Li Xiuying arrives in New York, Tuesday, July 26, 2039 at 17:35:04*.

Caleb needed more coffee, because that didn't make any sense. "Am I supposed to know who that is?"

Aidan's eyes lit up and he shook his head.

Oh. It *was* a historic image. Just not their history.

The revelation didn't have the same punch as seeing his own face. The strangeness crept up on him. It was one thing to live and work in a clandestine facility in space, and then to encounter a funhouse mirror version of that place. Facility 17 was *supposed* to be weird. But that park, those streets, this shabby little diner—all of it belonged to another reality.

Caleb took another gulp of coffee. It didn't help.

"I know, right?" Aidan said.

"I thought I needed to lie down *before*," Caleb said.

"I can't tell if I wish it were weirder and more obvious, or if that's the wrong thing to wish for," Aidan mused. He trained his gaze on the poster again. "More importantly, can you think of a lot of historical events that get dated down to the second?"

"No. There's no reason to record that," Caleb said, and then it dawned on him, "unless she came from somewhere far away only a few seconds before that."

"Yeah. And the caption says *arrives*, like that's noteworthy in and of itself. She has to be a runner. I can't think of a lot of establishments in our world that would put up celebratory posters of runners."

"If *you* can't think of them, they don't exist."

"Yeah," Aidan said. "In our reality, Quint was desperate to develop a suppressant that could disable runners. In this reality, they figured out how to give the ability to people who weren't born with it."

"Different priorities," Caleb said. "Though Quint would probably love to do that, too."

"He wants it for himself," Aidan said. "Not for anyone else. Not unless he could control it and profit from it."

"He'd find a way."

"He *won't*," Aidan said.

Their food arrived, briefly interrupting their conversation while Caleb demolished his whole burger without really tasting it. He was still hungry when he finished. When he looked up, Aidan was sipping coffee and staring at—no, not the poster. Aidan smiled ruefully at Caleb and pushed his plate across the table. The burger was untouched. He hadn't even eaten a fry.

This reality was backwards and upside-down in more than one way. Usually it was Caleb sitting in silence, waiting for Aidan to finish the frozen burrito or whatever he'd pulled out of Caleb's freezer in the middle of the night. Caleb kept his freezer stocked. He kept clean sheets and extra pillows on hand, too. Ice packs, bandages, pain pills. Aidan showed up erratically, and more often than not, he showed up in need.

In his more resentful moments, woken up in the middle of the night by the ding of his microwave, Caleb had grumbled to himself that Aidan would never return the favor. Aidan didn't have a place of his own, and even if he did, Caleb couldn't teleport into it at odd hours. The give-and-take of their relationship would always be Caleb giving and Aidan taking.

But this marked the third time Aidan had given him food without being asked. Caleb thought of Aidan offering him a hand up in the park, and of the hours of patience he'd demonstrated while teaching Caleb to get in and out of the Nowhere on command. He was a good teacher.

A good kisser, too.

Fuck. A good *friend*, that was what Caleb should be thinking. That kiss hadn't been real for either of them, no matter how clearly he could remember the warmth of Aidan's mouth.

The food, though, that was real. It was as solid a proof of friendship as anyone could ask for, and Caleb hadn't had to ask for it at all. This friendship they'd had their whole lives was precious, and not worth risking for the sake of one kiss.

"Thanks," Caleb said, picking up Aidan's burger and trying hard not to want anything else.

Oz Lewis lived in a long, low, uninspiring strip of an apartment building surrounded by an ocean of parking lot. The four-lane road outside was dotted with similar buildings, one of which was a motel. Caleb fell asleep on the bus ride there and Aidan had to shake him awake when they arrived.

"Wait, *this* is where he lives?" Caleb asked as they descended to the buckled sidewalk, stepping between puddles. The motel's molded plastic sign had almost no color left in its painted lettering. "Or are we stopping here? Because normally

I'd object, but I considered taking a nap on the ground earlier, so if it's reasonably clean, then it's fine."

"Unless you have the energy to jump us into a five-star hotel, this is what our cash gets us," Aidan said. "But coincidentally, yeah, Oz lives a few buildings down from this one."

Caleb cast a glance around, taking in the dented cars in the parking lot and the cinderblock apartment complexes across the road.

"It's not what I expected either," Aidan said as they walked to the reception desk. "But the tablet said Quint Services doesn't exist here, so he's not rich. That's good for us. It means he'll be more interested in our offer. But that can wait—you should rest."

Caleb needed to be able to jump them away from Oz just in case he turned out to be hostile. Aidan didn't mention that. It wasn't a restful thought.

"It's not check-in yet," said the woman at the desk without looking at them. Her voice creaked like she hadn't spoken in a while. A tablet on her desk was playing media of some kind. They must have interrupted her.

"Is there anything available right now?" Aidan asked.

She did glance up then, and she studied the two of them for a moment. Caleb's attention—what was left of it—was on the peeling grey-and-green wallpaper and he didn't notice. He slouched, his hands in his pockets. To Aidan, he looked pale and tired, but to a stranger, he must look disheveled and distracted, maybe high.

Beautiful, regardless.

The clerk smirked at Aidan.

She thought they were here to fuck.

It was a logical assumption on her part. Aidan was desperate for a motel room in the middle of the day, and he wasn't alone. An affair made a lot more sense than the truth.

Caleb had kissed him to fool Heath. This was minor in comparison, and lying in the service of a goal had never bothered him before.

He wished it wasn't a lie.

Aidan leaned forward, sliding another bill across the counter. "Please," he said, and found his mouth had gone dry. It came out quiet and conspiratorial. "We can't wait."

"Yeah, I bet you can't," she said. She slipped the extra bill into her pocket and tossed a heavy key ring at him. "Room 202. Keep it down."

"Uh," Aidan said, before coming to the blessed realization that he didn't have to say anything in response. He spun on his heel and reached for Caleb. He intended to tap him to get his attention but switched, at the last minute, to draping his arm over Caleb's shoulders.

The move was awkward and unconvincing—*please let the clerk be watching her show instead of us*—until Caleb leaned into him, not startled, but content.

"Did she say 'keep it down'?" Caleb asked as Aidan pushed open the glass door.

"Yeah," Aidan said, scorched with guilt everywhere they were touching. Caleb had told him to forget their kiss and here he was maneuvering them into another act.

Caleb twisted, caught her eye—she *was* watching them, shit—and winked. Then he grabbed Aidan around the waist and hustled them out the door and up the exterior stairs to the balcony before Aidan could respond.

Aidan jammed the key into the lock and gave the knob a violent turn. The room was dark inside, a vertical slit in the blinds on the opposite wall the only source of light. Aidan flipped the lightswitch to reveal faded orange carpet and pink walls. There was a similarly garish painting of a sunset bolted to the wall above the bed. The room was small and drab, and the remainder of its dented, sagging furnishings fit right in: two night stands, an armchair in the corner and a screen on the wall. Ugly as it was, the room was orderly, and when Aidan pulled the covers on the bed back, the sheets were scratchy but they smelled like detergent. Caleb had said cleanliness was his only requirement.

Caleb stepped inside and closed the door quietly behind himself, keeping his hands behind his back. "Hey, you're not mad, right? It was just a dumb impulse. A joke."

"Ha, ha," Aidan said. Hilarious, the idea of the two of them sleeping together. "And the kiss was a joke, too."

"No! The kiss was the only thing I could think of at the time. And it worked."

"You said you wanted to forget it, which is hard to do if you keep acting this way."

"But you were willing to let that clerk think we were—" Caleb paused, swallowed, and if the room weren't so goddamn dim and pink, Aidan would be able to tell if he was blushing.

"I don't see how it's different," Caleb finished. After a hesitation, he crossed the room to sit on the bed next to Aidan.

"It's one thing to distract people or cover our tracks when we have to. It's another thing entirely to make a game out of it," Aidan said. It was a bullshit distinction, but he couldn't say *every time you flirt with me as a joke, I die a little*. That would lead them into the minefield of his feelings, a place he preferred never to tread.

"Okay," Caleb said. "I'm sorry. I won't do it again."

Winning the argument felt a whole lot like losing the argument. Aidan wanted to blurt *no you should definitely do it again*, but that would be charging right into the minefield. So instead he said, "It's fine. You should rest."

"What are you gonna do?" Caleb asked, like he'd forgotten that Aidan wasn't tired. He gave the dull confines of the motel room a bewildered glance. There wasn't anything to do here except sleep or fuck, and they'd already firmly established that Aidan wouldn't be doing either.

Aidan lifted the stolen tablet. "Find out whatever I can about Oz."

"That's a good idea," Caleb said, yawning.

Aidan removed himself to the armchair in the corner so Caleb could stretch out. He typed "Oz Lewis" into the tablet's search engine and then rested it in his lap. The results fuzzed out of focus while he wondered, for a moment, if he'd been too harsh on Caleb.

Caleb had kissed him, and seized the opportunity to embrace him in front of the clerk, *and* gotten flustered several times when sex came up, or when they had to touch. They knew for sure that his double was attracted to men. Maybe Caleb was curious.

It wouldn't be so bad if Caleb kissed him again, even as a joke or an experiment. Sure, it would break his heart later, but it would feel good in the moment. There was precious little of that in his life now and the future didn't hold much promise. He'd have to disappear after taking down Quint. Even if they succeeded, Aidan was still a hated public figure, and Caleb would never be safe while he was around.

If he was planning to blow up his life anyway, why not take a little stroll through that minefield? What was he afraid of? It wasn't concern for Caleb stopping him. Caleb had made clear that he didn't have any real feelings for Aidan. Besides, he'd never had any trouble picking up the pieces after his girlfriends left. He'd be fine. He always was.

Aidan wouldn't be, but that didn't matter. Next time Caleb showed any inclination to kiss him, Aidan would volunteer for that experiment.

Oz Lewis didn't answer when they buzzed the main door of his apartment complex, but since it was six in the evening, two of his neighbors were coming home from work and Aidan and Caleb were able to slip inside. They found the door to 1E quickly, but had to knock four times before someone yelled "What?" from inside.

"Oz Lewis?" Aidan asked.

"Who's asking?"

"You don't know us, but I'm Aidan and my friend's name is Caleb," Aidan said to the door. He'd been less on guard against cameras in this reality, but he assumed there was one. There was always a camera somewhere. "We were hoping to talk to you."

Oz cracked the door open and peered out. "About what?"

"We have a proposal. We need your help."

Oz squinted, skeptical, and then opened the door all the way. He walked back into his apartment without inviting them in.

Caleb touched Aidan's hand, an unspoken question in his expression, and Aidan shrugged. It wasn't the ideal welcome, but they didn't need Oz to be nice.

He stepped into the apartment, a studio that was hard to see because all the blinds were drawn and the only light came from the screen of the wall display and the tablet in Oz's lap. He'd dropped into a slouch in the apartment's only chair, and in the blue light from the screen, he was even schlubbier in person than in his photo. He clearly hadn't shaved or showered in a few days, since he had the beginnings of a wispy blond beard and his long bangs were clumped into greasy ropes.

The room was stifling and stale, the overripe kitchen trash pervading the air. Once Aidan's eyes adjusted, he could see that there were empty beer cans and old food wrappers littering the kitchenette's counters, and Oz's armchair was surrounded as well. Other than the trash, the apartment was stark, with nothing on the walls and very little furniture. Oz didn't have a bed, only a mattress on the floor. It was bare except for a wrinkled top sheet and a black-and-white plaid blanket piled in the middle. Wadded-up tissues dotted the grey carpet around the mattress. Aidan shouldn't judge, since he mostly wandered from friend's couch to friend's couch, but still.

The drama playing on the wall display was the same one the motel clerk had been watching that morning. Funny that daytime soap operas were recognizable even in alternate realities.

"What do you want?" Oz asked. He didn't pause the drama or look up from the tablet in his lap.

Shit, this was already going badly. Aidan should have made Caleb do this part. Caleb could have used his superpower of figuring out what people wanted. He was charismatic and warm. People were happy to do what he said just to please him. Without him, Aidan couldn't have persuaded terrified, hunted runners to band together into a union to protect themselves—even when it was obviously the sanest, most logical course of action.

If Aidan were going to stick around after they were done with Quint, which he wasn't, he might try to get Caleb to come back to the Union.

How would Caleb persuade Oz? He'd use his beautiful face, the fucking cheat. Aidan couldn't do that, but he tried to give a friendly smile.

"Like I said, we need your help." He spread his hands. He felt awkward standing in the middle of Oz's apartment, but there was no other furniture, and given the state of things, he wouldn't have wanted to sit down. "It's going to sound strange, what I'm about to say next."

Oz looked up at last, blinking at them. He had startlingly blue eyes. There was an Oswin Lewis Quint double under there somewhere.

Oz gestured around the dark apartment, with its piles of dirty dishes and its rats' nest of trash. "How could you possibly need my help with anything? Are you looking to get yourselves deeper in debt?"

"Do you know about the Nowhere?" Aidan asked.

"Yeah, obviously."

"And do you know it can be used to travel to other realities? Worlds like this one, but not quite?"

"Get the fuck out," Oz said, and Aidan couldn't tell if he was expressing shock or a genuine demand.

"I'm serious."

"Did I not get enough sleep last night? Is this a prank?"

Aidan, having already expressed his seriousness, said nothing.

"It's not a joke," Caleb said. "And the reason we need your help is because you look just like someone in our world who's very powerful. A trillionaire named Oswin Lewis Quint."

"Ugh," Oz said. "I stopped using that asshole's last name the minute he left my mom and took all our money."

Aidan glanced at Caleb, wondering if he knew anything about Quint's family life, but Caleb was at a loss. He nodded sympathetically and said, "You're different people with different lives. I met my own double and it was disconcerting."

Aidan wondered if Caleb was extending the sympathy in his voice to himself. Was he reassuring himself with that "you're different people" line?

Oz picked up a bowl of instant noodles from the floor by his chair, a half-congealed dish Aidan had assumed was abandoned, and poked at it with a plastic fork. "Yeah, whatever. I don't believe you yet, but I don't have a whole lot else going on. Keep talking. Tell me your amazing plan."

Caleb continued gamely. "Like I said, you're not the same person. But you look the same, and that's what we need. Your double has, unfortunately, done a lot of unethical things. We're hoping you can help us by posing as him."

Aidan stepped in. "The police haven't moved to arrest Quint, despite significant evidence exposed in the press. We need to do something that will get their attention. If you could publicly confess to and apologize for what your double did, we think it could force the police to arrest him. As soon as he's sentenced, we'll switch you with him. He'll go to prison and you'll be free."

"Where's he gonna be, while I'm posing as him?"

"We'll take care of that," Aidan said quickly, and Caleb's composure slipped. He paled. Aidan continued, "Not with murder or anything, don't worry. We're just going to keep him somewhere safe for a while."

"You honestly think this scam will work?"

"I think it's worth a try," Aidan said. "This guy's rich and powerful. It's not going to be easy to take him down. But we might be able to catch him by surprise. Most people in our world don't know this world exists."

"What did he do? This guy who looks like me?"

Caleb stayed quiet just long enough for Aidan to realize that he had to be the one to answer this question. He didn't want to play up his victimhood, so he described his imprisonment and torture as briefly and clinically as possible. He imagined reading a bulleted list: abduction, starvation, cell in space, unauthorized experiments, violation of bodily integrity.

"Wait, people don't respect runners where you come from?" Oz asked.

"They do here?" Aidan asked, equally puzzled.

"Yeah, of course. They're heroes. Do you know how much better they've made the world? Can you even imagine life without them?"

Aidan exchanged a glance with Caleb. "You don't think of them as untrustworthy criminals? People who can't be made to obey the law?"

"What? No! We wouldn't even have space elevators or life in orbit without runners. They save lives all the time. What the fuck is wrong with wherever you come from?"

"I wish I'd grown up somewhere like this," Aidan said.

"So this amazing plan," Oz said. "The one part we haven't covered is what's in it for me."

"Because righting a wrong isn't enticing enough," Caleb said dryly.

"We can pay you," Aidan said. "Whatever's left of Quint's fortune when we're done, which will be significant. Our currency's different from yours but I assume rare metals like gold still have value here. That kind of payment can be arranged."

"Well," Oz said, putting aside his bowl of noodles and standing up. "You should have led with that."

[8]
HAREBRAINED SCHEME

It took Caleb two trips to return from the other reality to Facility 17, one with Aidan and one with Oz, and he collapsed as soon as he and Oz materialized in the room. Oz stood there, useless, so Aidan had to rush forward to catch him. He dragged Caleb to the bed, an ungainly movement. Oz didn't offer to help.

Caleb opened one eye as Aidan was pulling his shoes off. "You didn't ask."

Their little personal security system. "I think you remembering that is good enough for now."

"Deb's favorite doll," Caleb said, closing his eyes, "was named Lulu."

"You're right about that. Get some sleep."

Caleb didn't need to be told twice.

"Stay there. I'll be right back," Aidan said to Oz.

He went to retrieve Laila. Unfortunately, Laila wasn't in her room, but in the kitchen sitting across from one of the Facility 17 team members, a rangy woman with short brown hair named Clara Chávez. Aidan didn't really know her, and his dismay must have shown on his face because the smile she offered him was cut short.

"Laila, I need your help with something," Aidan said.

"Where the fuck have you been?" Laila demanded. "Kit came back almost twelve hours ago. He brought Lange back by himself. And now you just walk in and say you need my help?"

Right. He was being an asshole. Caleb reminded him about this sometimes, that he focused too much on his own plans and forged ahead without accommodating other people. "I'm sorry we worried you. And I'm glad that Kit and Lange made it back safely."

"That doesn't answer her question," Clara observed.

He'd been standing here for minutes and Oz was back in the room waiting for him. Aidan wanted to shift his weight from one foot to the other, or huff and roll his eyes, but he had to put Clara off the trail without antagonizing her.

"I'm sorry," he said again. "I just have a question for Laila about... our shared experience. In the cell."

There, that was private enough, wasn't it?

"What else could there possibly be to say about it?" Laila asked.

"Laila," he said through gritted teeth.

"It seems important," Clara said, stretching an arm across the table and laying her hand over Laila's. "Go talk. I'll be around."

Laila relented and they took their leave. As soon as they were in the hallway, she elbowed him in the side. "You're a terrible liar."

"I wouldn't have needed to lie if you'd just come with me the first time!"

"Next time you're flirting with someone cute, I'm gonna ruin it," Laila muttered, but she followed him back to the room. When he opened the door and ushered her inside, she stopped in her tracks and said, with no effort to keep her voice down, "Who the *fuck* is that?"

"Uh, hi," said Oz. He gave her a funny little smile that landed somewhere between embarrassed and hopeful. Aidan would bet all of Oswin Lewis Quint's trillions that the executive had never made that expression in his life.

"His name is Oz and he's the key to everything," Aidan told Laila. "And Caleb's sleeping, so be quiet."

"Oh, *right*, we're being quiet because Caleb is *sleeping*, and *not* because you have some harebrained scheme involving a Quint lookalike," Laila said. Aidan was only guessing, but something about her intonation suggested she didn't believe him.

"Do you think you could make him look more like Quint?" Aidan asked. He knew she could. He'd made a point of learning what all the runners in the Union could do in addition to being runners. He had some practice avoiding facial recognition himself, but his makeup skills were rudimentary.

To disrupt the algorithm, you had to treat your face like the canvas of an abstract painting, and Laila did museum-quality work. Aidan always thought of her personal style as *fuck you, I'm wearing makeup*. But she could do other, more subtle kinds, too. That was what he needed for Oz.

"I was really hoping you weren't going to ask me that," Laila said. "I was hoping you were going to say 'harebrained scheme? what harebrained scheme? *I* don't have a harebrained scheme!' and instead you were like 'hell yeah, harebrained scheme! I'm all in on *that*!'"

"It's going to work," Aidan said steadily. "We just have to do it right."

"You activists and your optimism," she said. "But sure, fine, I'll do what I can. I don't have anything here with me, though. I need supplies. And even then, if you want him to look like Quint, you need a kind of tailoring I can't afford."

"I'm hoping we can get into Quint's closet for that."

"You'd need to know where he lives—or where one of his many houses is, I should say. He's secretive as fuck. Most rich people are. They know we'd be coming for them with pitchforks, otherwise. And I'm just now remembering that I can't get into the Nowhere, and you can't get into the Nowhere, and Caleb's exhausted, and this plan seems to involve transporting a lot of people down to the surface."

"It won't be a problem."

"No. I don't care how much that boy loves you, you will not ask him to make three consecutive jumps down to the surface. Especially considering we don't know anything about the injection he was given and how long its effects will last. You need more people. We're telling Kit about this—and the rest of the team."

Aidan shouldn't have flinched when she said "loves." She meant it in a best-friend, brotherly kind of way. But paired with the accusation that he was exploiting Caleb's feelings for him, it hurt.

He wasn't doing that. Caleb had offered to help, and now his part in the plan was done. Someone would take him back down to the surface where he'd be safe.

Besides, even if Caleb did love him, there was nothing singular about it. Caleb loved everyone, and everyone loved him. He wasn't in love with Aidan. It wasn't going to break his heart when Aidan left, because he had so many other people in his life. Happier people. Easier people.

Some of those people were the people Laila wanted to tell right now. Kit's friends. They had no reason to like Aidan. Kit didn't—he'd refused to join the Runners' Union for years—and he wasn't alone in his dislike. At best, non-runners viewed Aidan as a shit-stirrer, and at worst, they wished him harm.

If these people wished you harm, they wouldn't have rescued you, he thought, and in his head, it sounded like Caleb's voice.

Fine. He'd talk to them.

And Laila had a point. Even with support from the Union, Aidan could use help here. Facility 17 was, as he well knew, an ideal prison.

"You're bossy," Aidan said.

"What I am is right," Laila said. "Come on. Let's go."

―――

CALEB WOKE up to a hissed argument in his room.

"He doesn't need to come," Aidan was saying. "Let him sleep."

"He's part of this. You can't exclude him now," Laila said.

Oz was standing apart from the two of them, wary and wide-eyed and silent.

Caleb swallowed to ease his scratchy throat and tasted sourness. He didn't know how long he'd slept, only that it wasn't long enough. He tried to lift his head as surreptitiously as possible, but his cheek was half-stuck to the pillow.

"Hi," Aidan said, his tone suddenly gentle. "You alright?"

Caleb sat up as proof. He repressed a yawn and refused to rub his eyes. Thankfully, he was fully dressed—still in his double's black clothes, since he'd fallen asleep that way. "What's going on?"

"Aidan's going to explain his plan to Emil and Kit," Laila said, and added, pointedly, "I thought you should be there."

"Yeah, of course," Caleb said, and got out of bed to follow the three of them to the common room, hoping his face and hair didn't look too obviously slept-on.

The common room was empty when they arrived. Oz sat down in one of the armchairs. Laila, bless her, marched right to the counter in the back of the room and started a pot of coffee. Caleb hovered behind her, useless and needy, until she turned around and touched his shoulder.

"Sit," she said, and all but pushed him toward the couch, staying close until he was settled on the stiff cushions. He caught a whiff of coconut scent from Laila's hair as she straightened. She cast a glance toward Aidan, who was pacing, the tread of his sneakers muffled by the grey carpet. "I know better than to tell you to sit. I'm going to get the others."

Aidan was agitated, but Oz's presence kept Caleb from asking about it. Revealing doubts in front of Oz might make him reconsider his participation. So Caleb listened to the percolating coffee maker until Laila came back with Kit, Emil, and one of the other team members, Jake, in tow. The big orange tom cat—Subrahmanyan Chandrasekar was its name, since it belonged to Solomon Lange—trotted at Jake's heels as though it was attending the meeting.

The cat was the only one who didn't stop to stare at Oz.

"He's not Quint," Laila said quickly. "Aidan will explain the rest."

Emil and Jake frowned at the same time, identical expressions creasing their faces. Kit's gaze sharpened with interest. He didn't need to be told that the blond man relaxing in the armchair wasn't the trillionaire. The real Quint wouldn't be caught dead with a stain on his shirt.

Kit sat on the other end of the couch from Caleb, while Jake and Emil remained standing. Laila crossed the room, retrieved a mug of coffee, and handed it to Caleb. Then she sat down in the middle of the couch and briefly leaned against him, the soft warmth of her body a gift.

Caleb didn't object to being comforted, but he wondered what had happened to make Laila worry about him.

"Everyone, this is Oz," Aidan said. "Quint's double from

another reality. He's agreed to help us put Quint away by publicly confessing to Quint's crimes. We'll switch him with the real Quint just before he goes to prison."

Emil sized up Oz. "I don't mean to be rude, but I'm sure you understand why I have to ask a few questions. What made you agree to any of this?"

"Money," Oz said easily. "Also, I don't have a lot going on at home."

"So you're not him and you know barely anything about him. Have you ever acted? Do you have any background in this kind of thing?" Emil asked.

"No," Oz said. "But one of you will coach me through what to say, right? You write the speech and I'll muddle my way through. I can read, at least, I've got that going for me."

"I can teach you," Caleb said. It came out too loud and startled everyone, but he had to say it. Now that they'd returned, Aidan would be in touch with the Union. He didn't need Caleb to get into the Nowhere anymore. Caleb refused to be sidelined. "To act like Quint, I mean. I'm good at that."

Aidan paused in his pacing to pull a grimace, but before he said anything, Laila patted Caleb's shoulder and said, "I think we should all wait to hear about how we're *not* going to end up in prison before we volunteer ourselves for this plan."

"Uh," Oz said. "Don't you know, like, dozens of people who can teleport?"

"Didn't help us last time," Laila said.

"Which is the reason we're doing this," Aidan said, his jaw tight. "So Quint can't hurt anyone else. The public here doesn't know about other realities yet. That's why we have to do this now."

"But we just got Lange back," Jake said. He didn't say much, but Caleb was always struck by how soft-spoken he was, for such a big man. "He's not in great shape. And there's still the problem of the breach."

"We do have a lot on our plate," Emil agreed.

"So you're saying it's not time to go haring off?" Laila asked, smirking at Aidan when he glared at her.

"There's a lot of people at this facility," Aidan said. "Surely we can tackle more than one thing. And Lange's presence is how we're going to get Quint up here."

Jake's shoulders shot up and Emil said, "What?"

"Call Quint," Aidan said. "Tell him Lange is exhibiting heretofore unseen symptoms and that you think he should come up here personally to observe. He'll want to be the first to study these interesting new effects, and he'll be the only one who can truly understand the full extent of their consequences. Say something flattering like that."

"You want Oswin Lewis Quint—the man at the head of the corporation that had you kidnapped and tortured—to come up here?" Emil asked.

"I need him out of the way. This reason for getting him off the planet has the benefit of being true. Lange is exhibiting heretofore unknown symptoms. Quint will be excited about that."

"You're gonna throw Lange under the bus?" Jake asked. "You know what Quint's willing to do."

"You'll keep an eye on him," Aidan said. "Show him Lange, but don't let him do anything but observe. Then if you could, say, break your comms for a week. And disable all your pods. And have your runners mysteriously absent or otherwise out of commission."

"You want us to keep Quint in a space prison," Kit said.

"It won't be anything like what he did to me," Aidan said. "But yes. Hold him here for a week, out of touch with the news."

Unexpectedly, Kit said, "Yeah, I'm not gonna lose any sleep over that. We're good. I like this plan and I'll do what I can to help."

Some silent conversation passed between Kit and Emil, a series of expressions Caleb could perceive but not interpret, and then Emil said, "Okay."

"Okay what?" Aidan asked. "You'll help?"

"Yes, we'll keep Quint here for you," Emil said. He glanced at Jake. "And we'll make sure he doesn't hurt Lange."

"Lange can defend himself, last I checked, which was when he almost killed me," Kit said. "Maybe we could just leave him and Quint alone together and see what happens."

"No," Aidan said firmly. "If Quint dies, someone at the company might continue his work. The world won't be any safer."

"You sure we can't kill him? Dump his body on the other side of the Nowhere in a place no one'll ever find it? It sounds nice." Laila smiled wistfully, like she was talking about a beach vacation instead of a murder. Then she frowned. "You're being so reasonable."

"I'm not," Aidan said. "I want to burn down everything he values—his company, his fortune, his name, his power, his freedom—and stomp on the ashes. And I want him to watch."

———

Right after the meeting, as everyone filed out, Kit caught Aidan by the elbow. The two of them stayed by the door, waiting for the others to leave.

Kit's posture and expression suggested a sulky penitence; his outfit left nothing to suggestion. Aidan could see his hipbones through his pants. He ignored that—it wasn't easy to ignore anything in that shade of electric blue, but Kit wasn't his type—and met Kit's eyes instead.

"I can help," Kit said. His arms were crossed so tight he was hugging himself.

Kit had been the first to support his plan in the meeting, *and* he was a runner. Aidan was already counting on his help. Kit must mean something else, though.

"Good," Aidan said. "We need all the help we can get. What are you offering?"

"You want a platform for your fake Quint to make a shocking confession, I know someone who can give you one."

Aidan's mouth dropped open. He'd been running through everyone he knew in the Union in his head, trying to figure out which of them might have that kind of connection. He could have run through that list a thousand times without ever guessing that neon-splattered, unfriendly, criminal Kit would know someone with a legitimate public career. Maybe the connection was through his adoptive mothers, since one of them had been a pop star in her youth. That felt tenuous, but Aidan couldn't conceive of anything else. "You know a news anchor?"

Kit curled his upper lip. "Not exactly. But she's got a big audience, and I know where she lives."

Shit. Aidan had just convinced a room full of people to go along with his plan, and here he was, stunned, thinking *this might actually work*. He walked back into the room to sit down on the couch and gestured for Kit to join him. If Aidan looked anything like he felt, his grin was feral. "Tell me more."

[9]
UPGRADE

"This is Oswin Lewis Quint," Caleb said, pulling up a photo on his tablet. He set the tablet on the bathroom counter so Oz and Laila could see it. Aidan hadn't come with them after the meeting and Caleb didn't know what was keeping him. "The man you need to impersonate."

"If he's my double and we have the same face, how come he's so much better-looking than me?" Oz asked, patting his scruffy jaw and cheeks as though it might answer his question.

"A lot of it's tailoring," Laila said. Privately, Caleb thought some of it might be hiring expensive personal trainers and chefs to oversee every aspect of Quint's diet and exercise regime, but they didn't have time to make those kinds of changes, so they'd have to hope that stealing a few of Quint's pricey suits would do the trick. "The rest is an expensive haircut and a very subtle makeup artist. Lucky you, I'm here."

Oz eyed Laila and the irregular starburst of black eyeshadow around her right eye. There was a rectangular bar of equally thick black color over her left cheek. Facility 17 didn't have a facial recognition algorithm to block, but her asymmetrical makeup was a kind of armor. She'd gone back to wearing it and curling her pink hair right after being rescued. How she'd found a curler on this asteroid full of short-haired, style-averse people was a mystery.

"Subtle," Oz repeated, skeptical.

"For you, I can be as boring as I need to be," she said.

"Clothes and makeup are only part of it," Caleb said. "You need to walk and talk like Quint for this to work. He's too private for interviews, but we'll work with what little video we have."

Oz groaned. "That sounds hard. Let's start with the haircut."

"There were already really nice shears in the facility, did you know that?" Laila asked Caleb, making conversation while she circled Oz like a sculptor studying a block of stone. "Chávez lent these to me. Since the team was supposed to be here for months, they had to think about this stuff."

Caleb and Laila spent the next half-hour treading in the blond fluff that had floated down to the bathroom floor in her first efforts, studying Oz from all angles, comparing his haircut to the tablet Caleb had brought in. There were few photos of Quint available to the public, and only three where it was possible to see the sides and back of his head.

"It's the front that matters most," Caleb said. Laila had done a nice job of trimming and arranging Oz's bangs so they mimicked Quint's carelessly dapper, sideswept style. "And as long as you get the behavior mostly right, people won't get too caught up in the other details. You need to shave your face. Do you have contact lenses?"

Oz shook his head. "Hate putting my fingers in my eyes."

"That's a problem. Quint doesn't wear glasses. We don't have time to fix your eyesight. How bad is it?"

"Bad," Oz said.

"Hm. Well, try not to squint, and if anybody hands you anything to read, pass it to me."

"Why would somebody be handing me things to read?" Oz asked. "Aren't we just going on some broadcast so I can make a speech? We're not actually going to his office..." Oz trailed off when confronted with Caleb's expression. "Shit. How much are you paying me, again?"

Caleb pressed a razor into Oz's hand. "Shave."

Clean-shaven and with his hair in Laila's best approximation of Quint's style, Oz was almost right. He was still wearing the stained t-shirt and shapeless old jeans he'd arrived in, but to fix that, they needed access to Quint's wardrobe.

"Stand up straight," Caleb said after evaluating Oz.

"I am."

Caleb poked him between the shoulder blades and helped him square his shoulders. It was a start. "Chin up. Now walk."

Oz walked to the other end of the bathroom, past the sinks and the stalls enclosing showers and toilets. He had a casual, shuffling gait, and by the time he'd returned to where Laila and Caleb stood, his shoulders had drooped into their usual rounded posture.

Aidan showed up then, pausing in the doorway to take in Laila sweeping up the hair cuttings while Caleb prodded at Oz.

"The haircut looks good."

"We're working on it," Caleb said. The way Oz carried himself, each vertebra piled on top of the one underneath, his arms hanging at his sides and now both hands jammed into his pockets, all of those were choices. Not conscious decisions, maybe, but still choices. Oz had to choose to mimic Quint.

"Straighten your spine and pull your shoulders back," Caleb said. Oz followed the instructions and ended up stiff and awkward, like a statue whose artist had read about human beings but never met one.

"Walk," Caleb suggested, and Oz marched like he'd been programmed to. "No, relax. But not that much."

"Which is it, relaxed or not? I don't know what you want from me here."

Clearly a different approach was required. Caleb chewed the inside of his cheek. He'd told everyone he could teach Oz to act. He'd actually said *I'm good at that* out loud. If he couldn't, Aidan would move on without him. Working with Oz would be easier if Aidan weren't watching.

"I think I've been explaining it wrong," Caleb said, clearing his throat. He could talk about this without giving specific examples of, say, successful kisses he'd staged. He *could*. "It's not about your posture, not really. It's about what you're feeling."

"I'm feeling like I don't get it," Oz said.

That much was obvious.

"You were good at pretending to be your double," Aidan said to Caleb, speaking up and smiling like he was being friendly and helpful instead of casually poking at a bruise. "How'd you do it?"

In a moment of desperation, Caleb ignored Aidan and turned to Laila for refuge. A mistake. At Aidan's question, she'd perked up like a cat that had smelled fish frying. God damn it.

"Look, watch this," Caleb said to Oz. "See Laila? See how she's standing? All the personality it conveys?"

"Uh," Oz said.

Laila had raised one thick eyebrow. Caleb resisted the urge to gulp. He'd chosen this path and it was too late to back off now. Besides, the fact that Laila was brimming with attitude made her perfect for this lesson.

"You see that face she's making at me, like she thinks I'm full of shit?"

"Mm," Laila said, shifting so her arms were crossed. "I don't remember agreeing to this."

"And now see how she's gonna kick me in the shins if I say one wrong thing about her appearance or her personality? That's the kind of expression we're talking about. She's doing some of it with her eyebrow, and some of it with her arms. And she's wearing those boots, too—that's why I said the thing about kicking me in the shins, because those look especially threatening. But it's not just her face and her arms and her outfit. There's more. Things you only perceive when you really think about how people use their bodies."

Caleb stood next to Laila, both of them facing Oz, and mimicked her pose. Arms crossed over chest, one hip jutting out slightly, feet planted. He raised an eyebrow.

"See?"

"You don't look anything like her," Oz said.

"That won't be a problem for you," Caleb said. "Stop thinking about the surface. Think about what's underneath. What do you see then?"

"It's assertive," Oz said after a pause. "Maybe a little challenging. But not outright aggressive. Kind of a wait-and-see pose. And she looks... like she might laugh."

"That's a recent development," Caleb said. He dropped the pose and went to stand by Oz. "But good, all of that was good. You know how I imitated her? I didn't do it by perfecting the exact configuration of my skeleton. I thought about the attitude she was conveying. I *felt* it. And you could see it, since you described her attitude perfectly just now. If you can make yourself feel it, the rest will fall into place. Your body knows what that feeling looks like."

Caleb stopped. Aidan had said something similar to him —*your body already knows how*—about jumping. A strange awareness, like Caleb's new sense of the pulse of the Nowhere, but warmer, rushed over his skin and made the hair on his forearms stand up. Aidan's expression was intense, his head tilted forward with interest and his black hair falling into his eyes.

"Well, this has been fun," Laila said. "But as we've mentioned, I'm a lot less subtle than Oswin Lewis Quint."

"The principle is the same," Caleb said. "You want to stand and walk and move like Quint? Feel like Quint."

"And how do I know what he feels?" Oz said. He gestured at the photo. "He's not giving a lot away. He's smiling."

"Right. And that's a posed photo meant for advertising purposes. He probably wanted to look friendly and trustworthy."

"Not sure he managed it," Laila muttered.

"You're right that this photo isn't much to go on," Caleb said. "Give me a sec."

He strode out of the bathroom. Emil wasn't in his room, but Caleb found him a few minutes later in the greenhouse. "Do you have a moment? Can you come with me?"

Emil looked perplexed at being dragged to the bathroom. Presented with the sight of Aidan, Laila, and Oz amid the detritus of their on-going makeover session, his confusion only worsened.

"You've met Quint," Caleb said. "Tell us about him."

"I'm not sure I know anything you don't," Emil said. "And I wasn't at my best during that meeting. He looks like that." Emil turned his hand, palm up, toward the display.

"How did you feel in the room with him?" Caleb pressed.

"Anxious."

Caleb turned to Oz. "What do you think it takes to make someone as confident and collected as Emil feel anxious?"

"I don't know that I'm either of th—" Emil started, but Caleb cut him off with a gesture and waited for Oz to answer.

"Power," Oz said. "But Quint's not bigger or stronger than

you—not if he really is the same size as me—so it's not a physical kind of power."

Caleb intended to validate this insight, but Emil was already nodding and saying, "He reminded me of a predator. And I had just been in a cave with this alien beast. A huge, muscular animal with six legs and two rows of very sharp teeth. The way it moved... Quint, even with all his polish, reminded me of that."

Oz frowned at Caleb. "How do I feel like a predator? I've never felt like one before. I'm a guy with four failed businesses who lives in a shitty studio apartment. My only social life is getting lunch with my mom every Sunday. Every girlfriend I've ever had has dumped *me*, not the other way around. Honestly, before you came to bring me here, I hadn't been out in... a while. The idea of leaving the apartment had become overwhelming."

Caleb met Oz's gaze and put his hands on his shoulders. "That's fear. You have to imagine you can't feel it."

"Oh, great. Sure. That'll be easy."

"Think of it like this. You're not trying to be Oz-with-no-fear. That's too complicated, too close to home. Don't even think of it as 'a guy like me, but fearless.' You have to pretend to be something else entirely. Oswin Lewis Quint isn't a person. He has so much money that he's untouchable. Practically immortal. He can have anything he wants at any time."

Aidan spoke up. "There are only two things he can't have in the whole universe, one of which is genuine immortality."

"What's the other?"

"Access to the Nowhere," Laila answered, her eyes meeting Aidan's for an instant. They must have talked about this in their cell. "Quint is so used to being able to have anything he wants, to having an unlimited amount of power, that it drives him up the wall that there are people in the world who have something he doesn't. And not just *people*, but *runners*. Nobodies from nowhere. Most runners don't have much family, and a lot of us grow up poor. We don't get the best educations, and many of us barely get jobs at all. But we can do something Quint can't. Something his private jets and spacecraft will never be able to do, no matter how much he pays for them. And that makes him so mad."

"How do you know that, if you've never met him and he doesn't give interviews?" Oz asked. "Not that he'd say those things in an interview."

"He put me in a cell and starved me for a week," Laila said. "I know him well enough."

"There," Caleb said. "Anything he doesn't have, he's willing to torture or kill to get. That's how you have to move through the world. Like other people's opinions and feelings—their *lives* don't matter to you. Like you own everything you've ever laid eyes on and will soon own everything you haven't. Like nothing can harm or hinder or even touch you, because that's how powerful you are. Like you left fear behind a few trillion dollars ago. Move through the world like that—fearless, careless, voracious with want. Oswin Lewis Quint is a monster in a human suit."

BEFORE QUINT ARRIVED, Dax herded Aidan, Caleb, and Oz into the supply closet now designated as a surveillance center. A grey table spanned the back wall of the room, and on the wall above it was a large display divided in four. One quarter of the display showed Lange's room. The researcher was lying motionless on his bed, the stretch of his long brown body interrupted only by the pair of blue plaid boxers that Caleb had cajoled him into wearing. The large orange cat was curled up next to him, while a tuxedo cat and a tabby were munching on cat food in another corner of the room.

All three cats were named after physicists, since it was Lange who had named them. Caleb hadn't seen them around the facility much, but he knew Kit had rescued them from the Nowhere. They'd had the same experience as Lange himself, but they didn't seem to share his trauma. Thankfully, the cats weren't manifesting telekinetic powers, either.

The other three quarters of the screen showed the kitchen, the common room, and the hallway outside Lange's room. Kit, Emil, and Quint were approaching the door.

Aidan sat down in the cheap grey rolling chair in front of the display, resting his hands on the table. There was a beat-up old keyboard on it, most of the letters worn off the keys, and a chipped mug, adding to the feeling that this set-up had been scrounged up from scraps. The mug was empty—Dax wouldn't let coffee go to waste—but the smell permeated the room, layered over the sterile, dusty scent of the closet itself. Oz moved to stand next to him, looking, as always, like he didn't know what his body was for. His hands dangled at his sides. Caleb took up position behind Aidan, settling one hand on the padding on the back of the chair.

Maybe it was the smell, or maybe it was the image on the display, but Caleb's stomach swam. They needed to do this, to show Oz the character he'd have to adopt, but it felt all wrong to be stuffed in a closet when Oswin Lewis Quint was a short walk away.

Caleb didn't know what he would do if he ended up in the same space as Quint, but at least he would have the option of doing something. Caleb leaned forward, as if being closer to the image would help.

Quint prowled into Lange's room, his dress shoes tapping

the floor. Caleb failed to find his voice for a moment, and then managed to say, "Watch his gait."

Oz nodded.

On the display, Emil was speaking in a low voice. "He just showed up here like this. We think he was trapped in the Nowhere. He hasn't spoken since he got back."

"You said he had telekinesis," Quint said, his eyes sharp with interest. He didn't look away from Lange until one of the cats got close to him. He made a pinched face and shooed the tuxedo cat away with a toe.

"We think he does," Emil said. "Objects move erratically in his vicinity. But he doesn't do it on command, and he hasn't been speaking to us. We don't really know what he went through, or if he'll ever be—"

Quint strode to the bed in two steps and prodded Lange in the arm as if he were a corpse or a mannequin instead of a living person. Caleb sucked in a breath.

He'd examined Lange twice since they'd brought him back, finding him slightly underweight and deficient in vitamins, but otherwise healthy. Lange hadn't reacted to the examination in any way, but Caleb had been gentle. It was his job. No. It was his obligation as a decent human being.

Watching Quint disregard that obligation so cavalierly made Caleb clench the back of the chair in rage.

Whatever Emil and Kit were discussing with that monster went unheard.

"Caleb?"

In the dim, bluish light of the room, Aidan's eyes were lit with concern. They shone, huge in his too-thin face, smudged with fatigue. Because *Quint* had imprisoned and tortured him.

"We should kill him," Caleb said. Somehow he'd loosened his jaw enough to speak.

Aidan had explained why he didn't want to kill Quint, but

reasoning evaporated in the heat of Caleb's anger. He could jump into that room right now and eject Quint into space. He'd be dead in two minutes. A couple of short jumps, a matter of seconds, and Quint would get what he deserved.

"Caleb." Aidan laid a hand over Caleb's, and at the warmth of his touch, Caleb's fingers relaxed. With great care and a steady gaze, Aidan said, "Step outside with me? On foot, I mean."

Oh. He'd been poised to jump.

Aidan kept a grip on him even after the closet door shut behind them. If Caleb was going somewhere, Aidan was coming with him. His fingers were locked around Caleb's wrist, a shade tighter than was comfortable. It made Caleb's heart race, and he couldn't say why.

It should have been a relief to enter the hallway, where the air was, if not fresh, at least fresher. But when Aidan leaned closer, the hallway didn't feel any more spacious than the closet.

"Promise me you won't jump into space," Aidan said.

"Not even if I have a *really* good reason?" Caleb said, adding a breath of laughter so it would seem like a joke.

"Not even then," Aidan agreed.

"He hurt you," Caleb said. It was the only explanation he could offer for his sudden bloodlust, but it felt monumental. Undeniable. More than enough.

"We could get away with it," Caleb added. Lots of people would notice Quint disappearing, but Oz's presence could confuse the timeline, make it seem like Quint was still alive.

"We could," Aidan said, not quite agreeing. He didn't say anything else, stroking his thumb over the delicate tracery of veins and tendons at the inside of Caleb's wrist.

"I wanted to kill him for a while, too," Aidan continued. "Every time I want to enter the Nowhere and can't, I think about it."

Every time I remember you strapped down and starving, Caleb almost said, but didn't. Aidan had been the victim. What he wanted was more important than what Caleb wanted.

"But he didn't kill me. I'm alive. I'm here." Aidan's thumb was still moving. The rage that had bolted through Caleb remained, but quieted, another feeling blooming in its place.

It was warm in the hallway. His mouth had gone dry.

The closet door slid open, framing Oz. "Hey, are you coming back in or what? I need guidance here. I don't want to screw this up."

Aidan dropped his grip.

"Yeah," Caleb said. "Yeah. Of course."

They crowded back into the room. Caleb glanced at the display, where Quint was still leering at Lange while Kit and Emil stood, stiff and frowning, a few feet away. The sight washed over him like acid, stinging and corrosive, but he didn't move to kill Quint this time.

No one was watching, so he reached for Aidan's hand and squeezed. "Let's fuck him up."

———

AIDAN MIGHT NOT BE able to get into the Nowhere himself, but now that Dax had put him in touch with the Runners' Union, he was almost as powerful. He'd asked Anna to come to Facility 17 this morning, and within five minutes of her arrival, she'd carried out a heist. Aidan was now in possession of one of Quint's suits and a pair of his dress shoes.

"Well, that was the easiest crime I've ever committed," he said, taking the suit from her and hanging it up in Caleb's empty closet. It was the one Quint had worn yesterday, charcoal grey and barely wrinkled. "I hope it's a sign."

"Does it even count as you committing it?" Anna asked. She

was less glamorous today than when he'd last seen her, in tight black exercise clothes with her hair in a single high braid. "I did the stealing."

"Hush," he said. "I'm the mastermind. Thank you, though."

"Anything for our dear leader," she said. "Oh, hey, I brought the stuff you wanted."

She pulled a black knit hat and a pair of glasses out of the pocket of her hoodie. The glasses were large, with thick black plastic rims, but the lenses weren't only for vision correction. The frame was embedded with tiny devices that would project different features onto his face.

Aidan didn't normally rely on this kind of tech to disrupt facial recognition. His previous strategy had been to avoid places with cameras if possible, and to be ready to vanish at a moment's notice otherwise.

That hadn't saved him from Quint's abduction, and now he was going to one of Quint's homes, which would be equipped with his own proprietary algorithm. Quint had made enemies of people who couldn't be deterred by locked doors, so his security system would rely on cameras all over the house, ready to call the authorities at the first sight of an unwelcome person. Aidan slid the glasses onto his face.

The hat was just a hat. He pulled it over his hair.

"What next? Need me to vanish?"

"If you don't mind sticking around, I could use your help, but don't feel obligated. I don't want to out you," he said. "Caleb's up here. You still haven't told him, right? There's a lot of other people around, too."

Anna nodded. "Thanks for thinking of me. I'm gonna go, but somebody else can pick up where I left off. I'll pass the word along. You sure you're safe up here?"

"I'm not staying. Next time I get in touch with the Union,

it'll be from the surface. I just need Laila to get Oz into character, and then we'll go."

"Where are you going? Or is that classified?"

"You'll see," Aidan said, and the arrival of the others saved him from further questions. Anna disappeared.

Caleb and Oz returned to the room, both freshly showered, and Laila and Kit came in a moment later. Kit was carrying a tote bag and a stack of clear boxes filled with makeup. It was hard to move among so many people.

Caleb and Aidan had been briefly separated, so according to their own rules, Caleb should prove his identity in some way. He hadn't had to do it in front of such a large audience yet. The tight downturn of Caleb's mouth reflected Aidan's own uncertainty. Neither of them wanted to do this publicly.

"The doll," Caleb said softly. "Deb's doll Lulu. I once hid her in a vent because Deb was being annoying and I was being awful to her. You didn't know anything about having a little sister, so you folded at the first sign of tears and rescued the doll for her. Then Deb told my parents that *both* of us took the doll from her, so you got in trouble just like I did. You didn't even defend yourself, you were so surprised."

"An early lesson in betrayal," Aidan said, smiling at Caleb. "Deb's always been trickier than she looks. Too smart for both of us."

"What's wrong with your face?" Caleb asked, frowning.

Aidan tapped his glasses. "Disruptor. You don't like it? Usually the default setting on these things is an upgrade. Smoothing things over, making them more symmetrical. Hell, it's probably straightening my teeth."

"Your face was fine the way it was," Caleb said.

"I feel like I'm not supposed to be watching this," Laila said to Kit, loudly enough for everyone to hear. "Do you feel like that?"

"Definitely."

"Well, I'd rather you watch them than watch me changing clothes," Oz said. He sounded cheerful enough.

At this reminder of their nakedness, a flush crept down Caleb's chest toward the white towel around his waist. Aidan always forgot how much chest hair Caleb had—not that he should remember a detail like that, or be looking in the first place.

"Be quiet and put that suit on, no one's looking," Laila said, turning her head. When he was done changing, she straightened his cuffs and collar. "You'll do. Now hold still while I put some concealer on you." Laila dabbed a little makeup under Oz's eyes. Once finished, she wiped her hands off and then combed her fingers through his hair. "You're gonna do just fine down there."

Oz gave her his slickest trillionaire's smile. Dizziness seized Aidan. Oz had gotten a little too good at acting.

Aidan couldn't show any doubt, so he nodded and said, "Let's go."

[10]
THE VOID

Kit had shoved Aidan out of the Nowhere and then vanished before Aidan knew where he was.

The scent struck him first. Something musky papered over with artificial flowers choked the air. He tried to breathe through his mouth as the rest of the room came into shadowy, soft focus. Caleb and Oz stood next to him, equally bewildered. Faded burgundy drapes in velvet blocked what must be floor-to-ceiling windows with an excellent view of the city. A sliver of daylight slit them. No matter that it was a sunny day, mid-afternoon—the living room was lit with dozens of candles, thick and thin, their lumpy wax in various shades of cream. They must be at least partly to blame for the smell.

The other parties responsible were a parakeet in a cage, a little cotton ball of a lap dog, and the famous spiritualist Miss Tallulah herself. She was a small woman in a silk dressing gown, a white brunette with brassy coloring in her short hair that suggested dye, and the pallor of someone who didn't go outside much. Aidan could smell her perfume—or maybe the lurid cocktail in her hand—from across the room.

Her mouth was rounded in shock at their sudden appearance in her living room. So much for her psychic powers. She'd sat straight up at the sight of him, nearly knocking the dog out of her lap and down into the plush carpet below. It had a floral pattern, as did the wallpaper and every other overstuffed furnishing in the room.

Miss Tallulah resettled the dog on her lap, brushing a hand through its fur and then through the loose waves of her own hair, the ends of which rested on her shoulders. Considering three strangers had materialized in her apartment, this was relatively little fuss. "I didn't invite any visitors."

Her tone was cool, but not outraged. Kit had said she didn't like runners, but maybe she just didn't like Kit. Then again, maybe she knew she couldn't do anything to them and was trying not to show any fear.

"My name is Caleb Feldman. We're here to offer you a chance to interview Oswin Lewis Quint on your show."

Her eyes flicked up and down Caleb, and she adjusted her silk robe, tightening the belt, pulling the sides closed. For an action ostensibly meant to cover her further, it drew a lot of attention to her body. Aidan bit his cheek.

"Why would I want that?" Miss Tallulah said. Even in the real Quint's tailoring, Oz couldn't impress her. "Why would *he* want that?"

"He's going through a spiritual crisis," Caleb said in a tone like an elbow to Oz's side.

"I need your help," Oz said, right on cue. "I've heard so much about your talents."

Miss Tallulah preened and then said, "I'm expensive."

"I'm rich."

Miss Tallulah bounced off the couch and began mixing drinks. Aidan declined his, more from habit than anything else. He could use a drink. The proffered cocktail was the first time Miss Tallulah had acknowledged his presence in the room. Caleb hadn't given his name and she hadn't asked for it. This whole setup made him uneasy. Before Kit's offer, he'd envisioned a newsroom, or at least a more traditional talk show.

Caleb and Oz graciously accepted whatever Miss Tallulah offered. Judging from Caleb's expression, it was strong.

"So. You want a séance? Who're we contacting?"

"No," Caleb said quickly. "Mr. Quint has some things he'd like to confess, and he was hoping you could offer him some guidance for how to make amends."

"A reading, then."

She'd agreed to that easily enough. Had Caleb researched her? They'd had so little time to plan this. Aidan had known he'd be good at this, but not how good.

"Live," Caleb said. "We want it to be broadcast live."

Miss Tallulah raised her eyebrows at that. "Most clients who can afford private sessions prefer them."

"I'm trying to atone," Oz said. "I don't want to do it in secret."

"Have it your way," she said. "I need some time to get ready. But before I leave a famous criminal alone in my apartment, maybe you could tell me what *he*'s doing here? Don't think that disruptor is enough to fool me. I know who that is."

Aidan wasn't worthy of naming. He merited only a single sharp tilt of her head.

Instead of Caleb, it was Oz who defended him. "He's part of the story. I need him here."

"This isn't some cheap prank? He's not going to jump behind me while we're broadcasting and make me shriek?"

Aidan struggled to avoid smiling or frowning; he couldn't say which. He could protest that he wouldn't do that, even if he had his powers. But now that it had been suggested, he wanted to.

"No," Caleb said, so solemnly that Aidan knew he was amused.

"Hmph," Miss Tallulah said. She considered the three of them. "You know I don't need anyone to be present except the person I'm reading for. It's disruptive to have two extra people here."

Oz was getting better at recognizing cues. He waved a hand. "I'll pay."

"I don't need you to confess anything, either," Miss Tallulah said. "The cards will show what they show."

"I know. But I need to."

"It's very unusual."

Disapproval weighed down her words, and Aidan had to cough to hide his laugh. This woman who billed herself as an old-timey spiritualist in 2093, with her candles and her silent-movie haircut, who ensconced herself in a fancy high-rise using the subscription fees of the poor saps who believed she could tell the future, who was romantically involved with some mob boss from Kit's past, she wanted to shame them for not following the rules?

"We're an unusual group of people," Aidan said. Miss Tallulah pinched her lips together and flounced out of the room.

As soon as she was gone, Oz eyed Aidan and Caleb. "What if she figures it out?"

"Hush," Aidan said. It was amazing how little it took for Oz's whole act to drop. One nervous eye movement, a single whispered sentence, and Oswin Lewis Quint was nowhere to be found. "She won't. She can't. You... don't actually believe any of this is real, do you?"

"I don't know. I came here from another reality. It doesn't seem all that impossible anymore."

Caleb put a hand on Oz's shoulder, and Aidan's gaze was drawn inexorably to that point of contact. His brain set about imagining what the touch must feel like—how warm, how tight, how reassuring—drawing from the database of all the other times Caleb had touched him. *Stop*, he thought, and it had no effect.

"I watched a few sessions before we came," Caleb said. He *had* done research. "She'll only answer the questions you ask. And whatever the cards are, you interpret them how you want. She uses a new deck, the one that's been in fashion since the sixties, so it'll have cards like The Void in it, just so you know."

"A new deck? The sixties? What?"

Caleb dropped his hand from Oz's shoulder, and Aidan was perversely glad.

"Right," Caleb said. "This was different for you. The first run was in the thirties, and it was a woman. Li Xiuying, right?"

"Yeah. Didn't that happen here? She's like, really famous. Everybody's hero."

Caleb shook his head. "The first publicly acknowledged run happened in 2058, and it was done by a man named Fehim Terzi. After that, the idea of the Nowhere freaked people out. Lots of religious leaders weighed in about whether it was some kind of limbo or gate to the afterlife. A lot more people started believing in ghosts and angels and whatever. And here we are a few decades later with spiritualists."

"Huh. I guess there's some mysticism surrounding it where I come from, but not like this," Oz said. "Anyway—you're sure the psychic won't figure it out?"

"No one will figure it out," Aidan promised. He didn't have Caleb's way with people, but that didn't mean he could abandon Caleb to do all the work alone. "Just tell your story, then look thoughtful when she does the reading."

"And don't worry if there's a card you don't recognize," Caleb added.

"Trust me, that's not the part of this that worries me."

Miss Tallulah reappeared in the doorway, wearing the same silk robe but with her hair slicked and her face made up. They stopped their quiet conversation when she appeared, and Aidan wished they'd smoothly switched topics to something innocuous. All Miss Tallulah said was, "Mr. Quint should follow me. I broadcast from in here."

To Aidan's relief, the next room in the apartment was cooler. The air had only a faint trace of the floral miasma in the living room. It was more minimally furnished, with a camera on a tripod trained on a round table and two chairs. Miss Tallulah gestured for Aidan and Caleb to stand off to the side, where they'd be out of frame.

The back wall of the room was a giant display, currently white, but as Miss Tallulah began to set up, it showed what the camera was recording. Oz sat in his chair with posture so good it made Aidan feel stiff just to watch.

The studio was carefully lit, not as dim as the curtains-closed living room, but not unflatteringly bright. Miss Tallulah lit a candle in the center of the table. She had skill with makeup, Aidan had to give her that. She'd done something to make herself not merely prettier, but sharper. More alert, and yet more mysterious. She laid the deck of cards on the table between herself and Oz.

"My subscribers received a notification that we'll begin streaming soon," she said. "We won't get the highest numbers at the beginning, so if you want more people to hear whatever it is you plan to say, you'll need to hold onto it for a few minutes."

"Will people be able to watch this after it's over?" Aidan asked.

"If they pay," Miss Tallulah said.

Hmm. That wasn't great for visibility, but this should be the first of a few appearances, so maybe it wouldn't matter.

She spoke to the camera in a lower, sultrier voice, one with an accent that seemed to come from every foreign country at once. "Welcome, friends, to today's session. I am honored to perform a reading for Oswin Lewis Quint. You may know him as the CEO of Quint Services, or..."

She turned to Quint, offering him an opening to say more about himself. The real Quint owned many companies, and was probably known to most people for the facial recognition algorithm that had earned him government contracts and made him rich at the age of twenty. Beside him, Caleb shifted in silence. Had they mentioned any of that to Oz?

Oz merely smiled at the camera. "All that matters today is that I'm here. Thank you for having me."

"I understand you have some things you'd like to say before we begin."

Caleb took hold of Aidan's elbow, turning him away from the two people at the table and toward the wall display. In the bottom left corner, it said *live* in fat red letters, and underneath that was an ever-changing number in white. Five hundred. Six hundred.

Six hundred people had dropped whatever they were doing in the middle of the afternoon to watch an unscheduled session with Miss Tallulah? How much were they paying for that privilege?

Enough that Miss Tallulah could afford this apartment.

Six hundred people wasn't enough to make his plan work, but he took a deep breath and reminded himself that it was only the beginning.

A few feet away on stage, Oz took a deep breath, too. "I came here today to confess to a terrible crime. My company, Quint Services, recently abducted two runners, held them against their will through starvation and sedation, and experimented on them without their consent. I make no excuses for this unconscionable violation of two innocent people, and I fully accept the blame. The two runners in question have now been freed, and no further experiments will be conducted, but I am here today because I feel lost. I need to know how to move forward. I know I may never fully be forgiven for what I have done, but I have to work toward that end regardless."

Miss Tallulah lifted her manicured eyebrows, but otherwise appeared to be taking this shocking news in stride. It must be bad for business, showing surprise. "Mr. Quint, if you don't mind, I have a few questions."

"Please go ahead."

"Have you considered that confessing to a crime on my live stream might result in authorities tracking you down and arresting you?"

"Yes. I plan to turn myself in shortly."

She raised her hands, palms facing the camera, and gave her subscribers and presumably anyone surveilling her a charming smile. "For the record, I had no part in this." Then she turned back to Oz, her gaze shrewd.

The robe, the cocktail, the little fluffy dog, the ridiculous decor—all of it combined had made Aidan underestimate her. He shouldn't have. Miss Tallulah was a force to be reckoned with.

"That's quite a confession, Mr. Quint," she continued. "What made you change your mind?"

"What do you mean?"

"Well, it's your company. You authorized those experiments, didn't you? At the very least, you hired the people who did them. Whether you let it happen or whether you helped it along, it doesn't really matter. Somewhere deep down, you knew something like this would happen. So what changed?"

"Ah," Oz said. Aidan detected the first creeping edges of panic in his tone and his rapid blink. Oz had memorized that little bit about his crimes, and they'd agreed that he'd just play his character—aloof, professional—if anything else came up. He was taking his time.

Come on, Oz.

Tallulah, conscious of the damage this long silence was doing to her viewer count, said, "Did you do this because of your mother?"

"My... mother?"

Damn. Aidan should have remembered: Quint's mother had passed away recently. Oz had mentioned his mother offhand, so she was still alive.

"Her death must have come as a shock to you," Tallulah pressed, like a predator who'd scented blood.

Oz swallowed and nodded, his wide eyes giving credence to that idea. Maybe he'd recover. Caleb had done his best to train him in the short time they'd had, and the role ought to come naturally, right?

"It did," Oz said, telling the truth and finding his voice at last. With fresh certainty, he added, "But I didn't do this for my mother. Someone else inspired me."

And then he turned his gaze toward Aidan and Caleb. Aidan froze. Where the hell was Oz going with this?

"Do you believe in true love, Miss Tallulah?"

"Of course, Mr. Quint. I see it between my clients and their departed loved ones all the time. And I've experienced it myself." The woman who'd ferociously dug into Quint's personal life on camera disappeared behind a dreamy smile.

"I wasn't a believer, but I've been converted," Oz said. "Do you know of a man named Aidan Blackwood?"

"The terrorist? What's he got to do with this?"

Out of view of the camera, Caleb put a hand on his arm, making Aidan realize how rigidly he was holding himself. He tried to relax his face, but the scowl just kept coming back.

Caleb stepped closer, as if he could put his body between Aidan and whatever was coming next.

"Some may call him a terrorist. I'm afraid that he was my victim in all of this."

"You mean the runner you abducted and tortured was *Aidan Blackwood*?" Tallulah mustered some shock for this point, even though Aidan had been standing feet away from her the whole time. "That's an important detail you omitted. But what does it have to do with true love?"

Aidan rolled his eyes at Tallulah's breathless professional-interlocutor schtick, and Caleb gripped his arm tightly. Aidan didn't need a scolding; outside of that lone eye roll, he'd behave himself.

Caleb tugged at his arm until Aidan turned. The number in the bottom left corner of the screen had changed.

Three thousand.

It ticked upward while he watched. Three thousand five hundred. Four thousand. Had the mention of his name done that?

"Yes," Oz was saying, "Aidan Blackwood was one of my victims, I'm ashamed to say. But you should have the whole story. Aidan was held in a cell in a secret facility for about a week, starved and sedated so he couldn't get free. Another runner was with him. I'll keep the second runner's name out of the story for now, but you should know that we calculated when we picked these two. We picked runners we thought nobody would miss. Yes, Aidan is famous, but it's closer to infamy. You yourself just called him a terrorist."

Miss Tallulah nodded, not daring to interrupt. Aidan wanted to burst in, grab Oz's mic, yell *stop telling my story*, but he was rooted where he stood. He couldn't reveal himself. He was a despised public figure. Quint couldn't make public amends in the company of a hated criminal. What the hell was Oz doing, bringing his name into this?

"This facility, I should mention, no longer exists, but it was top secret, and it was in space. We took precautions, since we were dealing with runners. Every detail I tell you makes me sick with guilt now, but it's important that you know." Oz took a breath. "It was impossible to get out of this facility, and it was very nearly impossible to get in. But one person did."

"A runner?" Miss Tallulah asked. A logical guess.

"No," Oz said. "Not a runner. A young man named Caleb Feldman. He'd taken a job with Quint Services about six months prior, working as a nurse in a clinic. He was an exemplary employee. I knew about him when he was hired, because he was a known associate of Aidan's. We had tried, in the past, to persuade Caleb to bring Aidan in. Caleb implied at his job interview that he would work on it. He never intended to. At Quint Services, we thought we were keeping an eye on Caleb, but really, he was keeping an eye on us.

"Caleb requested a transfer—he wanted to work in one of the clinics with the most cutting-edge research, he said. Because he was so good at his job, he was offered a position in one of the space facilities—the one I mentioned. Nothing in his file shows this, but I now know he wanted a transfer there because he suspected Quint Services of wrongdoing. Aidan had gone missing, and Caleb intended to find him. Caleb was ready to leave behind his family, his friends, and his entire life on Earth to go into space, working for an employer he knew might harm or even kill him, motivated only by this suspicion—this *hope* that he could save Aidan.

"When I heard that, I wondered—has anyone ever loved me that much?"

Beside Aidan, Caleb had gone eerily still.

Aidan couldn't speak to him, not here, not now, not to say *don't worry, I know it's not like that*.

At the table, impassioned by his role as storyteller, Oz continued.

"Is there anyone in my life who would throw away everything if I was in danger?" Oz shook his head sadly. "Now that my mother is gone, I can't say that there is. But what a force! That kind of love could fell empires. It could—and did—save lives.

"You may think that getting into the facility in space was the most difficult part, but it wasn't. Outside of the two scientists conducting this experiment, none of the personnel at this facility knew about the runners who were being kept there. They were kept in a room that was accessible only by runner. There was no door. Caleb kept working, solving this mystery, and through the sheer force of his determination, he found a runner who could get him in. Together they found Aidan and the other imprisoned runner, freed them, and brought the whole affair to my attention."

Oz aimed a beseeching, misty-eyed gaze at Miss Tallulah. The real Quint had probably never looked like that in his life, but it had the desired impact on their host. Her lip wobbled.

"So, you see, Miss Tallulah, I was so moved by this young man's heroism, by the overwhelming love that motivated him, and by the suffering that I myself had caused, that it turned my entire world upside-down. Now here I am, on your show, wondering what to do next."

Miss Tallulah reached out to put her hand on top of Oz's. "I can see that it changed you, Mr. Quint. And since it was such an incredible story, before we do the reading, I would like to invite the two guests we have in the studio to join us at the table."

Caleb was blushing scarlet, a nice complement to Aidan's

white knuckles. Christ. They had no choice but to play along. If they didn't, this whole thing would be a waste.

Despite his blush, Caleb was more present than Aidan, and he was the one who pulled folding chairs up to the table next to Oz. Before the two of them moved into the frame, Caleb tapped gently on the side of Aidan's glasses.

Oh. He had to show his real face for this.

Aidan folded up the disruptor and switched to his real glasses, blinking. He'd have to remember which face he was wearing from now on.

They sat close in the small space, made smaller by the camera pointed at them.

"I didn't do it alone," Caleb said. "I had a lot of help."

"But the story is true?" Miss Tallulah asked. "You really left your entire life behind to go search for Aidan in space?"

"Yes," Caleb said. "I just wanted to clarify that I had help."

That was the only clarification he wanted to make? Not "we're not actually in a romantic relationship, just very good friends"? Trapped, Aidan sat still and silent, clenching his fists under the table.

Caleb laid a hand on his shoulder. It was exactly the kind of comforting touch he might have offered in private. Now there was a camera on them, and Aidan couldn't trust it.

"Aidan doesn't usually stay in the spotlight for more than a few seconds at a time," Caleb said to Miss Tallulah, a wry allusion to Aidan's past. It was a bad idea to bring it up. People would remember they hated Aidan.

But Caleb gave her one of his dazzling smiles and she returned it, then said, "I'm so happy the two of you have found each other. Tell me, what made you go to such lengths?"

"I knew I couldn't live without him."

It had the ring of truth when Caleb said it. It didn't sound at all like he was playacting some grand love story for an audience, and yet a knife twisted in Aidan's gut. Why *had* Caleb put in such an effort to save him? They had a lasting friendship, sure, but Aidan had been a shitty friend in the past few years. Why hadn't Caleb given up on him?

Caleb pressed his thigh into Aidan's. Under the table. Where no one could see.

Aidan met his eyes. Caleb's gaze had some urgency to it, but the message was indecipherable.

Caleb took his hand and put it on the table. Right. Okay. A public display of affection. They needed to be convincing. Their romance had convinced a heartless trillionaire to give up his evil schemes and set out on the path to redemption. If a little fake handholding was all it took, Aidan could do that.

Caleb stroked his hand over Aidan's, a quiet show of comfort and intimacy. There was no such thing as *fake* handholding. Either you were holding someone's hand or you weren't.

He smiled, because no matter the circumstances, looking at Caleb made him want to smile.

It would be so, so easy to let himself believe this was real.

Caleb was telling a story now, a well-worn childhood scrape in which they'd gotten in trouble for trying to return a bike that other kids had stolen. Aidan's whole life was like that, he was saying—Aidan had a drive to do the right thing no matter what it looked like to other people. Sometimes you had to shout and trespass and break a few rules to do the right thing, but he'd never hurt anyone.

He's making me look good, Aidan realized. Caleb was doing this for him, because Aidan was incapable of doing it for himself. He didn't know how to be likable and charming. He certainly didn't have Caleb's flair for lying. Still, it wasn't right to make Caleb do all the work.

"Caleb is being so generous," Aidan interrupted. "He's

downplaying his own contributions, which is typical. He won't talk himself up, so I'll have to do it. Everything Oswin said about him is true. He gave up his family and his home and his life to come look for me, and if he hadn't found me, I wouldn't be here today. I don't even know how to express how grateful I am. How grateful I'll always be."

Caleb squeezed his hand. He knew acting didn't come naturally to Aidan. His smile was an affirmation that Aidan had done a good job.

Funny. Every word he'd said had been true.

"This is so touching," Miss Tallulah said. "I could let you talk all day. But Mr. Quint did ask me for a reading, and I think we should do one. We'll do a simple two-card spread to answer your question about how to move forward. Your first card represents the situation, and your second card represents a challenge."

Oz pulled out The Runner, which had an image of a human silhouette in white against a shimmering bluish-black background. The figure was upside down.

"The Runner, reversed," Tallulah said.

Aidan stared. He didn't believe in any of this, and yet, here he was: a runner, reversed. Was Caleb having the same reaction? His eyes were intent on Oz's hand pulling the second card. Aidan nudged him, but their shared glance passed too quickly to decode.

Oz laid his second card of solid black on the table. The Void.

It was a neat trick, if it was a trick. Not all the cards in the new deck had to do with the Nowhere, but Oz had drawn two that did. The second card was a rectangle of impenetrable black. What would Tallulah say about it? Quint himself was like a void—heartless, implacable, powerful—and in a way, so was Oz.

An imposter. An emptiness. A person with no ties, no roots, no history.

"Interesting," Miss Tallulah murmured.

Aidan had never participated in anything remotely like this. Would she question Oz to fish for clues? Would she hem and haw for a long time?

"I usually like to speak elliptically about these things. Poetically. But we're nearing the end of our time today and I don't want to keep you waiting, especially when the answer is so obvious. You've harmed people, Oswin Lewis Quint. You've harmed *runners*. As your solution, you drew The Void. You know what you have to do. You came here to confess—to pour out the poison you were keeping inside. To make space. Emptiness. You were right to do that. Keep doing it."

"What?" Oz said. Aidan was as puzzled as Oz. They hadn't discussed this with her beforehand. Caleb had been sure they'd be able to spin whatever she said.

Aidan hadn't expected her to fulfill all his wildest dreams.

Tallulah tapped the cards with a fingernail. "You did wrong, and maybe you can never make it right, but you can try. Empty your bank account and turn yourself in."

Caleb had the best poker face of the three of them, but Tallulah's bluntness had startled even him. Then Aidan saw what Caleb's wide-eyed gaze was focused on and realized it wasn't only what she'd said.

The red number in the lower left hand corner of the screen blinked every second as it refreshed. Twenty-two thousand people were watching.

[11]
FACT-CHECKED

The Inland New York offices of Quint Services were housed in a skyscraper, and the lobby was a sterile glass-and-steel affair, its hard surfaces echoing with the muted conversations of the staff and the authoritative click of high heels. The ceiling soared above them. It shouldn't have been so hard to breathe.

Caleb had pretended to be in love with Aidan in front of twenty-two thousand people. More importantly, he'd pretended to be in love with Aidan in front of *Aidan*.

For the third time.

A young woman in a severe black skirt suit with a chin-length black bob greeted Oz. She was brimming with on-the-clock concern and didn't spare a glance at Caleb or Aidan, who was wearing the disruptor again.

It had been nice to see his face.

"Sir. We weren't expecting you back so soon."

Caleb had to control his astonishment. Oz had Quint's face, so no one questioned them. They were just going to walk through Quint's entire life like this.

"You thought I'd want to sleep in a monk's cell in space?"

Oz said. He was enjoying himself too much, overacting the tyrannical executive. Caleb would have to tell him to tone it down once they were in private.

The employee didn't recoil, but Oz's tone alarmed her. She tamped down her startled motion and said, "Of course, that makes perfect sense. What can I do for you, sir? And your... associates?"

This was her only acknowledgement of Caleb and Aidan's presence. If she'd glanced at them, Caleb had missed it.

He had probably missed it. He kept nervously checking his side, like maybe if he was quick enough, he could catch sight of Aidan. He couldn't. The disruptor worked as designed. It was unsettling to be confronted with someone else's face.

If they were going to keep doing this, the only time he'd see Aidan's real face was when they were doing an interview, pretending to be in love.

Caleb scrutinized the woman's body language for a reaction. Was she the type of person to watch Miss Tallulah's broadcast? He didn't think so.

"Get me home," Oz said. He gave Aidan a disgusted glance. A nice touch, acting as if Aidan was the runner. "And not by runner! I've had enough of their kind for today."

Quint had kept his prejudices hush-hush from the outside world. It was unlikely he'd ever said anything so openly bigoted, and the employee's reaction confirmed it.

For a moment, Caleb thought the woman was going to ask Oz if he was feeling alright, but she decided against it and nodded instead. Questioning the boss's mood wasn't a risk worth taking today. Instead, she showed them to the underground parking lot. Caleb restrained his reaction. He'd expected Quint to have a driver—most cars were self-driving, but rich people did love to be served—and he'd thought that would solve the problem of Oz not knowing which car to take. There were eight cars parked in front of them, mostly sleek, black, modern machines. Did all of them belong to Quint?

Oz was already striding ahead. He'd chosen the most distinctive car, an elegant, vintage model in silver. It was a good bet that Quint would have picked something rare and special for himself, but Caleb panicked. That car might be too old to be self-driving. If it didn't know Quint's home addresses, it was no good to them.

The car unlocked at Oz's approach, its recognition algorithm more easily fooled and less given to doubts than the human employee's. A good sign. It might be a few decades old, but Quint must have updated its systems. It could probably drive them to wherever he lived.

Once the three of them were inside, Oz said, "Home," and the car called up a destination.

"That's across the state line," Caleb said. Quint apparently had some kind of estate in Connecticut. That was his nearest residence. "We don't have internal visas. We'll never make it through the border."

"What are you talking about? Visas?" Oz asked.

"Maybe they won't ask for them," Caleb said, seeking reassurance from Aidan, who shrugged. "New York and Connecticut aren't hostile to each other. Not like if we were trying to cross from Illinois to Indiana."

Not that Caleb would really know. He'd never needed a visa to go anywhere. He'd only ever traveled to other states via the Nowhere.

He was lucky to have Aidan as a friend. Most people never left their home state, whether they liked it or not. Or if they did leave home, it was to join the Orbit Guard.

"This place is weird," Oz said, since Caleb hadn't answered his question. "But by the looks of it, we have a couple hours until this becomes a problem, and meanwhile, that woman in the suit is still watching us and waiting for us to drive out of here. Cross that border when we get to it?"

Oz gave him a reassuring smile. Or maybe he was just pleased with his play on words. If Caleb had to spend a few hours trapped in a car with Aidan and a relative stranger, at least the stranger was easygoing.

"Nice work so far," Aidan said. "Let's get out of here."

Caleb had never driven out of the city, and he spent the first hour fascinated by the surrounding sprawl, which eventually petered off into a patchwork of open green space and wealthy little towns dotted with trees, all so different from the city streets where he'd grown up or the sterile claustrophobia of Facility 17. It was nice, being back on the surface, breathing fresh air and looking at the sky.

Then his body got the better of him and he fell asleep.

He woke when the car slowed. Aidan was asleep next to him, his head pillowed on Caleb's shoulder. Shit. They were at the border already? He should have planned for this. What would he say if they asked him who he was? He should have hidden himself in the trunk instead of napping in the back seat. Worse, what could he possibly say about Aidan?

At least Oz was awake and cheerfully alert in the front seat. He wasn't driving the car, but he'd still chosen the seat with the steering wheel, just in case.

A uniformed border guard peered in the window, saw Oz's face, and nodded respectfully. "Pass on through, sir."

They were already rolling away from the checkpoint by the time Caleb's brain caught up. The guard had barely glanced into the back seat. Aidan hadn't stirred, his face hidden against Caleb's shoulder. "They just… let us through?"

"I'm famous," Oz told him smugly. "I could get used to this, you know."

Caleb huffed. He recognized Oz's lighthearted intent, but

couldn't quite bring himself to laugh. Oz had sprung that love story on them during a live broadcast, and Caleb hadn't yet forgiven him. No matter the success of the ploy, it felt... dirty. Not because he was lying. Caleb liked lying well enough, or at least, he liked *acting*.

But Aidan had asked him to stop. Caleb wanted to respect that, and then he'd played along with Oz's idea. It was exploitative, and Aidan probably felt betrayed.

Caleb glanced down at his sleeping form, wondering when they'd get a chance to talk this out.

"He asleep?"

"Yeah."

"So I know this is none of my business, but... you and Aidan."

"Oh, now you want to talk about it? After you pulled that stunt on us?"

Oz's shoulders rose and fell. He didn't turn around. He wasn't driving; there was no need for him to keep his eyes on the road. "What did you want me to do, pull something from Quint's unknown backstory and wait to get fact-checked? If we get caught, I don't get paid. So I improvised. I watch a lot of soap operas. I know what makes a good story. And it worked. You were both great. So how much of it was acting?"

Out the window, an unremarkable blur of fields and towns passed by. Aidan slumped against his shoulder, warm and heavy, breathing peacefully.

Caleb didn't say anything for the rest of the drive.

As expected, the house had surveillance everywhere.

It was a sprawling and hideous hybrid of too many corners and columns in sand-colored stone, with a long loop of driveway curving in front, cutting through the manicured lawn. The gate slid open as they approached.

Quint had made his fortune in facial recognition algorithms, so it was only natural that his house was a nightmarish panopticon. Aidan's skin crawled as they crossed the threshold. Was there any greater proof that Quint was a soulless greed machine?

The door had opened as smoothly as the wrought-iron gate, but there was no one standing in the entryway to greet them. No sign of any staff anywhere.

"Hello," said the house, and Aidan jumped.

Caleb grabbed his hand and squeezed. Aidan couldn't tell if it was for show. He didn't want to like it, but he did.

"Hello," Oz said, too cheerful, like walking into what was ostensibly his own home was a grand adventure.

The house's voice was female, exceedingly polite and educated. "Welcome home, Mr. Quint. I wasn't expecting you. I apologize for the state of the house."

There wasn't a speck of dust in sight.

"Ah, yes, this visit is... spontaneous," Oz said. "These are my friends Caleb and Aidan, and they'll be staying here, so please give them access to the house. They'll only need one bedroom."

Oz smiled, proud of this bit of mischief. Caleb didn't react, his grip still warm and dry. Aidan removed his hand before his own slick palm became obvious.

He'd resolved to kiss Caleb, if Caleb ever seemed like he wanted to, but after today, he had no way of knowing what Caleb wanted. It could all be an act.

And now the house was always watching, and Oz had just forced them into an all-hours charade. Great.

"My apologies," the house said. "I'm having some trouble recognizing your friend on the left."

Aidan owed the Union so much for this disruptor. It was

already paying off. He'd expected Quint's house to have access to a database of unwanted visitors—his real identity among them, no doubt—and a much smaller list of approved guests. Apparently, it was broader than that. Even people arriving in Quint's company were scrutinized.

"He's foreign," Oz said. "He won't be in your database. But he's my guest."

"Thank you for making us welcome," Caleb said, speaking up. "How should I address you?"

"I respond to the name 'House'," the house said.

Somehow that made Quint seem like even more of an asshole, something Aidan hadn't thought was possible.

"Nice to meet you, House," Caleb said, with only the slightest hesitation. "Can I ask you something? What happens if there's a warrant out for someone and you recognize that person? Can you keep it to yourself?"

"I am obligated to log sightings in the state and federal databases."

"I see," Caleb said. "So even if Mr. Quint himself asked you not to, you'd still have to file a report."

"Correct."

"And if you don't recognize my... boyfriend, will that interfere with your functioning?"

"I cannot give him access to the house if recognition fails."

"But if he's with someone you recognize, he can get in and out with no trouble?"

"Correct."

"That's fine, then, House, thank you." Caleb shot him a significant glance, as if Aidan didn't already realize he had to keep his glasses on. He wondered if the AI had other types of recognition—some worked with body type or gait, and while he'd never heard a confirmed report of a smart house collecting samples from the people who lived in it, this stay would require some caution.

The house offered them a tour, which they accepted. Every room had been furnished right out of a catalog—albeit a very expensive one—with no personal touches anywhere in sight. No photos of friends or family. All the artwork blandly modern and shiny. It was almost like living in the sterile glass-and-steel corporate lobby, except there were more mahogany leather sofas.

And beds.

The master bedroom was palatial, but it didn't hold Aidan's attention. He wasn't going to be sleeping there. The guest room he'd be sharing with Caleb was almost as absurd, with its massive bed surrounded by empty space. The inside of the house wasn't as ambitious in style as the grand, grasping façade had led him to believe, and Aidan experienced some relief that the bedroom wasn't gilded or mirrored. It was, in fact, so boring that his eyes slid over everything without absorbing it. The walls, carpet, and furniture were in various shades of brown and grey, unrelieved by pattern or texture. There was a painting hung over the waist-height dresser in dark wood, a foggy landscape as drained of color as the rest of the room. The only color in sight came from the view out the glass doors: the pool was a searing turquoise, the lawn vibrantly green, the shroud of trees shades of red and orange.

The guest room was far away from where Oz would be sleeping. Good. Aidan didn't want him eavesdropping at night. The house was bad enough.

Not that any interesting sounds would emerge from their bedroom. Aidan might be willing to take this ruse that far, but Caleb had gone a little grey at the sight of the bed. Sympathy and hurt twisted in Aidan's gut. They'd been forced to improvise, and he wasn't looking forward to more public performances, either, but that didn't make it any easier to see Caleb looking so miserable at the thought of sharing a bed with him. If Caleb didn't want him, that was fine. Aidan knew how to behave himself, for fuck's sake. No reason to feel uncomfortable.

"Mr. Quint requests that you join him in his office," the house said, and Aidan was grateful for the interruption.

Oz was in Quint's office, sitting at a desk that was one massive pane of glass on a wooden stand and listening to the house read aloud all the messages he'd received that afternoon. There were a lot.

Aidan and Caleb sat down in the leather chairs facing Quint's desk. A young woman's voice played over the speakers, high and tremulous.

"Are you feeling well, sir? You cleared your schedule this week and then I see headlines about you on some psychic's private channel? I hope I'm not overstepping my bounds, but it's unlike you."

"Who is this?" Aidan asked, since Oz couldn't.

"Mr. Quint's assistant, Carrie Lee," the house said.

"—we've had eight requests for interviews just this afternoon," Carrie was saying. "I normally reject these kinds of things but, uh, I thought maybe I should ask? Anyway, let me know."

"Next message," the house said. "Today at 16:31, from Roger Somers."

A man's voice, his accent sharp with the city, began to speak. "Are you fucking kidding me, Quint? You want to start a charitable foundation and I have to find out about it from internet gossip about a fucking psychic? Have you lost your mind?"

The message ended there, and after a beat of silence, Caleb ventured, "And who is Roger Somers?"

"Mr. Quint's financial adviser," the house said. "The next

twelve messages are from members of the Quint Services board of directors."

"Right," Oz said. "Naturally. I think we'll skip those for now. Please write back to Carrie and tell her to accept all the interview requests. Don't care who they're from. Write back to Roger and tell him that he works for me."

"Please be more specific."

"Roger comma new line you work for me period your job is whatever I say it is period shut the fuck up and start liquidating assets period," Oz said. "No signature. I don't want to check for typos. Just send it."

Oz had really taken to this position. Aidan hoped to God that was how the real Quint spoke to his subordinates. But they were making it seem like he was having a mid-life crisis anyway, so maybe it didn't matter.

"Well, I think that's enough for today," Oz said. "I'm going to luxuriate in my ridiculously large bed and watch something trashy for the rest of the evening. I don't want to be interrupted."

He sauntered out, and Aidan and Caleb rose to follow him. Or Aidan rose and Caleb wobbled and caught himself on the chair.

"You need to eat," Aidan said. No wonder he'd been looking ill. He'd made a long jump earlier in the day and they hadn't eaten in hours. "House, show us the kitchen? I'd love to see it."

―――

Oz and Aidan both laid it on thick when they were acting. "I'd love to see it," *ha*. Aidan didn't give a shit about kitchens. He might love to vandalize it, but that was the limit.

Caleb couldn't tease him about it or tell him to tone it down. The house was watching. He'd have to couch whatever he said in other terms, and before he could, Aidan grabbed his hand and led him out of Quint's office, following the house's directions.

Aidan didn't seem distressed by the idea that the house might recognize and report him at any minute. Maybe it wasn't that different from the rest of his life. Caleb had always thought Aidan let his hair get long because he was too focused on his crusade to stop for a haircut, but maybe his unruly bangs were more strategic than that. Come to think of it, Aidan wore sunglasses on cloudy days and knit hats even when it was warm outside. He only owned about two-and-a-half outfits, but both were baggy, and one involved a hoodie. Aidan had a disguise just like Laila's, but Caleb had never noticed. That was just how Aidan always dressed.

It must be exhausting. Hiding all the time. Not having a safe haven of any kind.

Maybe while they were here, Caleb could divert some of Quint's money toward getting Aidan a place of his own. Nothing like this one, but somewhere to call home.

This house might be larger than all of Facility 17. It certainly had more open space. They crossed back through the obscenely large living room, with its couches that could sleep four people each. The kitchen was, if possible, grander. It was dusk, but in the daytime, those floor-to-ceiling windows must offer a view of the grounds.

Aidan let go of his hand. "What do you want to eat?"

"Literally anything." Caleb peered over Aidan's shoulder into the shiny, brightly lit fridge. It was mostly empty. Quint must have been living in one of his other mansions before he'd gone to Facility 17. He hadn't called ahead to say he'd be here—because he wasn't.

"Our options are pretty limited here. Can you call for delivery?"

Caleb paused until he realized Aidan was speaking to the

house. Once Aidan had ordered pizza, Caleb said carefully, "Our options *are* pretty limited here. I hope you're okay with the one we chose."

"The pizza?"

"Mmhmm," Caleb said, waiting for him to catch on, wishing the house wasn't listening.

"Oh," Aidan said. "You're worried I don't like *pizza*. But you don't have to be. I've been eating pizza my whole life."

"Sure, sure. But this pizza's not just any pizza. It's okay if you're mad at me," Caleb said. "I just didn't see a lot of other choices. There was no time to think of something better, and the... pizza was right there, so I made a split-second decision and ordered it."

"Yeah. You've done that a few times lately," Aidan said, and Caleb found a high corner of the room to stare at.

"Excuse me," the house said. "If you're unhappy with the pizza, I can provide you with a list of other takeout options."

"No, thanks," Aidan said. "We're going for a walk."

It was a long, strained walk down the manicured green hillside and into the cool, pine-scented woods. Caleb waved a hand in front of his face to clear away a few gnats, even that small motion taxing his poor, wrung-out body. It would be dark by the time they returned to the house, which now felt very far away.

"So. Pizza," Aidan joked.

"I think we're far enough from the house that we can say what we mean," Caleb said. He pushed the toe of his shoe into the carpet of pine needles. "I was trying to apologize for earlier today. You asked me to stop pretending, but when Oz went down that path, I followed him, and now we're stuck. I'm sorry. I should've thought of something else to say. I know you hate this."

"Yeah, but not for the reasons you think," Aidan said. He'd shoved his hands into his pockets, and he stared off into the trees before meeting Caleb's eyes again. "People *watched*, Caleb. That broadcast was weird and unexpected and—and *you*, people like you. You brought a lot to it. When all I did was tell the truth, you know, with evidence and serious journalism, no one cared."

"I think their caring was hindered by Quint burying the articles," Caleb said. "But point taken. It doesn't reflect well on us as a society that a real news story about torture goes nowhere, but as soon as you sensationalize it with gossip, the public's all in."

"If it works, I'll take it," Aidan said. "Unless you object?"

"I don't, not exactly. But..."

"But what?"

"It's not made up—or not all of it, I mean. The things Oz said about me leaving my life behind to come look for you, that's all true. He made it sound different. Grander, I guess. At the time, it was just a series of steps I had to take. Getting my job transferred to Facility 17, breaking my lease, putting a few things in storage. It never felt..."

"It never felt what?"

Caleb had gouged a long line in the dirt with the toe of his shoe. He kicked a few pine needles into it, but they failed to disguise what he'd done. He gave up and said, "Heroic. Romantic. Whatever Oz was going for with his story, it never felt like that."

"Oh."

"It felt urgent, but I don't remember panicking. You were missing. I did what I had to do." Aidan was staring at him, but Caleb had no better explanation. "Anybody would've done it."

Aidan shook his head, smiling a little. "That's definitely not true. But it's okay if you don't recognize yourself in the story Oz told. He was playing to the audience, just like you were. Oz is kind of a shit, but I'm not upset with you."

"Even though now we're gonna have to pretend all the time?"

"It'll probably be a gentler kind of publicity than what I'm used to," Aidan said. "And it's not all the time, it's only until we finish this and put Quint in prison. A week. You don't have to worry about me. If you're okay, I'm okay. So, are you okay?"

Caleb squinted at Aidan, who was still wearing his uncanny new face, wondering what he'd missed. The fatigue and hunger were making him stupid. "You didn't want me to pretend for two seconds when we were in the motel, and suddenly you're fine with a *week*?"

"Yeah. Are you? We can set some boundaries if it would make you more comfortable."

"Will you take your glasses off? I can't have this conversation with you if I can't see your face."

Aidan took off the disruptor. The sharp, slightly crooked shape of his nose re-emerged like a familiar landmark out of a fog, as did the freckle marking the high point of his left cheekbone. Caleb hadn't known it was gone, but now he would.

"I was serious about setting boundaries," Aidan said. "If you don't want to kiss in public, we don't have to."

"Kinda already crossed that line," Caleb said, his face warm. "But if you don't want—"

"I don't mind."

"Oh. Um. I don't mind either." He was too tired for his heart to be beating so hard. "So I guess we're both fine, then. Ready to go back to the house?"

"Yeah, yeah, of course, sorry to keep you out here so long. Let's get you something to eat." Aidan slipped the disruptor back on and his features blurred into someone else's.

Half an hour later, when three pizzas had arrived at the door, Caleb was stretched out on the couch trying to eat without dripping tomato sauce and melted cheese on himself. Caleb's entire apartment could have fit into this room, but having Aidan next to him warmed up the cavernous space and made it feel familiar. They'd done this a thousand times, sitting around with TV and takeout. Their talk hadn't changed anything between them—yet.

In the movie playing on the wall opposite them, a wizard disappeared from one spot and materialized in another. Not such a fantasy, that. Distantly, Caleb wondered how much pizza the wizard had to eat to sustain himself.

The next thing he knew, Aidan was nudging him awake. Caleb lifted his head from the couch—no, not the couch, Aidan's shoulder.

"Hey. We should probably move to bed."

"Mm," Caleb agreed, and followed Aidan to the bedroom, still bleary. He shucked off his clothes and crawled into bed without another word. A moment later, the other side of the bed sank under Aidan's weight. That was good. It was good to have Aidan here.

His presence meant everything would be okay. It had been that way when they'd shared a room as teenagers, and it was the same now. Caleb had grown used to the rustling of his movements as he settled into sleep, and the sound brought him peace. In the intervening years where they hadn't slept within hearing distance, Caleb had forgotten how reassuring—how *necessary*—it was to have Aidan in the room. Their time together in Facility 17 had brought it back to him.

They hadn't been sleeping in the same bed then. Half-asleep, Caleb couldn't find anything wrong with the new arrangement. Every time Aidan shifted, Caleb felt it. Sharing a bed was almost like touching. He smiled into his pillow and closed his eyes.

[12]
RABBIT

Aidan shot out of bed in the darkness, unsure where he was or why he'd woken, and then Oz flipped on the lights. He was grinning, already in a suit with his blond hair slicked back. What the hell?

"Learn to knock." Aidan lobbed a pillow at him, which he caught.

"No time. We have an interview to get to. We have *three* interviews to get to. Get up and get dressed." Oz's grin grew even wider as he examined Aidan and the rumpled bed, where Caleb was blinking blearily awake, his cheek still pressed to the pillow. Aidan had been spooning him.

Not on purpose.

"By the way, the public thinks you're 'surprisingly cute' and 'less of an asshole than I expected.' Those are direct quotes. People don't tend to write full sentences about Caleb, but I can show you some of the images if you want. There's a lot of women swooning and buildings bursting into flame."

Why had Aidan sat up? If he was still lying down, he could smash his face into the pillow and pretend this wasn't happening.

"Why is Oz in our room?" Caleb asked, still groggy but now sitting up. He was only wearing underwear. Aidan adjusted his glasses, which had been knocked askew when he'd sat up, and tried not to look. They hadn't discussed this—waking up half-undressed in bed together—in the woods yesterday. And Oz was watching, which made it weird.

"*Quint* is in our room because you're too damn charming and now we have to go on TV again."

"Oh." Caleb yawned. "But that's good, isn't it?"

Aidan grunted. He got out of bed and picked his jeans up off the floor.

"You can't wear yesterday's clothes," Caleb said, coming more fully awake. "If O—Quint is going to look put together, we should, too."

"I don't have other clothes. I wasn't expecting to become a public figure—at least not the kind people judge based on his clothes."

"You already were one. You think people were judging you solely on your ideology? Everybody gets judged on their clothes, whether they want it or not," Caleb said.

"Caleb is right," Oz said. "Besides, a lot of the commenters *really* don't like you, so whatever we can do to fix that, we should."

"I don't think new clothes are going to change much," Aidan said.

Oz ignored him. He turned toward the door and called over his shoulder, "Whatever you need for this, it's on me. We leave in an hour. Don't be late."

———

IN THE FIRST few years of the Runners' Union, Aidan had taken Caleb with him on some of his trips. Caleb had gotten to see more of the world; Aidan had gotten someone friendly and talkative to smooth things over with strangers. But the Union had grown, and grown more secretive, and now there were members Caleb didn't know.

Two of them—a white man with sandy blond hair and a Black woman with impeccably tight curls—had just appeared in his bedroom.

Well. Not his bedroom. A bedroom at one of Oswin Lewis Quint's many homes. If Caleb wasn't mistaken, the eyeglasses they were both wearing were disruptors. They knew the house might recognize them.

"Uh," Caleb said, glad he'd finished dressing a second ago, and then Kit and Laila showed up. Aidan hadn't warned him about this. "I guess some kind of announcement went out?"

"We heard you got famous," Laila said, and the two runners in disruptors nodded and held up the shopping bags in their hands with apologetic smiles. "And I heard we only have an hour, so let's get started."

"Hi Caleb," said the woman. "It's Lisa. And Craig."

Oh. He did know them, though it had been years. Squinting at their faces got him nowhere.

"Aidan said he needed our help," Craig said. "Other people called in favors from connections, but all I had to offer was my services as a delivery man."

The interviews. There were three lined up today not merely because the first one had gone viral, but because people in the Runners' Union had made it happen. Aidan had planned this. Caleb hadn't known any of that. It was bewildering, but also impressive.

"Now, if you'll excuse me, I do actually have a job," Lisa said. She vanished and so did Craig.

"I have way more than just one job," Kit said, cranky. "You've put us in a shitty situation, you know."

"We'll be as quick as we can," Caleb said, placating Kit on instinct more than anything else. A week was hardly any time to redistribute Quint's vast wealth, but it was an eternity to keep Quint at Facility 17.

Kit rolled his eyes and disappeared, leaving Laila in the room with them. She was already bending down to sort through the shopping bags, tossing things onto the unmade bed. "I'm staying," she said unnecessarily, since Kit had already left. "I'd rather be down here than up there sharing recycled air with—"

"Yes," Aidan interrupted. "We understand. The air in *this house* is much nicer."

"Oh, I bet," Laila said. She gave him a wicked smile, folding one of the thick black lines drawn down her cheek, further emphasizing the asymmetry of the abstract expressionist work she'd painted on her face. "I'm excited to take the whole tour. But not now."

She pointed toward some of the clothes she'd laid out. "Let's get you dressed."

CLEVER OF AIDAN TO call on the Union for help, even though he'd cringed through Laila's makeover. He shouldn't have—he looked good. Better, with the disruptor replaced by regular glasses. The familiar topography of Aidan's real face inspired a strange feeling in him, like passing by an old apartment, one he hadn't known he'd miss until after the lease was up.

Now that they were on set, Aidan was managing to smile for Jenna, their host, since the camera had turned its eye on him.

Jenna had a waterfall of impossibly glossy blond hair and a face that didn't move quite as much as it should. She sat in her armchair and directed her unchangeable smile at Aidan. "We've heard a lot from Oswin about how inspiring he found your relationship, and we've heard a lot from Caleb about when he realized he was in love with you. Aidan, I'd like to hear from you. Did you know you were in love with Caleb? Did you know he was in love with you?"

Caleb couldn't freeze, not when they were on camera, but his smile tightened. Even breathing shallowly, he could smell the strong solvents used to clean this set. Bleach wafted through the air. He gripped the arm of the couch, the knobby weave of its upholstery under his fingers, to keep himself from reacting further.

Of course one of their interviewers would eventually shift the focus to Aidan. Caleb couldn't control this forever. He had to let Aidan handle it.

Aidan crossed his legs and angled his body toward Caleb. On his other side, Oz perked up with interest, that drama-loving asshole.

Unlike Oz, Aidan wasn't wearing a suit. They'd decided it was out of character. His jeans weren't as ratty as normal, and his hair was wild in a more flattering way than usual. His shirt and jacket weren't wrinkled and baggy.

Caleb was loath to admit how much impact these slight changes had on him. He'd only ever thought of Aidan as *Aidan*, and all that entailed: fierce, scrawny, sharp, messy. He was still all of those things, or at least he would be tomorrow when no one was managing his wardrobe and hair for him, but there was something else there. Aidan didn't have the kind of beauty that made itself obvious at first glance, or all at once, but he wasn't bad-looking. It was a beauty that crept up on you, something that revealed itself in the angle of the light or the crook of his smile. Caleb found himself unmoored by this new knowledge; he wanted to stare at this person he'd known all his life, and it embarrassed him.

Then again, he was supposed to be staring. Playing it up. Might as well lean in.

Caleb had almost forgotten that Oz and Jenna were in the room, until she prompted Aidan by saying his name. Right. She'd asked Aidan a question. He gave her a weak smile. "I'm sorry, the truth is I don't know when I fell in love with Caleb. We were friends, and we were friends, and we were friends, and then... my feelings changed. I can't pinpoint the moment it happened."

Shit. What a disaster. That might be true but it was *too* true. It sounded like exactly what you'd say if someone had forced you to pretend to be in love with your best friend and you were a terrible liar. At least Aidan had been too reserved to sound nervous, but that wasn't much consolation. Caleb tried to catch Aidan's eye, to communicate some silent message about how to do better next time. *Put some feeling into it*. Aidan could be passionate about the plight of runners in the modern world. Why couldn't he conjure up some of that excitement for Caleb? When they'd been alone in the woods, he'd said he was fine with this arrangement. If that was true, he should commit to the role.

"And did you know Caleb was in love with you?" Jenna asked.

Instead of answering her, Aidan sought Caleb's attention and said, "Do you remember when Anna dumped you?"

Caleb blinked in surprise. The question was unexpected, and not in a promising way. "Dumped? Wait, which Anna are you talking about?" Probably Anna Keewatin, but there'd been an Anna Norris, too. And a third, technically, but that had only been one date.

"Right, because there have been so many women—it gets hard to keep track!" Aidan paused, smiled, and right on cue Jenna laughed, and the audience followed her lead. It was jarring to watch. His first answer had been so lackluster, and Caleb didn't know where he was heading with this. "And yes, I do mean *dumped*. I'm talking about Anna with the black hair and the high heels. You know, she was my favorite of your girlfriends."

Aidan was avoiding her last name. Then again, maybe it was wise to keep other people as far from this charade as possible.

Caleb said, "Oh, *that* Anna."

He hadn't always introduced Aidan to his girlfriends—for some reason, it rarely went well—but Anna had made the cut. Aidan was telling the truth about liking her, as far as Caleb could recall. She was a charismatic person. An actress, as warm in personality as she was beautiful. Caleb hadn't realized she'd made such an impression.

"I thought our break-up was amicable enough," Caleb added. They all had been. He didn't inspire strong feelings in anyone—including, it seemed, his best friend who was supposed to be pretending to be madly in love with him.

"So you don't remember what she said?"

Caleb did remember, and his stomach dropped. He couldn't say why. They'd already been mixing truth and lies for public consumption. It shouldn't make any difference to reveal one more thing.

He made a show of struggling to recall something, biting his lip. "I think she said—" he was getting good at blushing on command "—that the sex was good but that I had already made an emotional commitment to someone, and it wasn't her."

"Yes. That's exactly what she said." Aidan turned toward Jenna. "She was a really lovely woman, Anna. And great taste in shoes."

Where had that winning smile and sense of humor been earlier? And Aidan had never noticed anyone's shoes in his life. He'd grumbled about this morning's hasty styling session. Their host gave a tinkling laugh and Caleb smiled to hide his irritation.

"Perceptive, too," Aidan continued. "Anyway, Caleb was a little sad that this marvelous woman was ending things. He told me what she said mostly because he couldn't make sense of it. He hadn't ever been unfaithful. He wouldn't do that. So he didn't know what she meant."

When Jenna produced an "aww," Caleb nearly rolled his eyes. It wasn't cute, having your private emotional moments aired in public. Was this how Aidan felt yesterday when Caleb talked about him? Caleb should apologize.

As Caleb remembered it, he'd shared Anna's comment about emotional commitments because he'd wanted Aidan's reassurance. *She doesn't mean you, right? I mean, we're just friends. I'm allowed to have friends.*

The memory made him wince internally. What had Aidan said in response? Caleb couldn't recall anything beyond Aidan getting up from the couch and pulling a couple of beers out of the fridge.

"So," Aidan was saying to Jenna, not sounding nearly as chipper as he had at the beginning of this story, "that's when I knew Caleb was in love with me."

"Wow—" Jenna started to say.

"Bu that was *three years ago*," Caleb blurted, all thoughts of performance having fled.

Aidan put a hand on his knee and squeezed.

Caleb took a deep breath of bleach-scented air and felt a little faint. His urge to bolt might have stranded him in the Nowhere, except Aidan's fingers were digging into the flesh of his thigh. S*tay*, he thought, and almost burst out laughing. It was absurd to issue commands to his body like it was an unruly dog, and yet here he was.

Aidan and Jenna were talking to cover his silence, but they

might as well have been on another planet. It was one thing for Oz to twist the events of Caleb's life into some new shape to suit his purpose—Oz was a stranger, and they were paying him to lie—and entirely another for Aidan to do it.

Aidan had witnessed firsthand everything in the story he'd just told. There'd been a conversational flourish or two in the telling, but the facts were there. The sudden reversal put Caleb in mind of an optical illusion, as though they'd both been staring at the same drawing, one of them seeing a duck and the other a rabbit. Aidan had shown him the rabbit, and now he couldn't un-see it.

"Well, I think that's all the time we have for today," Jenna was saying, and then after a perfunctory goodbye, Aidan was ushering him off the set.

"Hey, did you mean that?" Caleb asked, before they were even really alone. A woman with a headset on rushed by, forcing them into the green room, a small, white-walled space furnished with a red couch and two matching armchairs around a low, round table. Neither of them moved to sit. Aidan shut the door, keeping his hand on the doorknob. His knuckles nearly matched the walls.

"I don't think it's wise to talk about what we *mean*," Aidan said in a low voice. "But no, of course not. I had to say something, and I'm not great at improvising, so that's what came out. If anything, it was wishful thinking on my part."

The whole room slid out of focus. "Wait, what?"

"You heard me." Aidan still had his hand on the doorknob, like he was poised to leave at any second, his whole body pulled taut. He kept glancing at the closed door.

Next to him, Caleb felt ponderous and slow. He quashed an

urge to lean against the door. "You... wish... I was in love with you? That's what you mean by 'wishful thinking'?"

"No, no, that's—no, I just meant—God, I feel like I'm crossing so many lines here, but that night was memorable, okay? Your girlfriend had just dumped you, you were looking for comfort, you came to me. It didn't go anywhere, but it could have."

"Oh. *That* kind of wishful thinking." Caleb laughed, but the explanation left him unaccountably disappointed.

The carpet was patterned in a dizzying grid of polygons in red, orange, and yellow. It was hideous, but the whole rest of the room carried with it the risk of looking at Aidan's face, or the certain knowledge that Aidan could see Caleb's face and every emotion that passed over it, which was worse. It was just jerking off, for fuck's sake. They both did it. He should be able to forget this, or at the very least, laugh it off for real.

Caleb wasn't going to do either of those things, and from the way Aidan was clearing his throat, neither was he.

"Sorry. I know that makes this—" his hand drew a looping squiggle in the air "—even weirder than it already was, and I know you're straight, and I won't ever bring it up again."

Caleb's head shot up at those words. "How do you know?"

"What?"

"How do you know I'm straight? Because I don't."

"Oh," Aidan said, far less panicked. "Okay. Sorry for assuming."

That wasn't the tone of someone finally seeing a rabbit after staring at a drawing of a duck. "You don't sound surprised."

"Do you want me to be surprised?"

Caleb wanted to grab him and shake him—or maybe he wanted to shake himself. "I don't know! What I don't want is for you to keep things from me. If you knew, you should have told me."

"Caleb," Aidan said, like Caleb was the unreasonable one here, when Aidan had been hoarding secrets for years. "It's hard to know what other people are really feeling, and even if you do suspect, people have to come to their own conclusions in their own time. If that's what you're doing, that's cool. Good for you."

"I mean, I—you're not mad? You don't think this is shitty timing? You don't feel like I'm using you?"

"I'm not mad and I don't think this is shitty timing," Aidan said carefully. "If you need to use someone, it might as well be me."

"Shit, Aidan, that's not what I meant."

"I'm serious. You know my work makes a real relationship impossible. This temporary arrangement is as close as I'm ever gonna get. It doesn't *all* have to be for public consumption."

Aidan smiled, a confident offer that rearranged his features into an unfamiliar shape. It made Caleb's heart bound in his chest with jackrabbit force.

Oz banged on the green room door, startling both of them, and called, "You two done in there? We have two more of these to do."

"Yeah," Caleb said, the door still closed, his eyes on Aidan. "Yeah, okay, let's do that."

[13]
TWO TRUTHS AND A LIE

"What are you two doing in here?" Laila asked, walking into Quint's massive kitchen like she owned it. Aidan and Caleb had just returned from their third interview of the day.

"Looking for something to eat?" Caleb ventured. He was far taller than Laila, and he had the access to the Nowhere that she lacked, but he clearly still found her intimidating. Aidan might have put it down to all that black makeup and spiky jewelry, but he'd seen Laila when she was only wearing a hospital gown. She was naturally commanding.

"No. No, you are not. You two have no idea how this works, do you? There are people up there trapped with—" She sucked in a breath to stop herself from saying Quint's name or something worse. Moderating her tone, she said, "You need to take advantage of your newfound fame. Go out. Be seen."

She turned away from them and opened the fridge, where there was one pizza box remaining from last night, containing two slices. Laila tore them apart and took one out.

"There isn't much food here," Caleb said in reluctant agreement. He'd been warm and talkative—almost excessively so—in their second two interviews of the day, after falling into silence during the first. He couldn't possibly want to go out and perform some more, but Laila had a point. Oz had talked to Quint's accountant, his lawyers, and the board of trustees of Quint Services, so their plan was in motion, but it couldn't hurt to make the most of their moment in the public eye.

"She's right," Aidan said. "Let me take you out."

"Pick somewhere *visible*," Laila said. She gestured at him with her half-eaten slice of cold pizza. Aidan looked considerably more put-together than usual—she'd dressed him herself—but he took her point. "I know what kind of places you frequent and none of them are acceptable. And spend some money. Quint's paying. I found a safe in the office."

She'd cracked a safe?

She added, "You were at interviews all day. I was bored."

"So you're... not coming?" Caleb eyed the pizza in her hand.

"No, I'm not coming on your *date*. Also—" She took another bite then waved a hand at herself while chewing. "Not into the public eye. Had enough of that already. Trust me, I am the wrong kind of famous."

"Right," Caleb said. He glanced at Aidan. If it had been fatigue shadowing his eyes, that would have made sense. Instead, they were wide and white. Aidan hadn't meant to scare him with that offer to fool around in private. "We'll see you later, I guess."

Aidan didn't know any trendy restaurants, but Caleb did. He jumped them right to the front door with no trouble, despite his nerves, and the host smiled and nodded at him. They were given a table right away.

Aidan slid into the seat opposite him and frowned at the menu, a short piece of paper with only five items listed. Every single one of them contained ingredients Aidan didn't recognize. He drummed his fingers on the blond wood of the table. Great.

"So, I, um, normally suggest the papas bravas to start? And they, uh, make really good cocktails, but I know that's not your thing." Caleb bit his lip.

The menu didn't faze Caleb. The host knew him. Caleb came here a lot, but Aidan had never heard him mention it. Because he brought his *dates* here.

A hurried server arrived at their table with glasses of water. She did a double-take when she saw Caleb, but that wasn't necessarily recognition. Aidan had seen plenty of women look at Caleb that way.

She smiled at Aidan, too, but that was customer service. "We'll have the papas bravas," he said, because Caleb wasn't saying anything. "And a ginger ale for me."

"A 'Two Truths and a Lie' for me," Caleb said. Aidan glanced at the cocktail list. He didn't know much about alcohol, but that one sounded strong.

She took note and departed.

Aidan nudged his foot under the table, startling Caleb. "Hey."

"What? Do you hate it? You hate it, don't you?"

Aidan took in the sleek modern light fixtures and the bustling open kitchen in the back corner of the narrow room. It smelled like frying oil and sizzling meat. The din of conversation surrounded them, but it was easy enough to talk across the tiny table. "I don't go out much, but I don't hate it. You don't need to treat me like this is our first date."

Caleb's mouth twisted into an uncertain shape. Not quite a smile. Smile-adjacent. His gaze darted to the side, checking the room. "Of course."

Shit. He thought Aidan was reminding him to keep up his act. That was the opposite of Aidan's intention. He touched the toe of his shoe to Caleb's ankle, forcing Caleb's attention back to him. "Tell me who you brought here."

"Wha—"

"C'mon. I know you brought women here. Did you bring any of the ones I knew? I know there were plenty I never even saw."

"You were busy," Caleb protested.

"And your dates never liked me," Aidan said, offering him a crooked smile. His current boyfriend was fake. His last boyfriend had been fake, too. As the world kept reminding him, he was a difficult person to like. "I don't hold it against you. I'm a divisive figure, so I hear."

"That's not why." In the soft, warm lighting of the restaurant, it was hard to tell if Caleb was blushing, but he took a long drink of water.

"I was *too* handsome," Aidan guessed, trying to make Caleb smile.

"It's... because of what Anna said. The story you told at the interview this morning," Caleb said, running his fingers through the condensation on the outside of his glass very intently. "I don't even know if I realized what I was doing. But after Anna said that, I stopped introducing my dates and girlfriends to you. I didn't want them to get jealous."

"Caleb, that's..."

"Ridiculous, I know."

"That's not what I was going to say," Aidan said. In truth, he didn't know what he'd been planning to say, but Caleb's confession made him feel a little unsteady.

Aidan should never have brought this up. He'd only wanted to distract Caleb from his nerves, not draw them deeper into trouble. He wasn't good at this—talking about feelings, being gentle, whatever it was. All he could do was ask the first question that came to mind. "How could you have a relationship with someone if you didn't feel comfortable introducing that person to your friends?"

"As you can see, I couldn't," Caleb said, sunny as always, clipping his words with a smile.

Aidan's stomach dipped, and then their food and drinks arrived. They ordered main dishes, and when the server was gone, Caleb took a gulp of his cocktail.

Aidan chewed his lip and opted to steer the conversation toward more harmless subjects: the food, the ambience, the neighborhood. When that ran out, he asked Caleb about his coworkers, trying to keep his questions in the domain of small talk without venturing into surreptitious intelligence gathering, which was his usual approach. He'd ask leading questions and then sift through the answers for clues that someone might be a runner, or might be prejudiced against runners. Caleb, on the other hand, talked about people because he liked them. The set of his shoulders eased as soon as Aidan led him to the subject.

"I didn't see much of Emil and Kit getting together, but the little bit I did see was pretty cute. Kit's so prickly, I didn't expect that from him. Remember all those times he rolled his eyes at us when we tried to get him to join the Union?"

"Vividly," Aidan said, pushing a piece of roast parsnip through the carefully styled drizzle of sauce on his plate. It was strange, eating with consideration for how things tasted instead of gobbling down whatever would take the painful edge off his hunger. Caleb had chosen a good restaurant, at least. "What do you mean, you didn't expect that from him?" *You don't think prickly people can fall in love?*

Caleb shrugged. "Falling in love makes you vulnerable. Kit always had his guard *all* the way up, you know? All those times we talked to him, he never softened, not even a little. And since they got together, I've seen them... smiling, flirting. Kissing."

Caleb reached for his cocktail, but the glass was empty. He

retracted his hand below the table like he'd been caught committing a crime. "Can I ask you something personal?"

"Yeah, of course."

"When did you know you were gay?"

When I accidentally transported myself through space to appear next to your bed in the middle of the night. "I think I sort of... always knew. I couldn't have articulated the feeling as a kid. Didn't have the words. I figured it out around twelve or thirteen."

"And how did you know? What made you sure?"

"I don't know how to answer that. I've never been any other way. What made you sure you liked women?"

Caleb pressed his lips together, and then said, "I'm trying to come up with an answer that doesn't sound crude." He laughed. "I guess it's the same as what you said. I always knew. That's why it's so strange to feel... something I didn't always know about. But since my double kissed me, I haven't been able to stop thinking about it."

Aidan's fork slipped out of his hand, clanging against his plate. He collected it sheepishly and then laid it down with care. "You didn't mention that."

"He caught me by surprise. I was embarrassed."

"Mm." Aidan would embarrass himself soon enough if he kept letting this play out like a movie in his head. Caleb's double had climbed into bed with Aidan and touched his thigh within minutes of encountering him. Apparently he'd been even more aggressive with Caleb. *He caught me by surprise.* Jesus. "I can see why you're still thinking about it."

"Oh, I didn't mean the kiss. I meant the rest of it, you know, feeling attracted to... men."

"Not just men who look like you?" Aidan asked. "Not that I'd blame you for setting yourself a high standard."

God, it was a pleasure to watch his Adam's apple bob as Caleb collected himself. "Aidan."

"What? It's a little late for me to pretend I haven't noticed. You're beautiful."

Caleb's many girlfriends obviously hadn't complimented him enough, if it was this easy to render him speechless. Aidan smiled, satisfied like he'd just stretched his legs after being cooped up for a long time. He didn't flirt often, but this—he'd been holding this in, and hadn't realized how much until just now.

Caleb was spared from further praise by the appearance of their server. He passed her a few bills, probably far more than what they owed. It was Quint's money, after all. Their server accepted the cash and then stopped in astonishment. Caleb leaned forward and gently closed her hand around it, saying, "We don't need change."

Aidan didn't miss the way she responded to Caleb's touch, extending her arm as he pulled his hand away, the unconscious motion an offer and a plea all at once.

People had assumed, back in high school and college, that Aidan was jealous of Caleb's looks and all the attention he received. If Aidan had been jealous of anyone, it was the women. They were allowed to go where he'd forbidden himself to follow. Watching their server gaze at Caleb, enchanted, he felt a pang of sympathy, and then relief. He was allowed now.

"It's true, then? He's really giving it all away?" she asked.

"Yeah," Caleb said, his eyes flicking to Aidan. "It's all true."

"Wow, that's—wow. Thank you. I can't tell you how much this—oh my God, sorry, I'm a mess." She sniffled, wiping the back of one hand across her eyes. "You two are cute together, by the way. I guess you know that. Everyone's been—I mean, obviously we wouldn't want to bother you, I didn't let anyone else come over here. But everybody, all my tables and everybody in the back, they've all been asking me about you all night."

"Thanks, we appreciate it." Caleb reached into his jacket for another stack of bills and handed that to her. She paused when their hands were touching, but this time it wasn't Caleb she was staring at.

Caleb pushed the money into her hands.

She nodded once and tucked it into her pocket, blinking rapidly, overcome.

"Hey, don't cry, I didn't mean to make you cry."

She hugged him as he tried to stand up. Caleb made bewildered eye contact with Aidan over her shoulder, and Aidan laughed silently.

"It's not even mine. It's pocket change to him. The world is fucked up and he should never have had it in the first place," Caleb was murmuring. "Just take it. Share it if you want, or keep it, it's yours now."

The room had quieted. People had stopped stealing surreptitious glances and were now staring. Someone's camera flash went off. Their server noticed and let go of Caleb. "Sorry, sorry, I didn't mean to make a scene. I won't tell anybody."

Caleb smiled and clasped her shoulder. "Tell whoever you want."

Aidan grabbed his hand on the way out of the restaurant, half for the benefit of the public and half because he wanted to. When the door swung shut behind them and they were alone with the streetlights, the distant noise of traffic, and the wind rattling through the dried leaves, he asked, "How much did Laila give you?"

"I didn't count it, but it's all hundred-dollar notes, so it's tens of thousands at least," Caleb said, heading toward the corner. It must be instinct pointing his feet that direction; they'd jumped to this neighborhood, and Aidan had assumed they would jump back. "I wasn't sure it was a good idea to carry around that much, but—"

"We could drop it down a drain and it would still be better than leaving it in Quint's safe," Aidan finished. "That was pretty slick, what you did in there. You're good at getting people's attention."

They had reached the end of the block, and Caleb turned away to check the oncoming traffic. It was an excuse. Aidan could tell by the way he shifted his weight from one foot to the other. "Thanks, I guess? I feel sort of weird and manipulative about it."

"You didn't do any harm in there, and I bet you did a lot of good," Aidan said. It was his fault Caleb was embroiled in this. "You wanna go home?"

"I'm still carrying a lot of money, and Laila said we should make sure people see us. We should go somewhere else. There's a bar around the corner."

Not exactly bursting with enthusiasm, but Aidan respected his dedication to their plan. He wished he could fix whatever was making Caleb sound so uncertain. He couldn't, of course. Even the *home* he'd mentioned was a lie.

Caleb knew the bar, another place Aidan had never been. It was even smaller and darker than the restaurant, its few lights reflected in the large mirror and glass bottles behind the bar. Every inch of space inside was taken up by absurdly attractive and stylish young people, perched on stools, lounging in leather chairs, leaning against the counter, and, in more than one case, pressing each other into dark corners, their hands disappearing into each other's hair and clothes.

Of course Caleb hung out here. He fit right in.

"I'm paying everyone's tab, with another round included," Caleb announced, using that long-ago high school theater training to project his voice loud enough to be heard over the music and conversation. The crowd parted. He strode inside and dropped two ludicrous stacks of bills on the polished wood of the bar. He winked at the bartender, an athletic young man whose hair was as artfully unkempt as his eyebrows were groomed. "Keep the change."

Caleb could carry off that kind of flirtatious confidence in public—God knew he had the jawline and the piercing blue eyes for it—but in private, if Aidan pointed it out in the right tone of voice, he'd fall apart. There was a thrill to being the only one in the room who knew the real Caleb.

The bartender set two shot glasses down on the bar in front of them and filled them with something amber. Whiskey, probably.

"Thank you, but I—" Aidan stopped addressing the bartender as Caleb curved a hand around both shots. A vision of Caleb drunkenly jumping himself into the Arctic flashed before his eyes. There was nothing to do but pluck one of the shots off the counter. Aidan could at least keep Caleb from drinking both of them.

Caleb watched him, surprise and skepticism taut in his expression. No backing down now.

Aidan had never taken a shot, but he was no stranger to swallowing. The liquor burned and his eyes watered, but he managed it.

"Alright then."

Was Caleb impressed or amused?

Before Aidan could decide, Caleb knocked his back. Tipping his chin up exposed the working of his throat as he drank. Aidan wanted to suck down a shot of *that*.

Caleb thunked the glass down on the counter and grinned at Aidan. Then he leaned forward, cupped Aidan's cheek, and drew him into a kiss.

Caleb had staged it perfectly—the approach, the angles—

but it was the parts no one else could see that interested Aidan. He swept his tongue into Caleb's mouth. Sweeter and slower than their first kiss, this one was laced with the liquor's subtle, smoky flavor, and it was just as potent. Aidan pulled Caleb closer, the smooth leather of Caleb's jacket sliding under his palms, and Caleb came willingly. Their bodies crushed together, one long hot line from lips to chest to hips. Thirst burned down Aidan's throat, and he drank and drank and drank.

Someone shoved past them, pushing them aside. They separated, breathless and glossy-eyed, barely aware of the people around them even after that reminder.

Christ. Aidan had to be careful. They were lying to everyone here, themselves included, drowning in a muddle of real and fake feelings. This had been a bad idea from the start and it grew into a worse one with every passing breath. Aidan still had to leave when this was over, because Caleb would never be safe while he was around.

Flushed and bright-eyed, Caleb beamed at the few people gawking at them. He inclined his head, one small drunken wobble short of actually taking a bow.

Aidan pressed his lips together like he could keep the taste of that kiss inside forever. His tolerance for alcohol was low and he could feel it swimming through him. But it hardly mattered. His preferred poison had always been doing things he knew he shouldn't, and Caleb was at the top of his list.

Aidan grabbed his hand and led him out of the bar. Once this scam was over, Aidan had to put some distance between them, but it wasn't over yet.

[14]
UNDISGUISED

Caleb wasn't that drunk, but Aidan insisted they take a cab home instead of jumping. Standing on the street corner, Caleb almost argued, but Aidan pulled him close. They glided into the kiss like stepping into the Nowhere, free and weightless. There was nothing except the sweetness of Aidan's mouth.

When Aidan broke away, Caleb was startled to discover they were still standing on the same busy corner. Pedestrians flowed around them. Late night traffic whirred by. Good. That was good. Another public display.

Aidan hailed a cab, the streetlight slanting across the sharp angles of his face, catching on the lenses of his glasses. When one pulled over, Aidan opened the door for him. Caleb shuffled himself into the back seat, ungainly, and Aidan keyed in directions to Quint's mansion and then sat back, paying no attention as the driverless vehicle pulled away from the curb. His eyes were on Caleb.

"There's no one watching us now."

"Right. No need to pretend." It was impossible to keep the disappointment out of his voice. He'd left the bar elated, but

Aidan's reminder had punctured his mood. There would be no more kissing, absent their audience.

"Mm," Aidan said, closing the space between them. "I told you it didn't all have to be for public consumption." He pushed Caleb's jacket off his shoulders. Surprised and intrigued, Caleb let it slip from his arms and fall to the floor.

Whatever Aidan was doing, Caleb was going to let him.

Aidan touched his face again, brushing his hair back, then slid his hands down Caleb's bare arms. That shouldn't have made him shiver, but it did. Aidan's fingers rested lightly against the insides of Caleb's wrists. Could he feel Caleb's pulse racing?

They had almost all their clothes on, they'd barely touched, and Aidan hadn't said a single dirty word, and yet somehow it was already one of the most sensual experiences of his life.

Aidan stroked a finger down his cheek, then from the hinge of his jaw to the tip of his chin.

Caleb's throat worked. He didn't say anything.

Aidan leaned up and pressed his lips to Caleb's. It wasn't rough or aggressive, the way Caleb's double had kissed, and it wasn't showy, the way their public kisses had been. It was powerful in its own way. Gentle, slow, and ruinously thorough, it was a kiss that said *I know what you want*.

Caleb couldn't argue with that. He couldn't even remember his hands, hanging idle at his sides, until the kiss left them both breathless. Caleb came up for air and dove back in, bringing his hands up to clutch at Aidan's back. Aidan pushed him down into the seat and got him drunk on whiskey-flavored kisses. It felt impossible. How could Aidan exude such power? How did they still have all their clothes on?

The lights of the city smeared in streaks outside the darkened windows until they dimmed into the sparser stars of suburban porches and windows, and Aidan didn't stop. He reached for the hem of Caleb's t-shirt, his fingers skimming the skin of his belly. Caleb raised his arms and let Aidan strip him.

His t-shirt floated down into the footwell. Distantly, it occurred to Caleb that he'd done that for women before, but he'd never asked any of them to do it to him. He wouldn't have. It wouldn't have fit.

Aidan slid his palm down Caleb's chest, steady and inexorable, like he could tame the pulse within. But that wasn't his goal. He dipped his fingers under the waistband of Caleb's jeans and Caleb twitched helplessly beneath him. Then he drew his fingers over the hard ridge of Caleb's cock under his clothes. Fuck.

Like a passing flash of headlights through the window, Caleb suddenly saw all his previous experience in terms of the role he'd played. Over and over, he'd cast himself as a caricature of how men were supposed to behave around women.

Now it was only him and Aidan, and there was no script. He didn't know how this would go. The freedom thrilled and terrified him, and he kissed Aidan for it, his fingers in Aidan's hair, their noses bumping together. Aidan kept his hand between their bodies, the pressure a promise. Aidan undid his fly and Caleb obligingly lifted his hips so Aidan could tug his jeans and underwear down his thighs.

Aidan gave him a look that seared right into him, so hot it was almost painful. The instant between the look and the touch stretched taut until Caleb wanted to say *do it, please do it*, but the words caught. Waiting was good. It hit him while he was staring at Aidan, still dressed and making a leisurely study of Caleb's nakedness. The restlessness he felt, the way he squirmed and shivered at every flick of Aidan's eyelashes, that meant the best was yet to come. Caleb wanted this to last, and if that meant he had to lie here dripping and aching while Aidan watched, he'd do it.

When Aidan finally touched him, one hand wrapping around the base of his cock, the jolt of it nearly liquefied Caleb. He gasped. Then Aidan bent down.

"Holy fuck." Caleb didn't mean to speak in a reverent whisper; he didn't mean to speak at all.

The wickedness of Aidan's smile registered for only an instant before he dipped his head and slid the length of Caleb's cock into his mouth.

Caleb had a lot more to say after that, but none of it was words. His breath stopped and started in a dozen little hitches and whines. He choked out praises and swallowed back pleas. It was a delicious kind of torment, being worked over by someone with such incomprehensible patience. Slick and slow, his lips locked around Caleb, Aidan gave him just enough to fuel his need for more, never enough to let him find release. Caleb's hips jerked. He could thrust into Aidan's mouth. It would calm the urgency tightening in his body, but it would also speed them toward the end. So he held still.

Caleb rested a hand on Aidan's head, not to hurry him along or exert control—Caleb was under no illusion as to who held all the power in this situation—but to feel the softness of his unruly black hair. It was a touch for touch's sake. Aidan was giving him a gift. Caleb responded with as much active gratitude as he could, given that his thoughts were reduced to the diameter of Aidan's mouth.

Aidan curved his free hand around Caleb's hip. His grip was just firm enough that his fingers indented the soft flesh there, and that touch—warm, encouraging, authoritative—tipped Caleb over the edge. He came with a sigh, spilling down Aidan's throat, fingers clenching in his hair.

Aidan swallowed and kissed the inside of his thigh. When he tilted his head back, his lips glinted with wetness. An unspoken challenge burned in his expression, so Caleb seized him by the shoulders and dragged him up into a faintly salty kiss. He didn't care. Aidan's tongue was in his mouth. What else was there to care about?

The car rolled to a stop. They'd arrived. A huff of laughter interrupted their kiss, and Caleb was glad he wasn't the only one who'd forgotten where they were. He pulled his clothes back on and paid for the cab, leaving another stack of hundred-dollar notes on the back seat. Something about the money made the whole experience feel sordid, but Caleb did his best to focus on the rest of it: the warm after-sex languor, the glee of having gotten away with something filthy and thrilling.

The cab drove off as soon as they'd exited. Thank God none of the house's other occupants would be awake to greet them at the door; the house itself was another question. As they stood at the edge of the long, looping driveway, far from the pool of yellow porch light illuminating the house's absurdly grand entrance, Caleb nudged Aidan. "Maybe if we make out the whole time, the house won't see your face."

"Not that I don't see the appeal of that plan, but I'm gonna have to breathe at some point, and I'd rather not go to prison for it."

"Well," Caleb said. "I guess we'd better use protection, then."

Aidan laughed and pulled off his glasses to exchange them for the algorithm-disrupting pair he was carrying in his jacket pocket. Before he could put them on, Caleb put a hand on his arm.

"Hey, just... give me a second."

"So we can stand here in the dark? I can think of better uses of our time."

"Shh." Caleb cupped his face with both hands, the skin velvet and warm to the touch, and mapped the arcing ridges of his cheekbones, softening and dipping under his eyes, then rising toward the peak of his nose. The disruptor could only change what he saw, not what he felt. "I want to know it's you."

He leaned in until their noses knocked together and their foreheads touched, until he could feel Aidan's breath on his lips when he said, "You will."

And then they were kissing again, deeply and at such length that when they came apart in the chilly night air, Aidan laughed and said, "Seriously, though, I do actually want to go inside."

He slipped the disruptor on, and they made their way to the door. If not for the gigantic mansion looming over them, it would have felt just like sneaking back to one of the many apartments Caleb had shared, trying to bring his date home without waking his roommates. They tiptoed through the hallway, hand in hand like they were navigating the dark. They weren't, since the house had lit their path, dimming the lights appropriately. Like so much technology, it was creepy and convenient at the same time.

Caleb forgot it as soon as the door clicked shut behind them. In the clean, climate-controlled air of the bedroom, the scent of sex clung to both of them, rich and heady, rousing some animal part of his brain. He pushed Aidan up against the door and kissed him again, reaching between them and gripping Aidan's cock through his clothes.

"Can I," Caleb started to ask, then interrupted himself to let his teeth graze the side of Aidan's neck.

"Yeah," Aidan said, pushing him to his knees with none of the careful deliberation he'd possessed in the car. He shrugged out of his jacket and tossed his shirt on the floor.

"I don't know what I'm doing," Caleb said. Aidan already knew that. There was no need to blurt it out. He blushed and glanced up.

Aidan carded his fingers through Caleb's hair. "I have faith you'll figure it out."

Aidan's glasses were crooked, but the illusion filter was still in place. It must be set to mask changes in the wearer's expression, since his cheeks were untouched by color, but a flush curled down his naked chest. High up his throat, a pulse beat rapidly under his skin, undisguised.

As Caleb undid Aidan's fly and shoved his pants down, his pupils grew huge and dark, leaving only a slender ring of green iris visible, and then reset to normal. Uncanny.

Aidan's body, at least, wasn't hiding anything. His cock was uncircumcised, hard and thick, its based surrounded by a nest of wiry black hair. Caleb had seen it before, but not like this.

It had never occurred to him that he wanted to look. That struck him as absurd now. He licked his lips. "I've wasted a lot of time in my life."

Aidan choked on a laugh, and then said, "Well, this isn't going to take long."

Caleb wet his palm, dragging his tongue along it to make sure, and then took hold of Aidan's cock.

"You liked it?" Arguably the answer was right in front of him. But he wanted to hear Aidan say it. Had that been different or special for Aidan? Maybe other people were having wildly transcendent sex all the time and Caleb had just never known it could be that way. "What we did in the car, I mean. You liked it?"

Aidan exhaled roughly as Caleb stroked him. "Yes."

"I liked it too," Caleb said. That didn't come anywhere close to how he really felt. He couldn't have come up with other words, not while he was gliding his hand back and forth, reveling in every tiny response he elicited: a shiver here, a hitch in breath there. His pale, slender body concealed nothing, and Caleb couldn't look away. Everything in Aidan that he usually thought of as *sharp* was rendered delicate, fragile, vulnerable. He was so beautiful. Caleb should have noticed before.

With great care, he leaned forward and took Aidan's cock into his mouth. It was heavy against his tongue. His first tentative, exploratory lick made Aidan groan and drop his head back against the door. Heat raced over Caleb's skin. He'd wanted this and hadn't understood how much.

Caleb moved, using his hand and his mouth at once, taking his cues from the rhythm of Aidan's hips. Aidan's hand fisted in his hair and Caleb took him as deep as he could.

Aidan's orgasm spurted against his tongue, sudden and hot. He trembled, breathing hard, but made almost no sound.

Caleb swallowed, wiped his hand over his mouth, and leaned his head against Aidan's thigh. Then Aidan pulled him up and kissed him, and the two of them stumbled into bed, shedding their remaining shoes and clothes along the way.

Aidan lay behind him, stroking his back, his fingertips leaving four trails of sensation in their wake. Something about the act—sensual, freely given—was almost more intimate than the sex. Caleb closed his eyes and melted into the mattress. He'd expected the sex to be fun, and it had been. He hadn't expected to feel *cherished*. This tenderness didn't fit into what Aidan had offered him, a few days of low-key fooling around in private, but maybe Aidan was like this with everyone. It must be great to be in a real relationship with him.

Caleb could feel his breathing and his thoughts slow down with sleep, drawn into the languid rhythm of Aidan's hand.

The strangest part wasn't that he'd given another man an orgasm, but that the man in question was Aidan. And there'd been so much that Caleb hadn't known about him. It was like discovering a new room in the house he'd always lived in.

[15]
SOLIDARITY

His idiot science-fiction twin had robbed him. Some cash and his tablet, nothing too important. There was more cash and an unloaded CX-93 locked in the bottom drawer of his desk, but neither the gun nor its ammunition had been touched. Caleb would bet all that stolen cash and more that his alternate self didn't know how to shoot.

He didn't know how to cover his tracks, that was for sure. The door log didn't show any new entries, which meant he'd used the Nowhere, at least. But *A Tale of Two Cities* had been lying face-down, open to the last page he'd read, and now it was closed, its black-and-gold cover face-up and as good as a signature. Someone who had the inclination and the time to flip through his book mid-robbery, but not pick the lock on the desk drawer in search of better loot. An idiot.

More of an annoyance than a real crime, the robbery still pissed him off. And those people on the other side, they'd fucked with him first. Going through that rift they'd ripped open had made his shakes worse. And they'd stolen the telekinetic from his cell. Spying was justified. Retrieving his stuff and scaring the shit out of his dumb twin would be a bonus.

So he'd crossed over. It had taken him days to get any traction. His first few visits to that other reality, his double hadn't been anywhere in sight. A search of his room—undetectable, because he was fucking good at his job—had produced the stolen tablet, abandoned now as if it was worthless, which it was, over here.

He'd spied on the other occupants of the asteroid, which they called Facility 17, enough to learn their names and jobs and a lot of other shit he didn't care about. For people who were destroying space-time, either accidentally or on purpose, they were boring. There were a couple of hushed, concerned conversations about the rift, but nobody took action. They mostly talked about someone named *Quint*, a name that meant nothing to Caleb. They didn't like this Quint, and Caleb, not liking them, figured the enemy of his enemy was a useful person to know. He wasn't stupid enough to make friends.

A tablet for a tablet, then. Stealth came naturally to him after years of practice, but he hardly needed it to steal a tablet from these people. Living on an asteroid, they weren't accustomed to worrying about petty theft, and they left their belongings in the common room all the time.

His twin's room was empty, the mattress that had been on the floor removed to somewhere else. His twin and the scrawny guy who'd been sleeping in here had left, and their absence felt permanent. They'd obviously done something down on the surface of his world, since they'd stolen cash, although not enough to get by for long. That meant they'd probably crossed back over.

On his newly stolen tablet, Caleb attempted a search: Oswin Lewis Quint. The same name he kept hearing in whispers over here.

At first, there was no signal, which struck him as unlikely. This was a high-tech facility in space; even if something went wrong with the array of antennae, they wouldn't leave themselves without communications for long. A broken connection might be the result of tampering. If the problem was physical, he was fucked. He wasn't equipped to go outside and fix the array himself.

Luckily, it wasn't physical. It still took him forty-five goddamn minutes to hack his way around it. This search had better be worth it.

Quint was rich as fuck in this reality, but his double was nobody. That meant Caleb's double was trying to run a scam. Interesting. He hadn't struck Caleb as the type. Too trusting. Too dumb.

There were a lot of videos in his search results. The one with the most views was behind a paywall, but whoever owned this tablet had a credit card stored in its memory, so Caleb charged it to them and watched, of all things, a psychic.

Caleb had once been sliced open in a fight and had to stuff a gleaming, bloody handful of guts back into the wound before he could jump back to Heath and have her patch him up. That hadn't fazed him. It was the job.

This video on the other hand... He didn't give a damn about Quint, or telling the truth, or love, or much of anything, but there was something disgusting about it.

His own face, looking like that, and it wasn't even real.

Caleb dredged up a reluctant admiration for his double's skill. He'd thought the other Caleb was a naive idiot, but instead, the man was so slick at lying that it made his skin crawl. Christ.

Caleb didn't want anything to do with that. His double wreaking havoc on a stranger's reputation wasn't his problem. The whole fucking multiverse was falling apart, and more importantly, so was he. When it came to the shakes, no amount of gritting his teeth and holding his guts in could save him. He didn't have time to fuck around.

The first time he'd encountered Aidan, Aidan had said something about not being a runner *anymore*. Either these people had a way to fix the multiverse, and possibly him, or they didn't. Caleb erased his browsing, wiped the tablet down, and stole back into the common room to return it to where he'd found it.

He was about to jump when he heard shouting in the hallway.

"You can't keep me here!"

"Seems like I can."

Caleb didn't recognize the first voice—male, imperious—but the second voice belonged to the short, purple-haired guy, Kit, one of the few people at the facility he hadn't immediately known. He was a born runner and had no double.

Kit continued, his tone nasty, "Or maybe you'd prefer I take you elsewhere? There's a whole lot of space out there, if you're feeling cooped up in here."

"One injection of suppressant and you'll never touch the Nowhere again," the other man said, quiet and icy. "You'll be just as stuck as me. Then we'll see how brave you are."

An injection that could un-make runners. Holy shit. Aidan had been telling the truth. These people had a cure for the shakes and they were using it to threaten each other. Caleb risked a peek into the hallway and was confronted with a face from the video he'd just watched, but redder and more disheveled. Oswin Lewis Quint.

"Uh-huh," Kit said, affecting nonchalance. The mention of the injection had scared him. That must mean it worked. "Good luck with that. We destroyed it all. Shot it right out the airlock with the rest of our trash. I'd be happy to demonstrate."

Caleb had to get his hands on that suppressant. Quint knew about it. He waited for the sound of their bickering to recede down the hallway, marking which way they went, and then crept after them. When Kit came back from locking Quint into his room, Caleb ducked into a storage closet only to discover a makeshift surveillance room. One of the screens showed the telekinetic lying motionless in an empty room and another showed Quint pacing a sparsely furnished bedroom. The telekinetic—Lange—was of interest to Heath, but she'd want a cure for the shakes just as much as he did.

It was worth a jump to get into Quint's room. He made sure to turn off the security camera first.

Caleb startled Quint, but he played it off, smoothing his suit jacket and radiating cool disdain. "You. The nurse."

"Whoever you think I am, you're wrong," Caleb said. He'd dressed in his double's scrubs for this visit, just in case anyone saw him, but now Quint needed catching up, which was irritating. "There are other universes with people who look identical to the ones here. They've got your double down on the surface, pretending you committed a bunch of crimes. There are videos everywhere."

"Everywhere except here, where communications have been down since I arrived," Quint said. "Who are you?"

"Someone who wants to make a deal," Caleb said. "You know how to make a suppressant for runners. I want it. In exchange, I can get you out of here and help you disrupt the scam they're running on the surface."

Quint had gone perfectly still. "Who are you? Why do you want the suppressant?"

A stupid question, he thought, and then came to the sudden realization that none of these people knew about the shakes. They'd developed a suppressant for the sole purpose of grounding people who'd been born runners.

Sinister shit, but that shouldn't bother him. So this world wasn't a nice place. Neither was his.

"None of your business," Caleb said. Quint wasn't getting an itemized list of his weaknesses, Jesus Christ. "We both know you're not getting out of here without me. Can you get me the suppressant or not?"

"I can," Quint said. "How soon can we leave?"

―――――

CALEB WOKE UP DESPERATELY HUNGRY, which was at least becoming familiar. Someone was pounding on the bedroom door. Not Oz, then. He would have just barged in.

"Kit's here," Laila called. "Meet us in the kitchen."

Caleb sat up. Aidan was still pressing his face, glasses and all, stubbornly into the pillow. Caleb poked him. "Come on."

Aidan turned over, his cheek marked with pillow creases, and Caleb's whole world wobbled. Holy shit. They'd slept together. And then... really slept together, pillow creases and all.

If this was an experiment, he'd confirmed his hypothesis. *I'm bisexual*, he thought, trying it on like a new set of clothes. It fit. After all his hand-wringing, it was nothing like getting injected and developing new senses and abilities. He didn't feel different.

Caleb glanced at Aidan, the messy nest of his black hair and the long, pale stretch of his naked back. Well. He felt *something*.

Emboldened, he slid one hand from Aidan's shoulder blade down to his hip. When Aidan made a pleased, sleepy noise into the pillow, Caleb felt the same pulse of satisfaction as when he'd touched other partners. It was a familiar cocktail of emotions—pride, tenderness, yearning to do it again—and yet it was new, too. He liked sleeping with men. He liked sleeping with Aidan.

Aidan hadn't spoken of the future, beyond putting Quint

away, and he'd only offered to fool around in private while they were also fooling the public. They'd be putting Quint in prison in a matter of days, and then there'd be no need for their romance act. A week wasn't long enough. Last night had been so good. Caleb wanted more of that.

To judge from Aidan's languid smile, so did he. Heat washed over Caleb's skin and he hurried out of bed. He finger-combed his hair into something halfway presentable and figured he'd leave the question of real clothes for later. Behind him, Aidan groaned and got out of bed.

Kit was seated on one of the bar stools at the kitchen island, wearing an atrociously green leather jacket and some kind of metal-mesh face veil, its headband buried in his violet hair. The veil was probably meant to deter the smart house's facial recognition, but since he was half-lifting it out of the way so he could drink a cup of coffee, Caleb wasn't sure how reliably it would work.

"Good morning," Laila said. She was standing by some very shiny appliance that must be a coffee maker, dressed all in black again, with makeup scrolling across her face like calligraphy. "Coffee?"

"Yes, please," Caleb said. He almost blurted *I'm bisexual*, because it felt momentous, worth sharing, but he couldn't say it here. They'd told the house Aidan was his boyfriend. Maybe the AI couldn't catch discrepancies in what they said to each other, but for all he knew, the tech was predicated on remote human observers. A distressing idea. His disappointment at not being able to tell Laila outweighed his concern. He would've told Kit, too, even though they weren't that close. Everyone in the kitchen was some flavor of queer, and Caleb wanted them to know he belonged, too.

"You okay?" Laila asked.

"Yeah."

Laila pulled a lever and the coffee machine whirred, and a second later she pressed a mug into his hands.

"Good morning to both of you."

"Morning," Aidan said. He perked up when Laila offered him some coffee.

"Kit scared the shit out of me this morning, nearly made me scald myself," Laila said, nudging him affectionately. "He hasn't told me why he's here yet."

"Why else would I be here? I'm here to talk about Q—"

"House," Aidan said loudly. "Where are the spatulas?"

Some of the under-the-counter lighting blinked, indicating a drawer. Aidan pulled it open and then gave Kit a significant look.

"Ugh," Kit said at this reminder that they were being watched.

While Kit contemplated how to rephrase whatever it was he wanted to say, Aidan kept opening cabinets and drawers. He looked just like he had in the other Heath's exam room, ransacking her drawers for possible antidotes, except here he was just hunting through a fridge. After a while, he must have found what he was looking for, because he turned to Caleb and said, "You want breakfast?"

"You're... cooking?"

Caleb had never seen Aidan cook. He'd never had a kitchen of his own—unless Caleb counted the six months Aidan had spent living with Brian, the ex whose name they never spoke. Caleb didn't know much about that period of Aidan's life. Maybe it had been domestic bliss. Maybe he and Brian had cooked gourmet meals for each other every night.

Even as Caleb recognized the absurdity of the thought, he had to swallow the sour taste it put into his mouth.

Whatever had happened with Brian, the rest of Aidan's adult life had been spent as an itinerant couch surfer. When he crashed at Caleb's apartment, it was literal. He was always on the verge of passing out. It fell to Caleb to cook for him.

Caleb wasn't a great cook, only an adequate one. He could keep himself—and Aidan—alive.

"You're hungry, aren't you?" Aidan said. He pulled out a mixing bowl and started measuring dry ingredients.

"Some of that better be for me and Kit," Laila said.

"Of course," Aidan said. "Solidarity and all that. Wouldn't let you go hungry."

"You know, I've been meaning to tell you, I think I'm—what, Kit, don't look at me like that," Laila said.

"Can we leave aside all this stuff about solidarity and personal anecdotes for a second?" Kit said. "I'm here to tell you that you need to move faster. Things haven't been going great for us."

They'd had Quint in space for four days and something had already gone wrong. A whole interview's worth of questions came to mind, but Caleb couldn't ask any of them. He stayed silent and sat on one of the barstools at the ridiculously large marble island in the center of the room, watching in fascination and trepidation as a pat of butter sizzled in the skillet and Aidan mixed pancake batter in a bowl. A sight rare enough to relish.

Caleb didn't want it to be rare.

"You know that... cat we adopted?" Kit asked, interrupting his thoughts. "The one with the shitty attitude?"

"Yeah," Aidan said. "Thanks for giving it a home."

"I'm not so sure we made the right choice," Kit said. "It's a little bastard and it wants out. Worst of all, I think it's about to figure out how to open doors and cause real trouble."

"Shit," Aidan said, flipping a pancake wrong and smearing batter across the skillet. "We'll be done soon, I think. We're, uh, moving some things around. But we'll be happy to take that cat off your hands in a few days and give it a forever home. Thursday, probably. Friday at the latest."

"It is Sunday fucking *morning*," Kit said tightly, like the number of hours in the day really mattered. "This has been the longest four days of my life and it's only been a week and a half since I got stranded in the wilderness and nearly froze to death. *Bad mood* doesn't begin to cover it. If you make me put up with that cat much longer, I'm gonna eject it into space."

"Okay, okay," Laila said, putting a hand on his arm. "We're all a little on edge. You can have the first plate."

"Fuck off. You're playing house down here and we are trapped up there."

Caleb stared at the counter, guilt closing his throat. He *had* been enjoying himself. It hadn't even been half an hour since he'd dreamily wondered if he and Aidan could prolong this week somehow. That wasn't fair to Kit and everyone else at Facility 17 who had to deal with Quint.

"Where is... Quint?" Caleb asked, glancing around like Oz might pop out at any moment. The grand floor-to-ceiling windows were open this morning, letting in brilliant daylight and offering a view of the mansion's manicured lawn. The trees surrounding the ground were a mixture of evergreen and yellow-orange fall foliage. The wind rattled their branches, showering the lawn with leaves.

"Asleep, I think," Laila said. "He keeps weird hours. Not that I'm one to judge."

"What was it you wanted to say earlier?" Aidan asked Laila. "You said you'd been meaning to tell us something."

She set her mug on the island and stretched luxuriantly. "I've been feeling good these past few days. Better. Like I could go anywhere I wanted."

"Because you're taking some kind of medication?" Aidan asked.

She shook her head. "No, I think it's more of a 'time heals all wounds' situation. Things going back to normal. You don't feel it?"

"I don't know," he said, staring down into the skillet.

"That's really good news," Kit said to Laila.

Aidan plated some pancakes, then passed them to Caleb along with silverware and a bottle of maple syrup.

"And mine?" Kit asked.

"They're almost ready, hold on a second," Aidan said, waving the spatula at him.

"Uh huh."

As Aidan was serving Kit and Laila, Oz walked into the kitchen with a jewelry box in his hand. He grinned. "Didn't know we were all doing brunch together this morning! Look what just came in."

He opened the jewelry box and pulled out a necklace so brilliantly yellow it could only be 24-karat gold. Everyone stared, and he winked in response. "I ordered a lot of these, among other things. Easier to transport, you know?"

"Smart," Caleb said, although the maple-syrup aftertaste in his mouth had suddenly turned sickeningly sweet. Was it just Oz's resemblance to Quint, their real target? Or was it something about the necklace he was casually tossing up and down?

Kit had already finished his pancakes. He pushed his plate away. "I have to go. But I'm coming back tomorrow, and I hope you have good news for me by then."

He vanished, and Laila sighed. "You want a cup of coffee, Quint?"

"Sure," Oz said, cheerfully oblivious to the tension in the room. Aidan grimaced and plated some more pancakes, then turned off the stove. "How was your date last night?"

Caleb struggled to control his face at the mention of last night. "Good," he said. "Public."

He'd almost forgotten the part where he gave away stacks of hundred-dollar bills. Aidan had eclipsed the rest of his memory. "We gave away a lot of cash. Is there more in the house? I think it would be good to keep that up. We can go out again this afternoon."

Oz frowned. "It doesn't seem necessary. We're doing all these interviews. That's enough, isn't it?"

"It can't hurt," Aidan said. "It's pocket change to you, anyway. What does it matter?"

Oz had stopped tossing the necklace and was now curling his fingers carefully around it, like one of them might snatch it out of his hand. "Sure. Of course. Why not? I'll withdraw some cash for you."

Oz left without eating, and the four of them shared a moment of silence.

"He's in a hurry," Caleb said, trying to lighten the mood. They could handle Oz. They could handle Quint, too. Things were okay. Things were good, even. Here he was, sitting in this palatial kitchen, eating pancakes and carrying out a scam with his best-friend-maybe-something-else-now, and strangest of all, it seemed to be working.

[16]
FORTY-TWO

Kit left and Laila volunteered to clean the kitchen, so Aidan took the opportunity to pull Caleb back into the bedroom. Caleb didn't resist being tugged down into a long, exploratory, faintly maple-syrup-flavored kiss, but he broke away as soon as Aidan started walking them toward the bed.

"Not that I object," he said, voice light with unreleased laughter, "but don't we have things to do? We're supposed to go out and be seen, and there's another interview later. We could save this for tonight."

"We have time," Aidan insisted. If Caleb didn't object, there was no reason not to press him down into the mattress, then ruck his t-shirt up over his stomach and reach for the waistband of his jeans, so Aidan did. "Why wait for later?"

"Good point," Caleb said, distracted by the play of Aidan's fingers against the spot under his navel. His skin was warm, and that pause to inhale between words heated something inside Aidan. He wanted to take Caleb apart, wanted to make him talk until he was wordless.

They kissed again, Caleb pulling him so they were both on the bed, their lips sliding against each other, breath slurring into moans. Aidan kept his hands between them, working Caleb's zipper and then yanking his jeans and underwear down his hips.

Caleb was hard already, and Aidan's own cock throbbed at the feel of it, rigid and satin-smooth, against his hand. He caressed it once, unable to stop himself, and then tore his attention away. He had *plans*. And Caleb wasn't naked yet.

"Take your shirt off," Aidan said, peeling Caleb's jeans off his ankles, and in one fluid motion it was gone. It was impossibly heady, the sense that he could speak whatever he wanted into existence, or maybe it was the sight of Caleb making him feel this way. There was so much of him to look at, and he was so beautiful—the rosy points of his nipples, the bramble of dark hair, the soft stretch of his stomach lifting and dipping in tiny, shallow movements.

"You alright?"

"I can't believe you just... walk around like this," Aidan said, simultaneously irritated at how stupefied he sounded and yet still stupefied enough to bask in it. He gestured. "All the time. Not just your face, but under your clothes—*that*. It's absurd."

"I think that's the meanest compliment I've ever received," Caleb said. "Do I get to look at you or are you keeping your clothes on?"

Aidan shrugged out of his clothes without grace or ceremony, being nothing much to look at. Then he caught Caleb grinning the kind of grin that Aidan had always had to pretend —until now—wasn't brain-melting. Dazzling. Whatever. Naked and gorgeous, Caleb was too much. Aidan made a strangled noise of appreciation. "God."

"Articulate," Caleb said.

"Shut up," Aidan said. He crawled on top of Caleb and then opened the top drawer in the night stand. He pulled out a bottle of lube, expecting to get mocked for planning this in advance, but instead he was met with an instant of wide-eyed silence. The color in Caleb's cheeks spoke volumes.

"Yeah," Aidan said. "We'll see who's articulate."

"Um, I thought we—I've never—what are you gonna do with that?"

"What do you *want* me to do with it?" Enjoying this probably made him a bad person; so be it. Aidan had only ever been with experienced partners, which was better, or so he'd thought. But initiating someone else into a new experience made him feel powerful, wise, like he was the keeper of some arcane secret. More than that, there was pride and deeply gratifying pleasure in finding something that Caleb had never tried with anyone else. Not one of his girlfriends had done this with him. Caleb obviously wanted it, but he'd never asked anyone.

He was going to ask Aidan.

The heat suffusing him was tinged with something selfish, jealous, and impure, and it was hot as fuck. He'd be thinking about the way Caleb looked right now—eyes trained on Aidan's hand, the red curve of his lower lip caught between his teeth, yearning inscribed in his posture—for a long time.

Caleb hadn't said anything in answer to his question. Relishing every second of slow movement, Aidan reached for the drawer again. "I can put it back if you're not interested."

"No! I mean, yes, I do—I am. Uh. Interested."

"In what?"

For a second, Aidan thought he wasn't going to say it. Caleb collected himself, so slowly and so physically it was as if Aidan could see the words take shape in his throat. "You, fucking me."

"Oh. Is that what we're talking about?" Caleb rolled his eyes and Aidan broke into a grin. "What a coincidence. I am also interested in me, fucking you."

Aidan positioned himself between Caleb's spread thighs, coated the fingers of one hand with lube, and set the bottle aside. With his other hand, he took hold of Caleb's cock, full and flushed and dripping on his stomach, and gave it a stroke.

Caleb sucked in a breath. Aidan could feel the same air being drawn from his own lungs. He wanted this very, very badly. Probably more than Caleb did, since this wasn't an experiment. The act held no novelty. Pressing a slick fingertip to the most intimate part of Caleb's body didn't qualify as *adventurous*, for him.

His heart was beating like he'd never done it before.

No need to think about that. He had better things to do. Aidan lowered his mouth to Caleb's cock, laving the head while still working his finger in small, gentle circles. He swallowed Caleb down to the root at the same moment he pushed in, the tight ring of muscle clamping around his finger.

He would have said all sorts of things—*yes, good, just like that, you're so beautiful, you feel so perfect, let me do this for you* —if his mouth hadn't been full. It was safer to use his tongue this way, licking and kissing, dragging it over the slit, than it was to let something irrevocable slip out of his mouth.

Caleb squirmed when he slid in deeper, a formless movement that took on form as Aidan curled his finger. Caleb bucked his hips, thrusting down against Aidan's hand and up against his mouth.

Aidan worked a second finger in and Caleb moaned. The sound thrummed inside Aidan like the missing note of a chord, and when it had gone silent, all he wanted was to hear it again. He was so hard he ached, the tip of his cock leaving wet smears against his thigh every time he moved, but he couldn't stop touching Caleb, who was breathing in fast, ragged gasps

"Aidan. Aidan, I'm gonna—"

Aidan thrust his fingers in and swallowed him to the root. Caleb's orgasm came crashing down, loud and forceful and hot, clamping around his fingers and spurting into his mouth. Aidan caught it in flashes—Caleb's eyes squeezed shut and the dark fans of his lashes against his cheeks, one hand clenching the sheets and the other in Aidan's hair—and thought he might die from how beautiful it was.

He was one ghost of a touch away from coming himself. One of his hands was free now, and he wiped his mouth, but didn't reach for his erection.

"Holy fuck. That was... you are really good at that."

"You're welcome."

"You didn't have to do that. We talked about you fucking me," Caleb ventured after a beat.

"Mm. Did we? It slipped my mind." Aidan shifted his fingers inside Caleb, and Caleb shivered. "Refresh my memory."

"I told you I wanted you to fuck me. I still do."

"Articulate," Aidan observed, and Caleb laughed. He'd been charmed by Caleb's earlier shyness, but he was equally as proud to have fucked it away. All these little details, the glassy darkness of his pupils and the sweat at his temples, Aidan had some hand—two hands—in making him look like that.

"You can go ahead," Caleb said. "You've been waiting. I already came, I don't need to come again."

Aidan raised his eyebrows. "I disagree."

With his still-slick fingers, he set a slow pace, listening to Caleb exhale. Caleb was satisfied, his cock lying soft on his stomach, and yet he was letting Aidan continue to explore his body. It felt like cheating, how easily they'd arrived here, like they'd skipped half a dozen steps. Maybe Caleb was this free and vulnerable with everyone.

Even as he thought it, Aidan knew that wasn't it. He couldn't think about that. Better to watch his fingers disappear into the tight clench of Caleb's body, letting the long, slow anticipation crowd out all his other thoughts. Sex was the only thing he liked to wait for. The taut, yearning stretch of the moment resembled nothing else in the frantic chaos of his life.

He wanted to touch himself, so he touched Caleb instead, gently stroking his cock back to its full hardness.

"Fuck," Caleb whispered.

That was as good a cue as any. Aidan removed his fingers and slid his dick in, sheathing himself inch by slippery, careful inch. It was tight and perfect, a knock-out rush of sensation. "Jesus," he said, then leaned forward until he could devour Caleb's mouth in a kiss. It was sloppy and hard, their tongues wild and their teeth nipping into lips, but Aidan's restraint was all focused elsewhere, driving into Caleb in deep strokes, making it last.

He was shuddering with the effort, his arms stiff and his muscles burning, by the time Caleb whimpered some breathless word that might have been "Please."

Fuck. He'd thought he was prepared for this and he'd had it all wrong. It should have been like the other times: something filthy and fun, a game he knew how to win, a way to show off. But that one little noise brought home all the feelings he'd been evading. His gaze caught Caleb's. No one else had ever drowned him in tenderness like this.

He kissed Caleb, plunging his tongue into Caleb's mouth, and thrust his hand between their bodies to bring him off. It was effortless. Inevitable. His orgasm was a flood of sweet relief, a flash of pleasure bright against the backs of his eyelids. He collapsed afterward, boneless and thoughtless, and nuzzled the side of Caleb's neck.

Caleb made an appreciative noise, combing his fingers through Aidan's hair. "Glad we did that. Now we can do it again later."

"You'll have to peel me out of bed first," Aidan mumbled, his mood deflated by the mention of *later*. There would be precious little of that. This arrangement would end as soon as Quint was in prison. Aidan would have to break up with Caleb publicly, of course. Otherwise disappearing wouldn't do anything to keep him safe.

"We could switch," Caleb said.

Aidan was so caught up in his own thoughts that he didn't take the meaning for a second, and when he did, it made him smile despite everything. He dropped a kiss under the corner of Caleb's jaw. "Could we," he said, and it wasn't a question.

They had a few more days. He was already in too deep, so what difference did it make if he dug himself in a little deeper? He had to enjoy his time with Caleb while he could. Once he left, he'd never have anything like it again.

———

They'd given away half a million by the fistful in a matter of hours. A barrage of hugs from strangers, tears, scorn, indignation, inappropriate touches, and some shockingly personal questions had prevented Caleb and Aidan from speaking to each other. Caleb had realized too late how easily a crowd like that might have turned into a mob, and he was relieved when they dispersed along with the last of the cash. He had to turn out his jacket pockets apologetically in answer to a few stragglers who approached them on their stroll through the park, but luckily no one got angry.

Aidan was quiet. Caleb reached for him, no longer pretending it was for any purpose other than his own pleasure. A long moment passed before Aidan took his hand out of pocket and accepted.

They didn't have to talk. It was a brisk, sunny day. He was happy to hold Aidan's hand and step on crunchy leaves in companionable silence.

He wasn't sure *Aidan* was happy, though.

"Have you read the news lately?" Aidan asked.

"To see what people are saying about us? I look sometimes. It's all pretty much the same, and a lot of it's wrong. But we're getting attention."

"A few states have launched criminal investigations into Quint Services," Aidan said. "It won't be long before he gets arrested. We need to make sure he turns himself in first."

So they'd have control over the situation and could switch Quint for Oz. Caleb nodded, not willing to say that out loud in public. "It's good that there are investigations. That's what you wanted."

"Yeah."

That didn't sound like the answer of someone getting what they wanted. It wasn't wise to discuss the details here, so Caleb let a little time elapse and changed the subject. "I can't stop thinking about this morning. It was so good. I'm glad we didn't wait."

That, at least, elicited a smile. "Some of us haven't had fifty girlfriends," Aidan said. "If you never know when you'll get your next chance, you learn to seize the moment."

"It wasn't *fifty*," Caleb protested.

"Fine," Aidan said. "Forty-two."

"Wait, really? I didn't even know that. How..." Caleb trailed off and examined Aidan, who'd blanched and was now staring resolutely at the distant edge of the lake. "I didn't introduce you to all of them."

"I knew anyway."

"You keeping a spreadsheet or something?" Caleb asked, the joke falling flat as soon as he'd said it. He was freaked out and couldn't identify why, and Aidan was obviously embarrassed.

"I was in your apartment often enough," Aidan said. He held still like a prey animal seeking camouflage in its surroundings—no, like a runner trying to get into the Nowhere. "There were always traces. I can't explain this in a way that doesn't make me sound like a creep."

"You're not a creep," Caleb said, distracted, wondering what Aidan had seen. Lost earrings and forgotten scarves. Soy milk in the fridge. Tampons in the bathroom trash, maybe. None of those things guaranteed a precise count of the number of women who'd come through his life in the last decade.

You'd have to be really invested to keep track. Caleb hadn't even known the number. He just said yes to beautiful women who wanted him.

In the fiction they'd improvised for their relationship, Aidan had gone into great detail about the moment he knew Caleb was in love with him. He'd obscured his own side of the story. What had he said?

I'm sorry, the truth is I don't know when I fell in love with Caleb. We were friends, and we were friends, and we were friends, and then... my feelings changed. I can't pinpoint the moment it happened.

Caleb had thought it was a weak answer at the time. Not the kind of captivating lie they were supposed to be spinning. It had slipped right past their interviewer's attention, probably by design. It had slipped right past Caleb's attention, too.

If you'd known someone all your life—long enough to keep a decade-long mental tally of that person's girlfriends—maybe you wouldn't know exactly when you'd fallen in love, just that you had.

And if the person you were in love with continually dated other people, you'd notice. Because you'd be hurt. Aidan's knowledge of the number betrayed a depth of feeling he'd never admitted to.

Caleb could have this all wrong. Aidan could just be weirdly observant. He could have been making up his answer in that interview. That was ostensibly what both of them were doing, or it was what Caleb had been doing at the beginning. Things had changed for him now.

It was a story, and it was a story, and it was a story, and then it was true.

"Hey," Caleb said, making Aidan turn to face him. He lifted his hand to Aidan's cheek, ghosted his fingertips down the side of his face, and said, "There might've been forty-two, but none of them are here right now. None of them stayed."

Aidan looked like Caleb had punched him in the gut. "Caleb, I'm not—this is fun, but it's temporary. It's not real."

Fuck. Caught between panic and anger, Caleb forced his voice to stay steady. Maybe he'd misunderstood. "Why not? It felt pretty damn real this morning."

"I can't *stay*, Caleb. You think Quint is the only person who'd lock me up and experiment on me? My life is dangerous. I won't get you killed. When this is over, I'm leaving. I'll have to find somewhere to hide. But I'll dump you in public so no one comes after you, don't worry."

"Don't worry? Don't *worry*? What the fuck, Aidan." Caleb intended to go on, but Aidan reached for him. Caleb didn't want to be touched, but the plastic smile on Aidan's face reminded him that they were in public. They had the attention of other people in the park just by virtue of being who they were. They couldn't afford to raise their voices and attract more.

"Let's walk," Aidan said, because they'd stopped moving after he'd revealed his bullshit plan to disappear.

"My life is dangerous, too, you know," Caleb said, keeping his voice low as they ascended a bridge that crossed the lake at its narrowest point. "This could all go south. We're committing fraud and who knows how many other crimes. We could both go to prison for a long time. And if we don't manage to put Quint in prison, he's going to kill us. Surely you know that."

"They can put us in prison, but they can't keep us there."

"Why, because your Union will get you out? Like they got you out of Facility 17? Aidan, that was *me*. *I* did that. I've been here—helping you, taking risks with you—the whole time. That doesn't have to change."

"Yes, it does," Aidan said, implacable.

They stopped for a moment because a couple at the apex of the bridge was getting photographed against the backdrop of the lake and the fall foliage. Then one of the women in the couple noticed them and smiled and waved, and the cameras turned their way. Caleb's face froze. Aidan stepped closer and put a hand on the small of his back, a touch he would have welcomed mere minutes ago.

It was Aidan who made polite, stilted conversation with the strangers after they'd finished the photos. It went on for too long because he wasn't good at extricating himself from social situations when he couldn't literally disappear. At least four opportunities went by. Caleb could have jumped in and made their excuses. He didn't feel like helping.

From the other side of the bridge, someone yelled "Caleb!"

Holy shit. Deb. Here. It didn't compute at first. His sister was one of the normal parts of life, totally separate from the life where he got his job transferred to space, visited another reality, and stole a trillionaire's fortune. He'd filed her away.

Except he only had one life. Deb and Oswin Lewis Quint were both mixed up in it. So was Aidan.

She was marching up the bridge, shading her round glasses with her hand. She'd cut her wavy brown hair short since he'd last seen her.

Before she got to where they were standing, he grabbed Aidan by the wrist and said "Sorry, we have to go," over his shoulder to the strangers while hurrying down to meet his sister.

"How did you find us?" he asked, breathless, searching for

some place they could talk without being seen. The park was disastrously open.

Deb didn't perceive his distress. She hugged him tight. Caleb hugged her back. It was almost enough to make him stop worrying for an instant.

"There's an app where people report sightings of you two," she said. "My own brother. In the city where we grew up. And I had to use an *app* to know where you were. You know I'm supposed to be in World Lit senior seminar right now? Not to mention I had to find out from some psychic's premium streaming channel that you and Aidan were finally dating! It cost me *ten dollars* and *all* of my dignity."

"So not that much, then," Caleb said.

She punched him in the arm with a force at the upper limit of what could be described as *playful*. Aidan had taught her too well.

"Ow."

"Hi Aidan," Deb said. "Don't think I'm not mad at you, too. But also congratulations, I guess. This has been a long time coming."

Aidan and Caleb shared a glance. Caleb said nothing, waiting to see what Aidan would say.

Admit you're in love with me, you asshole.

"Thanks," Aidan said, as quickly and flatly as possible, dodging the issue.

A generous interpretation of Aidan's answer was that he didn't want to lie to Deb about their relationship, whatever it was. Caleb wasn't feeling generous. They'd already lied to Deb. She'd watched the interviews. Lying to the public felt different when the public in question was family.

If Aidan dumped him in public, Deb would see that, too.

"This is the part of the conversation where *you* can ask what's going on in *my* life," Deb said. "I think I'm up to date on yours. Or you can take me back to the palace where you live and let me dive into your champagne swimming pool."

"It's a little cold for that," Caleb said.

"You mean the pool's not *heated*?" Deb asked with fake outrage. Then she grimaced. "On the other hand, the idea of a swimming pool full of warm champagne is pretty gross. Guess you'll have to talk to me instead. Let's go get coffee. You're paying."

She shoved her hands into the pockets of her brown leather jacket and strode off, expecting them to follow.

Caleb looked at Aidan. "If you don't want us to go with her, *you* have to tell her that. I'm not softening the blow for you."

"I don't think I'll be the one throwing the punch," Aidan said ruefully. "We can't tell her the truth, Caleb."

"And what truth is that, exactly?" Caleb asked. He could think of a few vicious follow-ups—*the truth that we're great together but you're too much of a coward to give us a chance*—but he kept them to himself out of some foolish hope that maybe Aidan would say the right thing.

"If we spend more time with her, it'll draw attention to her. She could end up in danger because of us. I don't want anybody else mixed up in this."

Deb saved Caleb from whatever he was about to say by stomping back up to them and saying, "What gives? Am I not cool enough to hang out now that you're rich and famous? My net worth is in the *high* double-digits, you know."

"We're really sorry, Deb, but unfortunately we have another interview later today, and we should get going," Aidan said.

Deb narrowed her eyes. Her suspicion was justified. Aidan had probably never been that polite to her in his life. After a second, she asked, "Rain check?"

"Yeah," Aidan said. "This should all be over soon."

Caleb didn't like the sound of that.

"Good, I'll hold you to that," Deb said.

Aidan gave her an uncharacteristically soft smile and said, "It was really nice to run into you, Deb."

He thinks this is the last time he'll ever see her. The realization tied Caleb in tight, anxious knots. It was barely a goodbye at all. Deb was practically Aidan's sister and he was just going to ghost her without another word.

Everyone left. Caleb knew that. All forty-two girlfriends had left, and sometimes it had hurt, but it had always been okay in the end.

Because Aidan stayed.

He was always there. Caleb had taken it for granted that he always would be. How cruel that just as Caleb had begun to understand how much he needed Aidan, Aidan wanted to leave. Forever.

Until now, Aidan had always had the power to go into the Nowhere, but Caleb had never genuinely worried about him disappearing. He always came back—or more often than not, he took Caleb with him when he went. Life without Aidan was inconceivable, the future a yawning void with no exits.

Whatever it took to make him stay, Caleb would do it.

[17]
INNOCENT

Aidan chewed a mint and paced around the green room while they waited to go on set. He couldn't sit on the couch next to Caleb. The loneliest place in the world, he'd discovered, was six inches from the person you'd hurt.

This interview would be a live broadcast, something they hadn't done since working with Miss Tallulah, but it should be similar to the other recent interviews in content. It would only be different because he'd upset Caleb.

It was too quiet in the room, only the sound of his shoes scuffing the carpet. Caleb hadn't flipped a magazine page in ages, and Oz was so absorbed in his tablet that he might as well not have been there.

"Are you going to to do it today?" Caleb asked, his eyes on the magazine, like he was talking about going to the grocery instead of getting dumped on television.

Fake dumped. They weren't really together.

"No," Aidan said. God, that made him feel like he'd swallowed a lump of ice. "It's too soon."

"Hm."

Oz would turn himself in on Friday, five days from now.

With Caleb treating him so coolly, it would be an eternity. *The bed's big enough that we won't have to touch*, he thought, and his throat closed up. He stopped pacing and dropped into an armchair. That wasn't what he wanted at all.

It didn't matter. He had always known this would hurt him.

He hadn't realized that it would hurt Caleb. All those ex-girlfriends, he'd always bounced back from them in a couple of days. This wouldn't be any different. More importantly, it would be worth it, because nobody would be coming to abduct Caleb. Nobody would ever hold him hostage in exchange for Aidan. Nobody would torture him for information.

You'll be safe, he wanted to say to Caleb. S*omebody else will love you.* History had demonstrated that over and over. Caleb was easy to love. He could have anyone. People would line up for their chance.

It just can't be me.

Aidan would explain all that later, when Oz wasn't in the room. Right now, they had to go on TV and pretend.

Aidan prayed Caleb was in the mood to cooperate. He was the best at this and they all knew it. Most of the questions would be the same. Quint would get asked about his change of heart and his plans for the future; Caleb would get asked about his heroics. If they were lucky, the host would ignore Aidan or only ask him softball questions about being in love with Caleb. If things got too close to a touchy subject, Caleb would slip in and turn the conversation toward some likable story—if he wasn't too pissed at Aidan, that was. He had such a talent for it. Aidan mostly remembered their wild adolescent hijinks as embarrassing and frustrating to the adults around them, but Caleb could make anything cute.

Aidan owed him so much.

As they exited the green room, Caleb rolled the sleeves of his blue-grey button-down to expose his forearms. Aidan didn't *want* to stare appreciatively—didn't have the right—but he couldn't help himself.

"Yeah," Oz said. "Do that in front of the camera and everyone'll love you."

"Fuck off," Aidan said.

They filed onto the set, where there was a leather couch at an angle to their host's wooden desk. His name was Ken Garnett and he stood to greet them, unfolding his legs from his chair and striding over. His suit emphasized the long lines of his body. He wore glasses and was grey at the temples, handsome and well-coiffed in a non-threatening, politician way.

Or, Aidan supposed, a talk-show host way.

Aidan shook his hand, trying not to inhale in the scent of his cologne, and then the three of them settled on the couch. Caleb slung an arm over the back of the couch, his hand landing on Aidan's shoulder.

Oh, thank fuck, he was in the mood to act. This would be easy. Aidan tried not to let his relief show while he listened to Oz's usual story about how he'd seen the error of his ways.

"Yes," Garnett said, something cool in his tone. "Interesting how quickly you turned around on the subject of runners. Do you still feel that they pose a threat to society? That was your position until recently, wasn't it?"

"I—"

"And for you to be associating with Aidan Blackwood now, it's very strange, isn't it?"

Caleb removed his arm from the back of the couch and sat up straight. He squeezed Aidan's knee, presumably as a sign not to engage with this hostile line of questioning. Aidan didn't need a reminder, but he understood why he'd received one. He'd always been most likely to start a fight.

"I don't know what you're implying," Oz said, once he'd collected himself. A good answer. Not confirming anything, but forcing Garnett into the light. "I have a great deal of respect for Aidan and I think runners are a valuable asset."

Aidan would have gone with *valued members of society*, but Oz was playing a recently reformed trillionaire, so maybe his word choice was more convincing. Regardless, it made Garnett lean in like a predator who'd smelled blood. He reached under his desk and pulled out a slim file.

Aidan's stomach flipped. He should have known one of these goddamn talk-show hosts would want to play investigative reporter. He couldn't afford to respond in his usual way—he had to be fucking *likable*, or their whole scam would fall apart. Christ.

If Aidan's access to the Nowhere was ever going to come back, now would be the time.

Garnett slid his fingers into the file and opened it with exquisite slowness. "Mr. Quint, I have here a list of Aidan Blackwood's inflammatory rhetoric and acts, perhaps I could—"

"Excuse me."

"Yes?" Garnett asked. Aidan tensed. What could Caleb possibly say to defuse the situation? There was no anecdote cute enough.

"Who's the most famous runner you can think of, other than Aidan?" Caleb asked.

Garnett wasn't expecting to be questioned. He spread his fingers and drummed them on the open file while he thought. "Fehim Terzi, I suppose. Or maybe the Franklin Station Bank robber."

"And what became of Fehim Terzi after the whole world celebrated his Istanbul-New York run?"

"Nothing much. He died young, didn't he? Most runners do."

Garnett's nonchalant bullshit made Aidan rage. He had to know what had happened to Terzi. Everybody knew. What was

Caleb doing? This wouldn't help anything. They couldn't talk about this; people didn't like him. People didn't like *runners*. He'd founded the Union with that in mind.

Instead of fidgeting, Aidan tried to project calm authority, like he knew exactly what Caleb was going to say, like they'd expected and prepared for all of this—or better, like he knew Caleb so well that he had perfect faith this would all work out. It was good to focus on something other than Garnett's smug, punchable face.

If Aidan could still jump, he would already have landed a hit.

"Yes, runners do have a shorter average life expectancy than non-runners," Caleb said acidly, not taking his eyes off Garnett. "In part because they're frequently the targets of hate crimes. Terzi—the most famous runner in the world, by your own account—died because he was *murdered*. Assassinated, even. Strange that you don't seem to know that, when you were about to present yourself as an expert on the subject of runners."

"Oh, yes, I do recall something about that now. But it's been decades, and it happened on the other side of the world. And it seems a bit of a stretch to call it an assassination."

"The world is a lot smaller than it used to be."

Aidan shivered, and he couldn't say if it was fear or excitement. He'd never heard Caleb—sweet, sunny, solve-all-the-playground-fights *Caleb*—sound so icy.

Caleb regarded Garnett, and then the audience, and spoke in a measured tone. "Fehim Terzi, the first runner to reveal himself to the world at large and a symbol of hope, was assassinated. He was poisoned. The killer's apartment was full of long-distance surveillance photos and equipment for listening to everything Terzi did. There was evidence the man was part of an organization that wanted to exterminate all runners, but he killed himself shortly after murdering Terzi and his contacts were never discovered. This all happened decades ago, and it's been forgotten by the world at large, but *runners* know it."

Aidan shouldn't be surprised. Caleb had cheered for every speech. Caleb had helped him found the Union. But it was still amazing, this proof that he'd really been *listening*. And he was willing to stand up for runners, even after Aidan had pissed him off. There was something in Aidan's throat.

"So that's one unfortunate incident. A violent crank. You don't have any evidence of an organization," Garnett said. "Meanwhile, there's plenty of evidence of crimes committed by runners. After all, I just said the two other most famous—infamous—runners are Aidan here and the Franklin Station Bank robber."

"If you saw someone shouting for help, would you scold them for being so loud?"

"No, not if they really needed it," Garnett said, obviously resenting this line of argument. Caleb had wrested control of the conversation.

"Runners can be denied jobs or housing just for who they are. Our society forces them to the margins and then pretends it's their fault. Do you know how many of the runners I know have been homeless at some point? Three-quarters, at least. That's appalling. We should all be outraged, and yet hardly anyone talks about it. When Aidan protests, people notice. He's doing the right thing."

"Is he? If there are so many homeless runners, shouldn't he be helping them instead?"

"He *is*. He does. Aidan is a hero."

Well. That was excessive. He opened his mouth to dismiss it, and Caleb cut him off with a hand signal. Aidan felt strange, sitting here in silence while Caleb argued. He'd never experienced anything like this. Caleb had been so serious and determined the whole time.

It didn't feel like a performance.

Aidan liked it way, way too much. He shouldn't. It wasn't making either of them seem harmless and cute. This wasn't what they'd come here to do.

It's not believable that I would dump him after this, he thought, an absurd flicker of panic. Worse, Caleb was making himself a target. Even if Aidan jilted him in front of the whole world, you couldn't say this kind of stuff in public without repercussion. Nasty articles and news segments. His defaced image on protest signs. Hate mail. Someone had once thrown a brick through the window of a house where Aidan was staying, after a photo of him entering found its way to the darker corners of the internet. Any of that could happen to Caleb. They would come for him too, now.

Caleb knew that.

Caleb had witnessed the aftermath of the abduction, categorically the worst thing that had ever happened to Aidan. He knew it could happen again—especially if they failed to put Quint in prison. He knew it could happen to *him*.

Aidan had tried to shield him from that. Had tried to choose for him. This was Caleb choosing for himself.

Aidan had hurt him and here Caleb was defending him despite everything. Caleb was on TV using his platform to talk about runners' rights.

"I understand you have a rosy view of Aidan, but surely you agree the Franklin Station Bank robber is a criminal?" Garnett said, desperate to regain some ground. "You can't argue that she's innocent."

"Yes, let's talk about her," Caleb said. "She was *fourteen* at the time she attempted the robbery. Do you know what happened to her?"

Panic overtook excitement. They shouldn't talk about Laila. She didn't deserve to be dragged through the public consciousness again, and more controversy was bad for their fragile plan.

"She went to prison, as people who get caught robbing banks usually do," Garnett said.

The audience was still, and the six-piece house band across from them hadn't produced so much as as a *ba-dum-tss* since they'd come on set.

All Aidan had to do was reach out and squeeze Caleb's knee. He'd get the message and back off as gracefully as possible. Maybe they couldn't salvage this interview, but they could wander around the city handing out thousands of dollars in cash to passing strangers. That would turn public opinion in their favor again.

Despite the nervous energy racing over his skin, Aidan's hands might as well have weighed two tons each. He couldn't move them. He was as rapt as everyone else in the studio.

Caleb stared down Garnett and said, "And how did they keep a fourteen-year-old girl in prison?"

"Not a girl. A runner."

Caleb ignored this. "Starvation, Ken. Starvation and sedation. That's torture. She was *fourteen years old*."

"She planned and almost succeeded in carrying out a bank heist. She was a dangerous criminal and she had to be stopped."

In the silence, Aidan could have sworn the temperature in the room dropped ten degrees. Caleb raised his eyebrows. "You support torturing kids?"

If they were going to blow it all up, at least it would be righteous. Caleb was brave as fuck. More passionate about the cause than Aidan had realized.

No, not just the cause.

Holy shit. He's in love with me.

Caleb deserved so much better than what Aidan had offered him. Aidan owed him the whole truth, every last terrified bit of it, from Brian and his surveillance photos to the nightmares where he was still in the cell. Caleb deserved to know how Aidan felt.

Aidan gave up on controlling his own facial expression and watched Caleb's instead. He'd narrowed his eyes at Garnett. He looked ferocious. Sure of himself.

It was hot as hell. Aidan shouldn't be thinking about that now.

Garnett spread his hands on his desk like his suit and his set could lend his horrific position some gravitas. He addressed the audience smoothly. "I support controlling a dangerous segment of the population. Extreme means are necessary. There are monsters among us."

"Unconscionable." Caleb nearly spat on the carpet. "I already told you how hard it is to get a job or an apartment in this country if anyone knows you're a runner. It's no wonder that some of them need to steal to eat. Runners made it possible for us to construct a space elevator, to build a civilization in orbit, and in turn, we've stood idle while radical ideologues hunt them down and murder them. We've used vile, abusive means to torture and imprison them. Worse, people like you have encouraged that."

Caleb paused and Aidan thought he was storing up to launch into another rant. Instead he slung one arm around Aidan, the other around Oz, dragging them close. He glared at Garnett and said, "Laila Njeim was a desperate fourteen-year-old girl who made a bad choice. *You're* a monster."

And the three of them disappeared.

AIDAN CAUGHT him before he hit the kitchen floor. Caleb stayed still and waited for his vision to come back. The jump shouldn't have been so hard—even with two people, it was the first time he'd entered the Nowhere all day.

It sounded strangely loud in Quint's house. Maybe the jump had screwed up his hearing.

Aidan pulled him fully upright. Caleb blinked. There were twenty people in Quint's kitchen.

What the fuck?

When he looked at them, still fuzzy and trying to figure out why they all had masks or makeup or veils on, they burst into cheers. Most of them had beers or wine glasses in hand, but a few of them were raising whole bottles. The specially insulated, glass-fronted wine rack under the marble island, he noted, was empty.

Someone pushed through the crowd. At least it was the one person whose strange makeup Caleb recognized, even with tears running down her face. Laila hugged him hard enough to hurt.

"Thank you."

"You don't have to th—"

She squeezed him sharply. "Shut up." She loosened her hold and then yelled toward the ceiling, "Someone get this man a drink!"

Another cheer went up. Shit, were they *chanting his name*? He was too dizzy for this. Caleb said mildly, "It's a little early for that, for me, I think."

"*I* heard the world is a lot smaller than it used to be," Laila said.

A moment passed. Why had she said that? She looked so expectant. "Are you *quoting* me?"

She laughed. "My point stands. 'It's five o'clock somewhere' is extra true when you can teleport." She kissed his cheek and let go of him. He wobbled, still dazed, but Aidan appeared at his side an instant later, a steadying presence. "If you don't want one, it's fine. But the rest of us are going to drink as much of Quint's cellar as we can."

"Fine with me," Oz yelled, hoisting a bottle of champagne over his head to more cheers.

Someone pressed an open bottle of champagne into Caleb's hand. He stared at it without drinking.

"Let's go back in the living room and watch it again," someone shouted. The voice was familiar. Without faces to match, it was hard to place people. Most of the Union members filed out of the kitchen and it quieted down.

"How did they all find this place?"

"I told them where it was," Laila said. "I started getting messages during the interview. And I was sitting in that giant living room alone and I thought, well, why not have some company?"

From the living room, Caleb heard his own voice, the recording turned to maximum volume. A cheer drowned out the recording. He blushed.

Laila patted his shoulder. "I have a party to attend. See you later."

"What's happening?" Caleb asked Aidan after she was gone.

"We don't get many victories, so we celebrate even the smallest ones," Aidan said with a shrug. "The Union is choosing to see this as a victory."

"You don't think I blew it all up?"

"Well, whatever else happens, we've given away a lot of money and we're about to trash this house. That wasn't really my goal, but it's something." Aidan walked one hand along the length of Caleb's shoulder, his fingers resting against the side of Caleb's neck. "And we got a handsome, charismatic man to give an impassioned speech about runners' rights on *Sunday with Ken Garnett*."

"Yeah? Who was that?"

Aidan rolled his eyes, smiled, and averted his gaze. "It occurred to me that I was kind of an asshole earlier."

"Oh?"

"I know that's been... a pattern, and I'm sorry. We should talk about it. There are some things I should tell you," Aidan said. He tilted his head toward the living room, which was now booming with music. "But maybe not with all these people here. And I don't want to gloss over your moment. I really was moved. It was good, what you did."

"It's not really my moment. I just said things you've been saying for years."

Aidan made a *stop talking* gesture. "You wouldn't let me protest being called a hero earlier, so you're not getting out of this. You did the right thing. Take credit for it."

A bunch of strangers chanting his name did nothing for him, but a couple of sentences from Aidan could make him weak in the knees. Caleb hid his reaction as well as he could. He hadn't forgotten this afternoon. "What did you want to talk about? You can't tell me we need to talk and then put me off till later. It's cruel."

One of the guests walked into the kitchen.

Even with a black veil slanted stylishly over her face, Caleb could recognize an ex-girlfriend. "Anna?"

Her smile dimmed from brilliant to sheepish. "There are some things I probably should have told you."

"That's becoming a theme," Caleb murmured. There was only one reason Anna would be in Quint's mansion right now. "You're in the Union?"

"Yeah. Please don't feel hurt—it's not that I didn't tell *you* I was a runner, it's that I didn't tell anybody. Not even Aidan. He guessed."

"I get it," Caleb said. After all, he'd just ranted at a TV host about the difficulties of living openly as a runner. Whatever small hurt he felt at not being told, it drifted to the bottom of the sea of other emotions swirling through him. "It's good to see you."

"Thanks. I'm really happy for you. Both of you. I had a feeling this would happen, and I'm glad it finally did. Cheers." Anna gave them both hugs and then left them alone.

Caleb had lifted the bottle he was holding, but he let his hand drift down without taking a drink. He still felt strange from his earlier jump.

Just like Deb, Anna had been expecting Caleb and Aidan to get together. She'd said as much when she'd broken up with Caleb, but he hadn't understood. She'd been right about him back then; she still was. It made him wonder what it was Aidan wanted to say, and whether this was the first time he'd tried to share it.

"Hey, let's go out there and say hi to everyone, and then you can go lie down if you want," Aidan said, nudging him toward the living room. "You look like you might need that."

"What I need is for you to spit out whatever it is you want to tell me."

"There won't be any spitting."

"*Aidan.*"

"Oh, it'll be mostly me acknowledging that you were right and I was wrong, followed by a lot of groveling. Don't worry, you'll enjoy it."

"Groveling, huh? What does that involve?"

"You gotta be awake for it," Aidan said. "I'm not wasting my groveling efforts on someone who's about to pass out. One victory lap and then you can collapse."

This many jumps would be hell on his body. He'd tried to get Quint to give him some suppressant up front, in the interest of not getting all of his matter unfolded, but Quint was too shrewd a negotiator for that. He needed a runner, and Caleb was the only one he had. Quint would keep him around as long as he could. Caleb took comfort in the fact that he could dump Quint in the ocean as soon as he had the suppressant, if the whim took him.

Caleb had spent a day and a half trapped with Quint. He was feeling pretty fucking whimsical.

He was standing motionless in the one corner of Quint's room that was invisible to the recently installed security camera. Caleb could have disabled the camera, but he didn't want to alert anyone else to his presence. Oz would text them at any moment, and then they'd be gone.

"How did you become a runner?" Quint asked, not for the first time.

Quint was relentless. Caleb was finally bored enough to answer. "Look, I don't know shit about the science, I just get the injection every two weeks and it works."

"Tell me everything you can," Quint said.

"Fine. I'll start at the beginning because I don't know how much you know—"

"A lot," Quint interrupted.

"—and we need to be on the same page, so you know what kind of questions I can and can't answer. It'll be mostly *can't*, I'm warning you now." He took a breath. "People perceive three dimensions, plus time, but there are more than that. The others are all folded up. All matter in this reality, your reality, is folded in a certain way. In my reality, it's folded differently. It makes no difference to our everyday lives."

"Except that the Nowhere is unfolded space, and anyone with two or more different foldings in their body can pass through it easily and painlessly," Quint said. "You can skip ahead a few steps."

Just to spite him, Caleb slowed down. "So you get the principle of how to make a runner: something in their body, doesn't matter what, that's folded differently. It has to be a significant amount of matter. Born runners get it from having their parents come from two different realities. I get it from the injections. The serum that Heath gives me, it has a dimensional prion in it. You know what a prion is?"

"A misfolded protein, but in this case, you mean matter that changes the folding of everything it touches," Quint said. "But we tried that and only had limited success. Why did it work for you?"

Caleb did actually know the answer to that. Heath had mentioned it, once, that not all dimensional prions were created equal. You needed a slow-acting one to ensure that the recipient had multiple foldings of matter in their body for a meaningful amount of time. In his case, it was two weeks. Instead of saying that, he shrugged. "Beats me."

Some people had spiritual crises about becoming runners—if this injection refolds all the matter in my body, what does that mean, who am I, am I just my atoms, do I have a soul, blah blah —but he'd only cared about access to the Nowhere. He hadn't bothered to learn any of this shit until he'd started showing symptoms of the shakes. It turned out the human body couldn't sustain having all its matter refolded every two weeks, if you hadn't been born a runner.

Caleb didn't share that with Quint, who was obviously after the serum. It was useful to know what people wanted, and Quint might not want the serum if he knew its long-term effects. Caleb had no plan to divulge his condition, either. As far as Quint was concerned, Caleb wanted the suppressant for the same reason Quint did: to ground any runners who were personally inconveniencing him.

"Every two weeks, you said?" Quint asked.

"The tablet's buzzing," Caleb said. It would be Oz's message.

They'd discussed the plan at length. It wouldn't be hard to make the switch, but they had to pick their moment. Oz had to be able to slip away unnoticed. Caleb had to make three *long* jumps back-to-back. Minimizing the amount of time Quint's room was empty meant minimizing their risk of getting caught. Yesterday's endless arguing between Oz and Quint had made the whole thing feel like that riddle about how many ferry trips you needed to get a wolf, a rabbit, and a head of lettuce across the river.

Oz was the head of lettuce, that grasping coward. It had taken nothing but the promise of more money to flip his loyalties.

Caleb listed the steps in his head: down to the surface with Quint, up to space with Oz, back down to the surface to get the suppressant Quint had promised him. He'd be in dire need of it.

Then he'd crash somewhere out of the way until he regained his strength. He didn't trust Quint enough to sleep in one of the man's absurd palaces, but after three jumps to and from space, his body might not give him a choice. He'd play it by ear. Once he was able, he'd go home with as much suppressant as he could get his hands on and never come back to this place.

"They're having a party in my house," Quint said, staring at Oz's message, then muttered, "Runners," like Caleb wasn't standing right there. Like his whole plan didn't depend on Caleb.

Like he didn't desperately covet the ability for himself.

Quint continued, "Oz will meet us in the garage. Have I

described the location accurately enough that you can get us there?"

"I'll get us there."

The first jump was unpleasant. He felt the Nowhere's strange push-pull more keenly that usual, and knew it was only a taste of what was to come. Hard to say how long he had until the glitching started. More than two jumps, he hoped.

The five-car garage was quiet except for the muffled sound of a raucous party happening on the other side of the wall, just as Oz had said. The din made Quint frown, so Caleb was fine with it.

Oz met them with a half-empty bottle of champagne in hand, tie loose and hair mussed. Wasted. He raised the bottle in greeting.

"You're not supposed to be *drunk*," Quint said, not so much emanating disapproval as whipping it directly at his double. "I've been in *prison*."

These two definitely weren't going to kiss. They might kill each other, though, and Caleb would happily watch that.

"I'll hide it," Oz said. "I'm a good actor."

Caleb waited while they switched clothes. Even after Quint methodically messed up his hair, it was still amply clear which one was which, but Caleb knew them way better than he wanted to. If they weren't side by side, it would be harder to tell.

When it was done, he grabbed Oz and said, "Don't fucking throw up on me."

Experience had taught him to warn passengers, especially drunk ones. The Nowhere was unkind to non-runners.

It wasn't all that kind to him, either. The few seconds in the void speared through him, leaving pain in places he didn't know he could feel pain. Christ. This might actually kill him.

They emerged into the room at Facility 17, which had been empty a scant few minutes since his departure with Quint.

Caleb's vision spotted black and his breath came in irregular gasps. He let go of Oz, who stumbled toward the bed.

Caleb didn't step back into the Nowhere so much as collapse into it. It was only his determination not to show weakness in front of Quint that kept him on his feet when he reappeared in the garage. Fuck, he ached. Needles all over his skin, weight on all his joints, and the persistent, unsettling sensation that everything inside him had been disassembled and put back slightly wrong.

"At last," Quint said, the ungrateful bastard. "Let's go in."

Quint could walk into his own home freely. Everyone inside would assume he'd stepped out for a moment alone and come back in, now that Oz wasn't there to confuse matters. Caleb would have to be more circumspect. He wasn't in a state to take risks.

"I'll wait here and you can bring me the suppressant."

"You have to come in," Quint said. "The suppressant's not here, anyway. We'll get it tomorrow."

God, his whole body was on fire. He was going to murder Quint as soon as he found the strength. "You lied."

"I didn't lie, I just didn't give you all the details. I need you for a few more days. Help me expose their crimes and I'll get you all the suppressant I have."

"That wasn't the deal."

"I'm offering new terms. Stick around for a few more days, pretend to be your double, and if you can get me some samples of the serum, I'll give you the formula for the suppressant so you can manufacture it yourself."

Caleb was in so much pain he had to drum his fingers against his thigh just to stay focused, to feel one sensation that didn't hurt. "Where will my double be, while I'm pretending to be him?"

"I don't know. Get rid of him. Isn't that what you do?"

"Jesus fucking Christ, Quint, I'm not a *contract killer*. I'm not going to murder an innocent person just because he's an inconvenience."

"He's not innocent," Quint said coldly. "None of them are. If you don't want to come in, you can sleep out here. I'll find you in the morning."

He walked up a set of three stairs and entered the house.

Caleb caught his breath for a moment in the silence of the garage, nothing but the ocean of poured concrete under his feet and the five huge, sleek cars. He quashed an urge to break all their windows out of spite.

It was a huge house. He could find somewhere to sleep without being seen. Everyone inside was drunk, so it would be easy.

He mounted the stairs, every step more awful than the last, and slipped into a hallway. At the opposite end, there was laughter and music and shouted conversation. Caleb crept down the hallway, checking each room for people, weighing his options.

Some paranoid need to survey everything propelled him to the end of the hallway where he could peek into the giant living room without being seen. He pressed his back to the wall and craned his neck to count twenty-three people, with Quint making twenty-four. His double wasn't in sight.

That should have been a relief. On the other hand, if he'd been there, at least Caleb would have known where he was and what he was doing. The unknown nagged at him.

He was just about to inch back down the hallway when someone said, "Caleb?"

Shit. Aidan. He was carrying a bin full of empty glass bottles and he set it down on the floor.

"Did you... change your clothes? Never mind. I thought you were going to bed. Are you okay?"

Fuck, fuck, fuck. Disappearing wasn't an option. Neither was his gun. In other circumstances, he might've just punched the guy, but he was injured and trying not to draw attention and he hadn't expected anyone to *hold his hand*.

Or touch his face and peer at him like—like—whatever that was. No one had ever made that face at him. He didn't want to think about what it was or why he'd never seen it before or why he was reacting this way. Not even the pain had fucked him up like this.

"You're really out of it," Aidan said.

"Yeah," he said, seizing the excuse. "I should go back to bed."

He slithered away, more reluctantly than he'd ever admit out loud, and went back down the hallway the way he'd come. But he didn't make it far.

"Caleb?" Aidan cocked his head toward the living room. "Our room's that way."

Where his double was asleep, no doubt. Shit.

"Maybe I should walk you there," Aidan said carefully, advancing until he could take Caleb's arm. He turned them toward the party. "What were you doing in this hallway, anyway? Going through the recycling?"

"I don't know," Caleb said. It wasn't hard to sound bleary and confused.

There was nothing to do but follow Aidan's lead. They cut through the party, and once it was quiet again, Aidan said, "Caleb. This is important. Did you jump there? I didn't see you walk through the living room. If you jumped in your sleep or by accident, I need to know."

"No, no, I walked. I just... I sleepwalked or something. I didn't jump. I'm too tired for that." *That* was true.

"Okay," Aidan said. When they arrived at the closed door to

the bedroom, he chewed his lip and said, "I guess I should have done a security check."

Caleb already knew how unsecure the house was. "Mm."

"I know you're tired. I don't need much. Maybe just... tell me what we talked about earlier."

Oh, *that* kind of security check. God fucking damn it. After a split-second of panic, some combination of training and instinct kicked in. The hand-holding, the face-touching, the concerned questioning, that look. Things had changed since he'd last run into Aidan and the poor guy had been scandalized by a hand on his thigh. His double and Aidan had fucked. Recently.

Caleb could work with that. He didn't need a gun or the Nowhere to solve this problem. It didn't matter that he wasn't at full strength. He knew how to use his face.

He conjured up a smile. Stalling for time, he drew a finger along the underside of Aidan's jaw.

"You said..." he started, and then stopped. He couldn't provide any actual words. Better to be vague. "You made me a promise."

"Yeah, I guess I did."

Jackpot. "About when we were alone together," Caleb added, growing more confident. He slipped his finger under the collar of Aidan's shirt and traced the delicate stem of his clavicle.

"I *also* said it should wait until after you'd rested," Aidan said.

Caleb yawned, taking advantage of his natural inclination and turning it into something theatrical. "You were probably right. Go back to the party. I can find my way from here."

He pushed lightly on Aidan's shoulder. Tried not to think about how warm he was. The sooner he was away, the better, since Caleb had to wrangle his goddamn double once he got in the room, and who knew what that would sound like.

"Okay. Get some sleep." Aidan pressed a kiss to his mouth. It was quick, over before Caleb knew what was happening, and then Aidan was gone.

Caleb touched his lips, like an idiot, and then shook it off and went into the room to find his double.

[18]
CONFESSIONS

THE PARTY CONTINUED FOR HOURS AFTER THE SECOND time he'd shepherded Caleb into their room. When Aidan finally shooed the last of his comrades out of the living room and kitchen, Laila had long since gone to bed. He debated leaving all the party debris in the house out of spite, but he couldn't manage it. They were living here at least until Friday. What if Caleb got up in the middle of the night and stepped on broken glass? So Aidan collected and threw away all the takeout containers—he found one from Lima, another from Taipei, and a third from Franklin Station, people had gotten a little wild with showing off—and then went in search of empty bottles, which clinked as he deposited them in the recycling. He swept up all the shards of glass, shedding no tears for Quint's expensive barware.

Aidan made one last survey of the kitchen and was surprised to find Oz, still in his suit and remarkably put-together for someone who'd downed so much champagne, leaning against the doorjamb and watching him.

He had the look of someone who'd been there a long time. That was no reason for the hair on the back of Aidan's neck to stand on end. *It's Oz*, he reminded himself. *You found him surrounded by old candy wrappers and dirty laundry.*

Aidan nodded at Oz. "Night. See you in the morning."

"There's an early interview," Oz said, his tone flat. Aidan couldn't say he relished the thought of another interview either. "Don't miss it."

Aidan left the lights off in the bedroom and got into bed as quietly as possible, but it was no use. Caleb stirred.

"Oh," he said. "It's you."

"Yeah. Who else would it be?" Aidan joked. "You feeling any better?"

"A little," Caleb said. "Why? You planning on keeping your promise?"

"It's a lot less sexy than you're making it sound," Aidan said. "Not that I won't make it up to you. But if I start at the beginning, it's not going to put either of us in the mood."

"I want to hear it."

Aidan lay on his back and stared up into the darkness. Maybe this would be easier in the dark. He could tell Caleb to rest, or that they'd get to this in the morning, but that was cowardice, and he'd had enough of it.

"Do you remember that night I showed up in your apartment at like three in the morning?"

"Uh."

"I know, I know, I need to be more specific." Aidan had developed a few bad habits in his life, and dropping in on Caleb at inopportune times was one of them. He'd only recently realized it was kind of an asshole thing to do, constantly showing up in the middle of the night with some nightmare problem dogging your heels. "I'm talking about the night I broke up with Brian."

"Oh," Caleb said. "Brian."

"You never asked for any details. You probably thought it

was my activism—or maybe my personality—that drove us apart."

Caleb did him the courtesy of exhaling a silent laugh at this weak joke.

"Anyway," Aidan said, collecting himself. He didn't really want to tell this story. Maybe it was the memory of the small hurt Caleb had done him that night—something so trivial it shouldn't have made a difference, not after what Brian had done, and yet the sharp point of it was still buried deep in his flesh.

But Caleb deserved to know.

Aidan had fled the apartment he shared with Brian, their fight still echoing in his ears, and materialized in Caleb's living room and kitchen area. It was dark, of course, being three in the morning. Normally Aidan knew his way around the place just fine, but that night he was out of sorts. He'd knocked his shin into the wooden edge of the coffee table, then missed the couch entirely, landing on his ass on the wood floor. He'd been cradling his bruised shin in his hands, his head leaning against the couch, when Caleb had trudged into the room. He'd been wearing a faded grey t-shirt and blue plaid boxers. Even in the dark—even when he was wounded—Aidan registered these things. The moment had such clarity because Aidan, hurting in every way, had experienced a second of relief. *There's Caleb*, he'd thought, *now I'll be alright*.

Caleb had rubbed his eyes and grumbled, "This isn't a fucking all-night truck stop, Aidan. It's not a motel. You can't just show up whenever you want."

Aidan had sucked in a breath like somebody had kicked him. He didn't think of Caleb's apartment like a motel or a truck stop. Those places were way stations, temporary reprieves. This was home.

Even when he'd been living with Brian, this was home.

"Shit," Caleb said, finally catching sight of Aidan on the floor between the couch and the coffee table. "Are you hurt? Let's get some ice on that."

Caleb had helped him to his feet and set him on the couch, then returned with an ice pack wrapped in a dish towel. He'd pulled Aidan's leg into his lap and applied it. They'd sat there in the yellow light cast by a single table lamp, not speaking, until Caleb had observed, "You look worse than a little bruise can explain. Am I gonna see headlines about this tomorrow?"

"No."

"Okay." Caleb had grasped right away that it must be trouble with Brian, and Aidan had been grateful he didn't have to explain. "You wanna talk about it?"

Aidan had shaken his head. Caleb had offered him tea or coffee or "something stronger, even though I know that's not your usual," and Aidan had declined it all. Then Caleb had removed the ice pack and said, "You take the bed, then."

"No, I can't—"

"If this is about what I said earlier, I'm sorry. I think I'm entitled to a moment of irritation when a crash in my living room drags me out of bed. I didn't really mean it, and you're obviously having a shitty night, so how about you let me do this one thing to make it up to you? Take the bed."

Aidan hadn't had the energy to argue, but as he'd lain down in Caleb's bed, the sheets long since gone cold, he'd wondered about that phrase *I didn't really mean it*. Brian had lied to him for months and he'd had no inkling. How could Aidan be sure of who *really meant* anything they said?

It had been a memorably bad night in so many ways.

"When I broke up with Brian," Aidan said, restarting his story while Caleb lay beside him, waiting in expectant silence, "it was because we had a fight. I found evidence he'd been lying to me. Our whole six-month relationship was a sham. He was working for someone. Quint, I assume. Brian was trying to find a way into the Union, trying to locate more runners. In retrospect, it's clear they would have ended up as experimental subjects at some place like that cell in Facility 17."

"Shit," Caleb said.

"I was... angry. I know. You think that's my default state. But I've never been angry like that. Caleb, he had... files. Recordings. Long-distance surveillance photos."

"Creepy," Caleb said, detached, as if Aidan were telling a ghost story instead of recounting something that had actually happened to him.

Creepy didn't cover the half of it. Aidan took a breath. "Some of them were of you."

"But *I'm* not a runner," Caleb said at length. "Or... I wasn't a runner when this happened."

"Right. He was considering using you as leverage. I knew then that I had to distance myself from you, that you'd never be safe as long as the world knew we were friends."

Caleb had been strangely quiet for this whole conversation. Into the darkness of the bedroom, he said, "Wow."

"I couldn't ever really stay away from you," Aidan said. "Even when I knew every moment we spent together was putting you in danger, I still wanted to see you. You probably thought I was ashamed of you. I know it seemed like I was exploiting you, showing up in the middle of the night and asking for help. And I guess maybe I was, but the truth is that whenever I was in trouble, you were the first person I thought of. The only safe person. And I always wanted to see you. I like you too much. I love you, I guess I should say. That's always been true."

"Oh."

That was a little discouraging, as responses went, but it was okay. Caleb could probably tell that he wasn't done yet.

He continued, "And ever since you got me out of that cell, I haven't been able to stop thinking about it. The cell, I mean, but also the photos. That could've been you, Caleb. The worst thing that has ever happened to me could have happened to you. And it would be my fault. Anyone who abducted you or tortured you or tried to kill you, they'd be doing it because they were after me."

"I don't think it would be your fault," Caleb said. "If someone else attacked me."

"It would feel like it. And I'm terrified of that, Caleb. I don't want to be the cause of anything happening to you. I thought maybe I could keep you safe if I left you. But then you said all that stuff on TV today and... God, you scared the shit of me, but you were brilliant. Once I saw you choosing for yourself, I realized I'd been trying to choose for you. I shouldn't have done that and I'm sorry."

"Good."

"So that's what I wanted to tell you. I love you. It's terrifying and I don't know what to do, but I love you."

It was a relief to speak the words.

It was not a relief to hear Caleb say, "Well." A silence followed. "You're important to me, too."

Not the response Aidan had been hoping for, not after the day they'd had. But maybe, after what he'd just revealed, it was the response he deserved.

———

AIDAN WOKE up feeling like shit. As usual, he'd had nothing to drink at the party. It was an emotional hangover.

Caleb's side of the bed was cold.

Strange that he'd gotten out of bed so early in the morning, considering how tired he'd been. Aidan had given him a lot to think about, he supposed.

He got dressed and went into the kitchen. Caleb was there, an empty plate of what had been eggs and toast sitting in front of him. It smelled like bacon, which was strange, because Caleb didn't eat that. The Feldmans didn't keep kosher, but they also never had pork products in the house, their food traditions having endured far longer than any others.

Laila was Muslim, and about as religious as Caleb—barely at all—but it was still hard to imagine that she'd been the one to cook the bacon. Then again, while they'd been in the cell together, she'd rhapsodized about the barbecue she could have been eating in Nashville if they hadn't been abducted to space. Aidan gave up on conjecture.

He was in a bad mood and it was making him suspicious, that was all.

Oz wasn't there, even after he'd lurked in the kitchen to remind Aidan of their morning obligation last night.

Laila, wearing a huge pair of sunglasses in addition to the black makeup stippling her face like she was a greyscale comic book character, mouthed *are you okay* at Aidan from across the room. Whatever his face looked like, if she was already asking that, it must be bad. He poured himself coffee and shrugged.

"What's this interview about, again?" Caleb asked.

Aidan and Laila glanced at each other.

"The same thing as all the other ones," Aidan said.

"No, I mean, who's it with?"

"Uh. Mandy Dawson, I think? It doesn't really matter. She won't be hostile like Ken Garnett was, I don't think, although she'll probably ask about yesterday."

"It's been all over the news," Laila said. "They've been replaying clips all morning."

"Sorry," Aidan said. "I know you don't like having your name brought up like that."

"It's the first time I've ever seen anyone say anything nice about me on TV," Laila said. "It's okay. Besides, look at this."

She instructed the house to turn on one of the wall displays, and a panel of two pundits in suits, a man and a woman sitting behind a table, appeared. They were in conference with another person, a bespectacled man whose face was shown in a rectangular frame in the rightmost third of the screen.

"He experimented on U.S. citizens," the woman was saying.

"He experimented on wanted criminals," her co-host said. "Besides, the crime was committed outside U.S. jurisdiction—and not by him, we should specify. Jennifer Heath and Vaughn Winslow are already in prison."

"So you don't think authorities should pursue him at all? I don't think that's an option, Jim," said the man in the glasses. "Quint is clearly dangerous. He can't be allowed to continue."

"Caleb Feldman is clearly dangerous, going by that unhinged tirade we were all treated to," Jim, the male co-host, answered. "And Quint has shut down Quint Services. He offered everyone working for him a generous severance package. Would someone as villainous as you think he is do something like that? The man promised to turn himself in, for God's sake, let's give him a little credit."

"He hasn't done it yet," said the woman. "And frankly I don't see why we should trust him to. If the authorities have the evidence, they should knock down his door like they do everyone else's."

"I doubt they do," her co-host scoffed. "If Quint were really involved in abducting and torturing people, he would've been caught a long time ago. The whole thing's a hoax."

"House, turn it off," Laila said, and the screen went dark. "I know it's annoying to hear it debated when we *know* what happened, but at least they're talking about it."

"I don't think anyone's ever called me dangerous before,"

Caleb said. It was the first time Aidan had seen him smile all morning.

"We have time to take a car to the studio," Aidan said, finishing his coffee. He was troubled by the implication that the police might come for Oz early. The plan depended on Oz turning himself in at the time of his choosing, so two runners could be on call to get him out of prison and put Quint in. But Aidan couldn't talk about that with the house listening, so he addressed Caleb instead. "It'll save you the jump. I know you didn't feel great after the one yesterday."

"Yeah, and then I can come with you," Laila said. Aidan frowned at her—she'd already provided a styling consultation, so she didn't need to go—but far be it from him to stop her.

"Thank you," Caleb said. "We'll be glad to have you there, as moral support."

What the hell did that mean? It sounded like Caleb had asked Laila to come with them, but Aidan couldn't figure out why he would have done that. He picked up his mug like the answer might be in his coffee, but that was gone, too.

Confessing his feelings had been a terrible idea. Aidan stared out the window all through the car ride and saw nothing. He'd have to overcome this during the interview, but that felt impossible. How could he pretend to be happily in love with Caleb when he was desperately, miserably in love with Caleb?

Oz wasn't making his usual irritatingly cheerful small talk this morning, so the atmosphere in the car was frigid. Laila played a game on a tablet she must have picked up somewhere in Quint's house, seemingly unbothered by the silence.

Things didn't warm up after they arrived. Aidan slipped into the green room to catch a moment of solitude. He sat heavily on the couch, grabbed a bottle of water, and took a desperate gulp. A little hydration wasn't going to fix anything, but he wanted to believe it could.

Someone stepped inside after him. Only the change in the light from the door shutting alerted him. Aidan turned.

"Caleb."

He didn't smile. But why would he? "Hey, Aidan. You ready for this one?"

"Yeah," Aidan said, taking another swig of water. Caleb had been acting so fucking weird since—well, since Aidan had tried to change their entire relationship. There was a logic to Caleb's behavior, seen in that light. It was natural to be a little chilly.

Logical or not, it had blindsided Aidan. Caleb had wanted this, yesterday, or so he'd thought. And then in addition, Caleb had stood up for him and for all runners on TV. He'd nearly tanked their whole plan because he felt so strongly. Aidan had finally been sure they felt the same way about each other.

They'd known each other for two decades and Aidan had never misread Caleb so badly.

The cold, faintly cucumber-flavored water in Aidan's mouth went down the wrong pipe, and he curled over in a coughing fit.

Caleb watched. He didn't take a step forward or reach out or say *raise your arms*.

Throat still raw and eyes watering, Aidan sat back up and said, "You remember that time after prom when we both got really drunk and threw up a disgusting amount?"

"Yeah," Caleb said. "Why?"

Shit.

"I feel kinda like that, that's all," Aidan said. That, at least, was true. His empty stomach roiled. The coffee he'd drunk this morning threatened to spew right out of his mouth. He'd been fucking oblivious.

The man standing in front of him wasn't Caleb.

Frantic, he filed through all his recent interactions, seeking the moment. It had to have been when he'd found Caleb—the wrong Caleb—in the hallway on his way to take out the recycling. Aidan had kissed the wrong person. He'd confessed to the wrong person.

Where the hell was Caleb?

Oz—no, *not* Oz—poked his head through the doorway. "We're up. Let's go."

Somehow the real Quint had gotten free from Facility 17. He must have encountered Caleb's double while the latter was sneaking around and then convinced him to help. Sometime during yesterday's festivities, they'd made the switch.

God, Caleb. Had they killed him? Aidan's heart dodged a beat and stuttered. He could almost sense the Nowhere. His urge to disappear rose fast and hard. He didn't know if he could jump yet. If he ran, how would he ever find Caleb?

He followed Quint and Fake Caleb out onto the set.

Quint wasn't going to say *and by the way I murdered the love of your life* on a live broadcast, but maybe there would be some hint.

This one was similar enough to all the others, with a live audience in the studio, an attractive host—Mandy Dawson turned out to be a brown-skinned brunette in a pink sheath dress, her slender fingers pinching a sheet of paper with notes on the interview—and an arrangement of leather armchairs. The leather was white this time, and there was a deep blue carpet with an irregular grid of thin yellow lines running through it. Aidan's shoes sank into it when he sat down. He dragged one toe through the pile, disrupting the pattern with a line of lighter color.

"You three certainly made a splash yesterday," Dawson said. "Caleb, can I ask what motivated you to do that?"

"Actually, Mandy, I have something to say and it can't wait," Quint said. "I was coerced into giving that confession, and none of it's true. Aidan Blackwood has been stealing my fortune and holding me hostage."

Mandy Dawson's mouth formed a perfectly made-up O. This hasn't been in her page of interview notes. "That's quite an accusation, Mr. Quint. Aidan, what do you have to say for yourself?"

"I'd advise him to say nothing until his court-appointed lawyer arrives," Quint said. "The police are already on their way."

Aidan didn't have to reply. Laila materialized in front of him and yanked him into the Nowhere.

[19]
DO WHAT I'M TOLD

"What the fuck are we going to do?"

The words burst out of him as soon as Laila brought him back to the world. It had been cloudy in Inland New York, but here, the sunlight pouring through the window was so warmly yellow that it was almost as sticky as the air. Aidan recognized the seashell-pink living room of a Runners' Union safehouse in Florida.

"Breathe," Laila said. She walked into the kitchen and started rummaging through the cabinets. There would be a stash of non-perishable food somewhere.

Aidan checked the fridge. If someone had stayed here recently, there was a chance they'd have left a few things. He found butter, eggs, sliced wheat bread, and orange juice.

Before he could ask if Laila was interested in any of that, Kit showed up in between them, his eyes wild.

"I was in the green room, waiting to tell you he was a fraud," Kit said, still catching his breath. "Or, I mean, that Caleb was a fraud. That Quint was the real one."

"We figured it out," Aidan said dryly.

Kit glared at Laila. "I jumped to that green room *from space*.

And then you made me come all the way here! Make it a little easier on me next time."

She shrugged, tucked the unopened peanut butter jar she'd found under her arm, and opened drawers until she found the spoons. She sat up on the counter and ate a spoonful before saying, "I had to get us out of there. What was the one thing I said? The one condition I had for participating in all this nonsense?" She shook at her spoon at each of them in turn, punctuating her words. "*I'm not fucking going back to prison. And neither is Aidan!*"

"I know," Kit said, softening. "You won't. I won't let that happen."

"Neither will I," Laila said, eating another heaping spoonful of peanut butter. "The only person who's going to prison is Oswin Lewis Quint. Plan A is fucked. What's our next move?"

"I don't know where Caleb is," Aidan said, sounding faint even to himself. "I don't know if he's alive."

"So we find Caleb," Kit said. "And then we deal with Quint and Fake Caleb."

Laila, having demolished most of the jar of peanut butter, put it aside and got down from the counter. She went through the cabinets a second time. "I forgot what it was like to be this hungry," she said. "Fuck, I missed jumping. But why are all the snacks in this stash so boring?"

Kit reached into the black messenger back he was wearing and pulled out two candy bars with red packaging. "Here, Laila." He tossed them to her.

She caught them and beamed at him when she read the wrappers. "Zings! Kit Jackson, you soft-hearted fool."

He rolled his eyes.

Laila pushed herself back onto the counter. She ripped open the wrapper and bit into one of the chocolate bars, revealing the wafer and spicy red filling inside. "You really do love me. Now, how do we find out about Caleb?"

"Quint and Fake Caleb are the only ones who'd know where to find him," Aidan said. "I think our best bet is to go back to the mansion—if we move fast, we can probably catch them before they relocate to one of Quint's other properties."

"I wish I could help, but I'm done for the day," Kit said, finishing off a protein bar and then crumpling the wrapper in his hand. "I'm gonna rest, but I'll stick around in case you need me. Oz is still up in Facility 17, but since he's a lying asshole who flipped the instant that real Quint offered him more money, I'm guessing you don't really care when or how he gets dumped back in his reality."

"I don't," Aidan confirmed. He didn't have time to feel disappointment in Oz. He glanced at Laila. "How do you feel? If you can't do it, we can contact the Union. We should let them know regardless."

They were all in danger. Aidan couldn't seem to do anything without putting people he loved in danger. The thing he'd been most afraid of had happened. Someone had kidnapped and possibly harmed or killed Caleb in order to get to him. Nothing was worth feeling this way, guilt and fear souring in his stomach. He hadn't even told Caleb the truth. He might not ever get a chance to. If they found Caleb, he would give up his career. That bargain was more than fair.

He couldn't say what he'd do if they didn't find Caleb.

"Give me a couple hours and I'll be good," she said. "But if we find Fake Caleb, what are we going to do with him? What if he doesn't want to talk to us?"

Aidan couldn't answer that question. From what little he knew of Caleb's double, the man was dangerous. And he'd chosen to align himself with Quint, which didn't speak well of his conscience. "He can't run from us, not if you get close enough to grab him. We might have to threaten him. Do you have any weapons?"

Laila shook her head. Kit sighed and flipped open his messenger bag. Instead of a candy bar, he pulled out a knife sheathed in a brown case. He passed it, handle first, to Laila, while she struggled not to laugh.

She pulled off the sheath, revealing a partially serrated blade of about five inches with a wickedly sharp tip. "Is Emil making you carry this around?"

"It's for *wilderness survival*," Kit said, not looking at her. "But I'm guessing it's fine for stabbing, too."

"Amazing. Tell that man I love him." Laila put the knife back in its sheath and hopped off the counter. "I wouldn't bet on myself in a fight against Caleb's double. I guess we'll just have to take him by surprise."

―――

A NASTY TASTE furred the inside of his mouth. The outside was duct-taped shut. He'd woken up with the scratchy pile of wall-to-wall carpet half-embedded in his cheek, and his wrists and ankles were tied. He was lying on his side on the floor of a closet, based on the pant-legs and dry-cleaning plastic hanging down around him. It was dark.

Caleb couldn't remember how he'd arrived in this position. He remembered an interview, and a party, and going to bed before Aidan. Someone had dragged him out of that bed to put him here, in this closet in an unknown location, but he must have been forcibly sedated first.

The only other time that had happened to him, it had been done by his double.

Shit. His double had replaced him. Aidan wouldn't know he was gone.

A closet full of clothes suggested a house. The same house, possibly. It was risky, not moving him somewhere farther away. This wasn't a cell or any place devoted to holding prisoners. If it was his double who'd drugged him, why not take him into the Nowhere and stash him somewhere unfindable? Caleb didn't plan abductions for a living, but that tactic had almost worked when Quint Services kidnapped Aidan.

Maybe his double had been feeling as shitty as him. If he couldn't jump, that would explain the closet.

It wouldn't explain what he wanted. Caleb had nothing to do except contemplate that, but he went in circles.

The closet door slid open, flooding the space with light and making him squint. His double crouched down, put a finger to his lips, and then ripped the duct tape off Caleb's face. It *hurt*. When Caleb made a noise to that effect, his double slapped a hand over the raw skin around his mouth.

"What part of—" he put the same finger to his lips again "—was unclear to you?"

Caleb said nothing. He could bite his double's hand. Minor violence might satisfy his spite, but the thought of sinking his teeth into his double's flesh unsettled him. He didn't want to know what it tasted like.

"I told Quint I killed you," his double said, removing his hand. "So we have to stay quiet."

"Why didn't you?"

"I need you. You're gonna be me for a little while. Go with Quint to one of his labs, pry some suppressant out of his greedy hands, bring it back to me."

The plastic tie was digging into his wrists. The pain rendered his double's lack of apology conspicuous. "Why would I help you?"

"Well, you're not getting untied unless you agree to, that's one reason. But our interests align."

"Drugging me and tying me up was a weird way of showing that. Is Aidan okay? Did you hurt him?" A horrifying possibility dawned on Caleb. "Did you sleep with him?"

"No. He's fine," his double said curtly. It was as much of a relief as having the tape removed from his mouth, and it hurt about the same, because Aidan wasn't here, and Caleb really, really wished he were.

"Listen to me. Quint is expecting to go to this lab in Tennessee as soon as I—meaning you—leave this room. If I give you the coordinates, you can find it, right?"

"Yeah," Caleb said. He'd found alternate-reality Des Moines, or close enough. Agreeing was his best chance of getting free. "Explain how our interests align and then untie me."

"You don't like Quint, I don't like Quint," his double said.

He leaned over Caleb to snip the tie. Caleb pushed himself upright and then rubbed at his wrists.

His double cut the tie around his ankles and said, "I'll help you take care of him if you'll do this for me. Go with him, pretend to be me, get as much suppressant as you can. He won't give it to you willingly, even though we had a deal. You'll get to the lab and he'll show you he has it, then he'll demand that you provide him with the dimensional-prion serum. He'll be expecting you to take him to Heath, probably, because he won't know you already have some. Preempt him."

His double pulled a rectangular case in black leather out of his pocket, then unzipped it to reveal two vials of clear, colorless liquid and a syringe.

Caleb stared. The end of the world came in a small, unassuming package.

"I'm sorry. Are you telling me to give Quint something that will allow him access to the Nowhere? Something that will allow him to make anyone he chooses into a runner? You said our interests aligned, but this will make Quint unstoppable. How is that 'taking care of him'?"

Caleb should have asked what *take care of him* meant earlier. Should have objected to the implication of murder. But it was Quint, and someone else was offering, and he found he couldn't care. All he had to do was think of finding Aidan in that cell, and the idea of killing Quint became perfectly acceptable. Murder didn't trouble him; giving Quint the serum did.

"Look at my hand."

His double's hand, stretched flat to display the case, was trembling. No. It wasn't a tremor running through his body, something simple and physical, but Caleb didn't know how else to interpret what he saw. The edges of his double's hand shifted and blurred, a millimeter to the right, then two to the left—phasing in and out, uncontrollably.

"We call it the shakes," his double said, voice rough. "Another few jumps, I won't be able to stay in place anywhere. Doesn't take too long to die after that happens."

Caleb forgot Quint for a moment. "Is that going to happen to me?"

"No. One injection's not enough. Neither are two, not unless you take both at once and OD on prions."

"And you want me to make Quint do that? That's not going to work. He's not going to inject himself with an unknown substance once, let alone twice."

"He will if we set things up right," his double said.

"We're going to poison him," Caleb said faintly. Ridiculous, that his qualms about murder returned once he realized it required his direct participation. It wasn't ethics, just squeamishness. Again, the thought of Quint's crimes laid his hesitation to rest. A syringe was nothing. He'd do it with his hands if it came to that.

"Please. He's going to poison himself. Don't get all weepy,

you know he deserves it. If any of that shit you and Aidan said on TV was true, he deserves worse."

It was strange to imagine his double watching him and Aidan in those interviews. That wasn't important. He focused. "Why are you doing this?"

"Are you still sedated? Pay attention. I need the suppressant to live, and so do lots of people at home. I can't make another jump right now, but I suspect you're a decent enough person to get me what I need. Steal whatever he has on hand. If you can find the formula, even better. If not, if you get enough samples, Heath can figure it out."

His double got out of the closet, stood up, and stripped off his shirt.

Caleb's first bewildered, useless thought was *he's hotter than me*. "What—"

"You need my clothes," his double said, continuing to undress. "Now. Listen. Quint and I don't have any affection for each other. I'm gonna give you an earpiece so I can listen in and talk you through it, but it won't work in the Nowhere. Your best bet is to talk as little as possible. Except when Quint is trying to renege on the suppressant, then you *have* to take control. And for fuck's sake, don't apologize or smile."

"I'm better at acting than you think," Caleb said, mildly offended. When he stood, he was stiff from spending the night on his side in the closet. He started picking up his double's discarded clothes. When he pulled the shirt over his head, it felt and smelled unsettlingly familiar. "How will I find you afterward, to get you the suppressant?"

"Let's pick a place to meet. Not too far away—I have to be able to get there without the Nowhere. You have a driver's license, right?"

Caleb shook his head. "I grew up in the city and my best friend was a runner."

"Too bad. It's always good to follow the little rules when you're breaking the big ones. Where can I meet you? Do you have an apartment?"

"Gave it up when I went to Facility 17 to search for Aidan," Caleb said. He picked up a pad and a pencil from one of the tables by the bed and started writing. He gave the new address since Laila had promised she was almost done with the paperwork. "Stay here and I'll come back for you. If more than three days pass and I haven't made it back, look for me here."

———

WHEN CALEB WALKED into the living room, Quint said, "You finished powdering your nose?"

"Roll your eyes," his double said into the earpiece.

Caleb didn't need that instruction, which made it even easier to follow. "Let's get this over with."

His double had been willing to switch clothes, but not to hand over any of the arsenal that he carried on his body. "You have the Nowhere, you don't need a weapon," he'd said, which made Caleb wonder about his life, since usually his double would have both. "You'll just shoot yourself if I give this to you."

Caleb hoped Quint didn't notice the difference when they came into contact. When he put his arms around Quint, the man stared at the ceiling to pretend the whole thing wasn't happening. His powers of observation weren't at their height.

"Going into the Nowhere has been miserable for me lately," his double said. "Quint doesn't know that and I've been working as hard as I can to hide it. Anything you feel, you have to hide it. Good, bad, painful, doesn't matter."

Stop giving me notes. Since Caleb couldn't say that out loud, he entered the Nowhere instead.

Before he'd become a runner, he'd always thought of the

sensation of travel through the Nowhere as a punch in the gut. Sudden and violent. It was the easiest way to conceive of it, since actual descriptions never made sense—too hot *and* too cold, like drowning and being sucked dry at the same time, it stretched you out and crunched you up. Since the injection, the void hadn't affected him, but today it was creeping back into him, tugging at his skin. The ability was fading.

He shoved Quint away from him as soon as they were out, then pretended he wasn't catching his breath and checking his surroundings. He ignored the familiar ache of hunger. They were in a long hallway with cinderblock walls and no windows. He hoped it was the right one.

"Not as precise as usual," Quint observed. "Perhaps you're feeling ill?"

"You're back," said his double in his ear. "You must have made it, if Quint's being a dick."

Caleb didn't respond to either of them. Quint took off down the hallway, entering one of the unmarked doors. The large, unoccupied room was a lab packed with scientific instruments Caleb couldn't identify, its walls lined with black formica benches covered in glassware. There was a sink at the end of one bench, and a surprisingly dated computer at the opposite end.

The cabinet above the sink was locked. Unlike the other cabinets, which were made of wood, this one was metal and had a keypad in its lower right corner. A safe. Quint tapped the metal door with a finger. "The suppressant's in here."

"I don't see you unlocking it," Caleb said.

"Do it now," his double said.

"I know you want the serum," Caleb said to Quint, irritated at having his lines fed to him. Luckily, *irritated* was his double's default state, so it played well.

His double went silent, giving him free reign at last. Caleb made unrelenting eye contact with Quint and said, "I can offer you some, but you have to pass me the suppressant first. All of it. Everything you have on hand."

"Or what?"

"Or I shoot you, Oswin. You think I can't crack a safe? We've spent enough time fucking around. Give me what you owe me."

"Holy shit," his double said. "You don't have a gun *and* I guarantee you don't know how to crack a safe. More chutzpah than I gave you credit for."

Laila knew how to crack a safe and she would help him if he needed it. His double should acquire more friends. He was right about Caleb's lack of gun, though. They'd be screwed if Quint called his bluff.

"You can offer me the serum?"

Thank God. "Yes."

"Are you able to take me to it right now? To meet your version of Dr. Heath?"

"You'll get it when I get mine," Caleb said. "Open the cabinet."

The safe beeped as Quint keyed in his code, one hand curved around the keypad so Caleb couldn't see what he was doing. The latch thunked and the door popped open. Quint pulled out a rack with twenty vials and set it on the counter. The clear, colorless liquid inside sloshed with the movement.

In Caleb's ear, his double growled, "Get the fuck away from me" at someone Caleb couldn't see.

Laila landed them in the bedroom Aidan and Caleb had been sharing, but it was empty. They crept through the rest of the house—the living room furniture was still at strange angles from the party, which felt long ago now—until they heard sound coming out of one of the previously unoccupied guest bedrooms.

They pressed their ears to the closed door. Fake Caleb was pacing and talking to someone. He must've been on a call, because it was only his voice.

Laila reached for Aidan, silently offering to jump them inside. It was their best chance, so he stepped closer.

They materialized next to him, Laila with the knife in hand. Instead of vanishing, Fake Caleb raised both hands. His expression didn't suggest a fearful surrender.

"Get the fuck away from me," he said, his voice a low rasp.

"No." They stood to either side of him. Laila wrapped a hand around his upper arm. "Wherever you can go, I can follow," Laila continued, her sweet tone at odds with her clenched jaw. "So don't try it."

Gratitude and envy twisted Aidan's insides. He needed Laila. He was glad for her help. But when would *his* power come back?

"Do I look like I'm about to try it?" Fake Caleb asked mildly.

"Did you kill him?" Aidan demanded. "Where is he?"

"I didn't kill him."

Oh, thank God.

"I'm talking to him right now, you idiots. He's with Quint, doing a delicate operation, and you're distracting us both," Fake Caleb said.

"He's with *Quint*?" Aidan said, raising his voice in horror.

"He's wearing an earpiece," Laila said, then shoved her fingers into his ear and pulled it out, offering it to Aidan. "Find out if Caleb's on the other side."

Aidan put it in his ear, in such a rush that he didn't bother to wipe it off. "Caleb? Are you there? Where are you? I'm with Laila, we'll come find you and get you out."

"He can't answer," Fake Caleb said, exasperated. "Quint will hear him and know something's up. Quint thinks he's me."

"So where is he?" Laila asked, still holding his arm and now pressing the point of the knife into his side.

Fake Caleb rolled his eyes at her. "I could snap your neck. You can let go of me, I'm not going anywhere."

He was wearing Caleb's clothes. Aidan had almost gotten used to his face, but being so close to him and smelling a mixture of Caleb's laundry detergent and sweat was strange.

It wasn't the first time they'd been close. This man had kissed him. They'd slept next to each other. It made him want to shudder, but he didn't.

In the earpiece, he heard Quint's voice. "There you go. Twenty vials of suppressant. Now hand over the serum."

"How do I know this is what you say it is?" Caleb asked.

Caleb. It was really him.

"Inject yourself if you really want to know," Quint said. "I'd offer to let you examine it with one of the instruments, but I'm sure you wouldn't know what to look for."

It was hard to focus on their conversation, since Laila was talking to Fake Caleb. "I'm not letting go until you answer us, O Neck-Snapping Badass. Where is Caleb? What the fuck are you up to?"

"Shh," Aidan interrupted. "He was telling the truth. Caleb's with Quint. They're negotiating. Quint's offering Caleb twenty vials of suppressant—the company promised to stop manufacturing it, but of course they didn't."

"Has Caleb given him the serum yet?" Fake Caleb asked.

"Has Caleb *what*?"

"Shut up and listen to me. As soon as Caleb offers him the serum, we call the authorities and report Quint's location, tell them he's a flight risk."

Aidan had never called the cops in his life. He'd been

willing to work with the criminal justice system as a way to punish Quint, but after that last, disastrous interview, the cops were just as likely to arrest Caleb as they were Quint. This was a bad idea.

In his earpiece, Caleb said, "Pleasure doing business with you," in a tone that suggested the opposite. "You satisfied, or you want a ride home on top of everything else?"

"I'm surprised you're still here," Quint said.

"Well," Caleb said. "I wouldn't want to get in trouble with you."

Caleb hadn't emphasized the phrase *get in trouble*, but he didn't need to. Aidan knew it was for him.

"You're causing me trouble just by being here," Quint said. "I'm working. Go away. Unless, of course, you're too weak to do that. Runners so often are."

"I'm fine," Caleb said, which was reassuring, although he hadn't jumped away from Quint yet, which was what Aidan wanted. "I guess I should *do what I'm told*."

"For once in your fucking life," Quint said.

Aidan motioned for Laila to let go of Fake Caleb and put the knife away, which she did. Caleb wanted them to work with his double. Aidan didn't trust Fake Caleb for a second, but he had to trust the real Caleb. He should have trusted him far more, starting a long time ago.

"Then again, the work you're doing is fascinating. Maybe I'll stay to watch," Caleb said.

"No," Aidan said, unable to keep the thought to himself. "Get out of there, Caleb."

"And maybe when you're done, I'll stick around and sightsee in your version of Tennessee. Is there anything worth seeing, other than this underground lab?"

"Will you shut up?" Quint said.

Aidan looked at Laila. "He's in the underground complex in

Tennessee. I don't think he would have said that unless he was worried about his ability to jump out. Kit's been there, right?"

"Yeah," she said. "I'll message him for coordinates."

"We need to call the authorities right now," Fake Caleb said.

"I hate this," Aidan said, his stomach roiling with fear. He was willing to sic the cops on Quint, but Caleb was still with him. "But Caleb asked me to do what you said, and I trust him."

"Wow," Laila said. Her personal experience with the police was far, far worse than his, but she didn't tell him not to. "Okay."

"You people and your fucking feelings," Fake Caleb said. "Let's finish this."

[20]
KNEES, ELBOWS, FINGERS, TWIST

The seconds stretched out, invisible and eternal, as if each one contained hidden dimensions folded within it. Caleb had heard Aidan call the cops—a thing he never thought he'd witness in any form—to report Quint's location, but no one had arrived. The lab, entombed under the countryside, remained silent.

It was not fascinating to watch Quint dole out tiny amounts of serum into whatever instrument he was using now, but Caleb couldn't look away. With each drop gone, he worried the amount left wouldn't be enough to give Quint the shakes. He'd make himself a runner, no one would ever catch him, and it would be Caleb's fault.

When the pounding came, it nearly startled him into the Nowhere. He barely stopped himself from making a fatal, uncontrolled jump. The sound thundered through the walls, making the twenty vials of suppressant clink in the rack he held.

"What the hell is that?" Quint asked, narrowing his eyes at Caleb.

"Sounds like someone trying to get in," Caleb said. "Maybe you should get a doorbell."

"Why the fuck are you still with him?" his double hissed in his ear. He must have reclaimed the earpiece from Aidan. "When I said we should make sure he did it, I meant we'd watch by hacking the security feed, not that you'd stay in the same goddamn room. Fucking hell, Caleb, I didn't give you a gun!"

"No one knows where this place is," Quint said.

"Don't look at me. I've been with you the whole time," Caleb said, trying not to be distracted by his double muttering some combination of insults and plans.

He had the energy for one more jump. He had to. Even if he couldn't get all the way out of this complex, he could at least get away from Quint. The police might catch him, but Aidan or Laila would get him out. He took a breath.

He couldn't do it. His sense of the Nowhere was gone.

Something went crashing down outside, and the sound of sirens and loudspeakers pierced the hallway. A moment later, booted footsteps echoed off the concrete.

"The police," Quint said, darting toward the two vials of serum he'd left on the bench. The black leather case was lying open next to them, a syringe still tucked inside it. Quint prepared it, then shoved his sleeve up his arm and stabbed.

One down.

Quint closed his eyes. Nothing happened.

He rounded on Caleb. "How do I do it? Why isn't it working?"

"You just think of where you want to go," Caleb said. "It should be working. Maybe it wasn't enough, after all those samples you took."

"It takes a few minutes, normally," his double said. "Don't know how fast the shakes will get him."

So helpful.

Quint loaded up the syringe with the second vial and pierced his vein a second time. He jerked it back out, wild-eyed, and threw it down on the bench. Then he made a pained grimace and held still.

He didn't go anywhere.

"You lied," he yelled at Caleb, hurling himself across the room. Caleb flinched, pushing the precious rack of suppressant vials out of danger, dimly aware that his double was yelling "Tell me what's happening!" in his ear. He couldn't think of an answer, but it didn't matter. The hit never came.

Aidan was standing in front of him.

Quint's hands were around his neck and Aidan was pulling at his grip, trying to get free. Caleb cut across the lab, picked up an Erlenmeyer flask, and bashed Quint over the head just as Aidan brought his knee up into Quint's stomach.

Quint vanished. The spray of glass shards scattered to the floor unimpeded.

"God, I'm so glad to see y—" Quint wrapped an arm around Caleb's neck from behind, cutting off his air.

Aidan had gone pale with terror, looking almost as drained of life as he had in Quint's secret space prison. *Fuck that.* Caleb's double could get out of this, and so could he.

"Choke," he rasped.

"This one's the one you like," Quint sneered at Aidan.

His double's calm voice in his ear drowned out the rest of what Quint said. "If the hold is from behind, don't lean back. You need to bring your weight forward. Drop to your knees, elbow him in the groin, jab your fingers in his eyes, then grab his arm and twist out of it. Got it? Knees, elbow, fingers, twist."

Quint was still talking. Threatening him, gloating at Aidan, something like that.

Knees, elbows, fingers, twist.

Caleb lurched downward, the hold around his neck tightening painfully. His elbow missed Quint's groin but landed hard enough in his belly for Quint to grunt and release him. By the time he jabbed over his shoulder with his fingers, Quint had disappeared.

Caleb dropped to the ground. He tried to catch himself and instead caught his palm on the pile of glass shards. He lifted his hand, a triangular piece of glass sticking out of his palm, its edges red.

"That work?" his double asked.

"Yeah," he said. Aidan was kneeling in front of him, holding his wrist and gently removing the piece of glass. It stung.

"The suppressant," Caleb reminded Aidan, and he fetched the rack off the lab bench before returning to where Caleb was sitting.

"Now get the fuck out of there," his double snapped.

Aidan couldn't hear anything he said, but he grabbed Caleb and pulled them into the darkness.

―――

They ended up in a house Caleb had never seen. He squinted out the living room window and saw a small scrubby yard and a quiet street dotted with more palm trees than street lights. A few houses away, the dark water of a sluggish canal lapped up what little light the stars cast. Tangled mangroves bordered the water. They weren't in Tennessee or New York.

"Kit and Laila are probably asleep," Aidan said quietly. He put the suppressant down on the kitchen counter and then shepherded Caleb into the bathroom. He rinsed out the cut in the sink, then applied stinging, cool antibiotic spray to it.

When he got out the gauze, Caleb noticed how well-stocked the first-aid section of the medicine cabinet was. This was a Runners' Union safehouse.

"Quint got away," Caleb said as Aidan was draping a bandage over his palm.

"I don't care," Aidan said, wrapping one end of the bandage over the base of his thumb.

"He's got access to the Nowhere now—wait. You don't *care*?"

"He doesn't have you," Aidan said. He tied off the bandage, but kept his hands on Caleb's wrist. "That's all I care about. We can be done, Caleb. I will give it all up and we can move somewhere remote—another reality, if necessary—where nobody has ever heard of Aidan Blackwood or Oswin Lewis Quint."

"Aidan," Caleb said. He brought his uninjured hand up to Aidan's face, saw Aidan track the movement in the mirror behind them. He kissed Aidan, because they were alive and together and because he could. It was quick and sweet, because he had more to say. "It means a lot to me that you would even consider that. But I don't want to do that, and I don't really think you want it, either."

Aidan's face fell. "I don't. But I don't know how to live like this."

"Like what?"

"Like I'm in love with you and terrified that I'll be the cause of something bad happening to you," Aidan said, his fingers tracing the edge of Caleb's bandage.

"Aidan. It's a cut."

"He had his *arm* around your *throat*."

"And I got out of it," Caleb said. "You saw that, right?"

"You got out of it thanks to me," said a voice in his ear. "You're welcome, by the way."

Caleb yelled, "Stop listening, you fucking creep!" Then he pulled the earpiece out, opened a drawer in the vanity, dropped it in, and slammed it. After a moment of collecting himself, he sheepishly remembered that it was the middle of the night and other people in the house were sleeping. He said, "Can we revisit the first part of that thing you just said?"

"You sure he can't hear us?" Aidan asked, eyeing the drawer.

"Aidan."

"I said I was in love with you. Am, I mean. In love with you." Aidan's cheeks colored. He stared at Caleb's hand like he wished it needed another twenty yards of bandage. "I've been kind of a dick about it. And I think I did this better the first time, with your double. I said all this stuff about how I'd been trying to make your choices for you, and that's not right, and then I tried to do it again just now because seeing you in harm's way makes me panic. I'm sorry. This is hard."

"You don't have to apologize," Caleb said. "This time, you said '*we* can be done' and '*we* can move somewhere remote.' I'm counting that as progress. It's way better than 'Caleb, I'm going to leave you forever and you get no say in the matter.' Also, I'm trying not to be weirded out that you accidentally told my double you loved him."

"Oh, don't worry, he broke my heart hard and fast," Aidan said, smiling ruefully.

"Not to interrupt this very important conversation, but I'm so hungry I could die. It's been a long time since I've jumped. Come into the kitchen with me?"

Caleb followed Aidan into the kitchen. The fridge was stocked and there were brown paper grocery bags folded flat on the counter. Kit or Laila must have been out recently.

He peered over Aidan's shoulder into the fridge. "You want a sandwich? I'll make you a sandwich. Two sandwiches, even."

The corner of Aidan's mouth quirked.

"Or more," Caleb offered, feeling a smile come unbidden. It wasn't all that funny, but it made him want to laugh anyway. They were alive. Together. Making sandwiches.

He didn't even know what town they were in and this kitchen felt like home.

Caleb hadn't properly appreciated all other times they'd peered into a fridge or stood around discussing what to eat. Aidan had taken care of him when he'd been hungry, and Caleb would do the same. He couldn't believe he'd ever been upset about Aidan showing up unannounced in his apartment—except he could, because Aidan had always *left*. He hadn't liked that.

The part where they took care of each other, he loved that.

"Hey," he said, wrapping both arms around Aidan. "I'm in love with you, too. You know that, right?"

Aidan touched his arm. "Yeah. Still nice to hear it. Nice to hear you shout at a talk show host for me, too."

He kissed the back of Aidan's neck. "Any time."

"I'll make my own sandwiches, though. You're injured. Go sit."

"Barely," Caleb protested. He sat on one of the barstools on the opposite side of the counter while Aidan sliced avocados and cucumbers and started assembling sandwiches.

Soothed by having something to do with his hands, he said, "There's something I never told you," and launched into a story about his ex. Aidan really only had one ex, and his name was Brian.

"So, that's that," Aidan finished. "He'd been lying to me and tracking you. Surveilling everyone I had contact with, really, but it was the idea of endangering *you* that upset me the most. And that's why I've been... the way I've been, ever since then. Not wanting to be seen in public. Never using your front door. Showing up in the middle of the night."

"I know."

Aidan's mouth dropped open. "Wait, you *know*? You knew this whole time?"

"I didn't know about Brian," Caleb said. "And I'm so sorry you went through that, and that you felt like you couldn't talk about it. It must have been awful. But I knew, in a more general way, that you were trying to keep me out of your life. That was obvious."

"I was trying to *protect* you," Aidan protested. "That's why I was so unhappy when you took that job with Quint Services. And then you showed up at Facility 17—"

"We could have an argument about which of us needs protecting," Caleb said, watching Aidan stack a second sandwich with haste and plop it onto a plate. "Or we could just agree that we're in this together and be done with it."

Aidan came around to the other side of the counter, set his plate down, and took the stool next to Caleb's. "I think I'm beginning to get that. I'm just a little slow." He smiled. "But what I was going to say is, having something bad happen to *me* that I couldn't predict or prevent or get out of, that made everything worse. I was scared for me *and* scared for you. I don't know how not to be. I care about you *so much*, Caleb."

"I know," Caleb said, putting a hand on his knee. "I care about you, too. And I know I might not really get the extent of your fear, but... it makes sense, after what you went through."

"Yeah."

"I'm scared for you—for both of us—but your work is important. I want to do it with you. I always have, even before I knew what an evil piece of shit Quint was. Being alone doesn't make either of us any safer, but being together might. And putting Quint in prison definitely will."

"You're right. If we don't find him, someone else will. But where do we even start?" Aidan said. "Either he's a runner in good health and can go anywhere he wants, or, if Fake Caleb was right, he's got the shakes and will appear randomly."

"No one is better equipped to find him than us," Caleb said. "You know almost every runner in the world. Get the word out to the Union to report any sightings. He might not have the shakes yet, but he will soon. I believe my double about that. Also, did you call him 'Fake Caleb'?"

"Well, yeah. You're the real one."

Caleb smiled. It made him feel warm and almost weightless. Aidan was in love with him. They were in love with each other. They could do anything.

———

AIDAN WAS USED to sleeping in unfamiliar beds—or couches— in unfamiliar places. Squatting in Quint's house had been more luxurious than normal, but just as temporary. He'd come to think of sleeping next to Caleb the same way, as a luxury that wouldn't last, something he was borrowing that he'd eventually have to give up.

Slipping into bed in the safehouse, he folded himself into the curves and angles of Caleb's body. So tired he was half-dreaming, he thought *we could do this every night*. They didn't have to stop. He didn't know where he'd be living when this was over, or what tomorrow looked like, let alone next week, but he could fall asleep with Caleb warm and solid against him. That mattered more than all the rest, so much that it made him giddy. His eyes were already closed, but he felt himself smile, buoyed by thoughts of the future for the first time in years.

With his nose pressed into Caleb's shoulder, he mumbled, "D'you want sex?"

"You have the energy for sex right now?"

"You want it, I'll find it," he promised.

"Nah, I'm good." Caleb pulled Aidan's arm over his waist and intertwined their hands. "This is all I want right now."

"Yeah," Aidan said. "Me too."

[21]
THERE'S ONLY ONE YOU

"Are we seriously discussing rescuing that man?" Kit asked. He grimaced into his coffee.

Clear early morning sunlight poured in through the living room window. The four of them had gathered in the combined kitchen and living room in the center of the house, unable to sleep in with the problem of Quint unresolved.

Kit continued, "Can't we just let him suffer his fate? It only took *me* a few uncontrolled jumps before I almost died. Either he'll end up in space eventually, or he'll die of starvation because he can't stay still long enough to eat. Feels poetic."

"I didn't say *rescue*. I said *find*," Caleb said. "If we don't, someone else will. He'll wriggle his way out of the problem like he always does. We spent some of his money, but he's still a rich man. Our goal is the same: put him in prison."

"We're the only ones who can," Aidan said. "We have the suppressant. All we need is Quint. We'll offer to save his life in exchange for him turning himself in."

"Good luck with that," Kit said. "You know he'll still be a threat even in prison, right? You can take away his money, but he'll still be Oswin Lewis Quint. He's gonna spend every minute inside scheming to get out, and he's gonna come straight for you when he does."

"I also owe my double some suppressant," Caleb said, changing the subject. "He helped us. I have to get it to him. He's still in Quint's house in New York, which is as good a place as any to start looking for Quint."

"You'd better go soon," Laila said. She turned on the news, which was switching between aerial footage of a collection of vehicles parked outside the Quint Services complex in Tennessee and shaky body-cam shots from inside the hallways.

"Oswin Lewis Quint vanished from a Quint Services facility late last night after authorities were alerted to his presence there," said a voice-over. "He has not been seen since. In the hours since his disappearance was first reported, eight properties owned by Quint or Quint Services have experienced an attempted break-in."

The video switched to more aerial footage, this time of a burned mansion. Aidan didn't recognize it; it wasn't the house in New York. "At least one of his homes was looted and then burned."

"Can't feel too bad about that," Laila said, looking up from her second cup of tea. Her tablet lay on the counter in front of her and she scrolled through it idly with her thumb. "How awful does it make me if I want to lay bets on the outcome of this?"

"I'll be awful with you," Kit said. He was seated next to her, his eyes on the news. "Fifty bucks says when he finally turns up, he's a corpse."

"Plenty of people would still cry at his funeral," Aidan said. "I'd rather see him in disgrace and in prison before he dies."

"We'll put him there. Unless he's dead. That would suit me fine," Caleb said, his tone so steady it was alarming.

"Wow," Kit said. "I always thought Aidan was the one to

watch out for, but you and your evil twin have more in common than I thought. Maybe you're *both* the evil twin."

"He saved my life," Caleb said, only to be ignored.

"Nah, our Caleb is definitely the good twin. I know because the scruffy murder-y thigh-holster one's hotter," Laila said. "The evil twin is always hotter."

"Aww, I like our wholesome version," Kit said.

"We all know what kind of wholesome nerds *you* like," Laila said.

Caleb was pretending to be riveted to the wall display, which was looping the same footage over and over while some reporters discussed it.

Aidan patted him on the shoulder. "She's wrong, don't worry."

Caleb's jaw worked. He turned away, but Aidan could see the tips of his ears were pink. He swallowed and said, "I don't think she is, actually. My double has abs."

"Wait, you saw him *naked*?" Laila asked.

"You are so nosy," Kit told her. "But did you?"

"We switched clothes," Caleb said primly, laying their speculation to rest. Then he smiled. "He is a good kisser, though."

Laila yelped "what," and then burst out laughing. "Get the fuck out."

"Like you wouldn't kiss your double if you had one," Kit said. "You know you would."

"I've had better," Caleb said, nudging Aidan, obviously pleased with himself. "And we were just going."

———

Fake Caleb was sprawled on his stomach on the gigantic couch in the living room, reading a leather-bound book chased with gold that was in pristine condition. It had probably never been opened before. The only light in the room came from the high skylight, cool and long-shadowed even in the middle of the day. He hadn't straightened any of the living room furniture, and Aidan suspected the number of dirty dishes lying around the room was motivated by spite.

At least the dirty dishes were evidence of life. The emptiness of the rest of the huge house rendered it obscene and desolate, a ruin still standing. Aidan wanted to get out.

Fake Caleb lifted his head and put down the book when he saw them. "You got it?"

"We did," Caleb said. He produced a syringe, still in its packaging, from his pocket. He'd insisted on buying new ones. "You gonna apologize for dragging me out of bed and tying me up?"

"Getting you out of Quint's clutches doesn't count?" he asked. He glanced at Aidan and added, "You can take that thing off your face, by the way. I disabled the AI."

"How?" Aidan asked. He wished they'd done that sooner, but he'd thought it was impossible. Quint had made his fortune in that kind of tech.

"Cut the power."

"Oh." When Aidan put on his regular glasses, the first thing he saw was Fake Caleb smirking at him.

"Still waiting on that apology. Helping me not get choked was basic human decency. You can do better," Caleb said.

"Sorry. I was improvising. I needed some time to think through my options, and I couldn't do that if I got caught."

"That's a C-plus apology at best, but I'll take it," Caleb said. "Here you go."

"You'll get me back there, right? Because I'm not going anywhere after this," Fake Caleb said, sitting up to accept the syringe and the vial of suppressant.

Aidan felt a pang of sympathy. Maybe he should think of

Caleb's double in some kinder way than *Fake*. He'd helped them, and he was about to experience a loss Aidan knew all about. "Yeah, I'll take you home."

Caleb's double loaded and used the syringe with efficiency, a series of motions born of long practice. "Don't look at me like that," he said, laying the syringe on the coffee table and not making eye contact with either of them. "This is better than dying from the shakes."

"Thanks for your help," Caleb said, and Aidan was grateful he'd intervened, because he didn't know what to say.

"That's a C-plus thanks at best," his double said. He stood up from the couch, and then, after a moment, picked up the book he'd put down. "I'll take whatever suppressant you have left. Other than that, I'm ready to go."

"You can have seventeen vials," Caleb said. He handed over the box where he'd packed them in old newspapers. "One's for Quint and the other's back-up."

"That's fair," his double said. Clutching the box and his book in one hand, he took hold of Aidan with the other. He was casual about it, unafraid of where they were going.

Then Quint showed up.

He lurched forward on one foot, and before Aidan had even registered the gun in his hand, a shot blasted the wall behind him. Other Caleb yelled "Get down!" and forced Aidan to the floor.

Quint's suit was stained all over with mud and water, his formerly white shirt peeking through the ripped shoulder seam. There was blood on his collar. His blond hair stood up in stiff tangles and his eyes were veined red above the deep, shadowed hollows below.

It hadn't even been twenty-four hours since they'd last seen him.

Clutching the gun in both hands, he swung his arms. Aidan

couldn't make sense of it. He had the impression that his brain had filled in missing pieces of the movement, like it was an animated sequence with frames missing.

There was an ugly purple bruise spreading across Quint's face, and a smear of red across his teeth when he opened his mouth to speak.

"Where is it? Where's the suppressant?"

The box Caleb had packed was hidden from sight because his double was lying on top of it. Caleb must have pocketed the remaining two vials. Aidan tried to memorize the carpet in front of his face so his gaze wouldn't betray him.

He was the only one in the room who could jump in a controlled, precise way. He could solve this. He just had to pick his moment.

"Fix me," Quint said. "Or I kill you all."

Get right in his space. Get the gun. Hope the second you spend in the Nowhere isn't long enough for him to shoot Caleb. Fuck. No. Not good enough.

"We can fix you," Caleb said from his position on the floor, his voice soothing. "Put the gun down."

Quint aimed at him. *No, no, no, fuck no.*

Other Caleb kicked Aidan in the ankle, made a second of fierce eye contact—what Aidan wouldn't give to be a mindreader—and then stood up.

"*I* can fix you," he said. "I have the suppressant. He's lying."

Quint twisted toward him, his movements strange. When he'd aimed the gun, Aidan jumped. He showed up inches from Quint's face, breathing in the blood-and-sweat smell of him. There was a rotten note to it, muddy and sickeningly sweet, but also something so sharp and acrid it almost knocked him out. Stale piss, probably.

He grabbed Quint's wrist in one hand and the hand that held the gun in the other, forcing his arm away and wrenching the gun down. Quint's trigger finger twisted with an unnatural crack. A shot fired. The floor reverberated under his feet. Then Quint grabbed his throat, his fingers digging into the soft flesh under the hinge of Aidan's jaw.

Aidan kneed him in the balls. Quint grunted in pain but didn't let go. He clenched Aidan's throat harder and Aidan brought his knee up again, missing this time. He couldn't breathe. His hands were still tight around Quint's gun arm, but slippery with sweat now.

Quint shuddered under his grip. They exited the world together, the Nowhere a flash of black, and then reappeared in an intersection, headlights and honks bearing down on them. Quint tried to shove him to the pavement. Cars screeched toward them. Aidan dragged them both back into the Nowhere, no air in his lungs, chanting *living room, living room, living room* in his mind like a prayer.

It worked. They returned to the room. Then Quint twitched under his hands.

The Nowhere. A humid forest at daybreak. Quint slammed Aidan into a tree trunk, and the pain blinded him for a moment. He dropped his grip on Quint's hand, flitted into the Nowhere, and materialized behind Quint. Aidan tackled him, sending the gun flying from his injured hand.

The living room again. Quint left a streak of mud and blood on the white carpet while he struggled beneath Aidan.

Aidan's body burned from back-to-back jumps, but Quint had to be worse off. He'd lost the gun. He had to give up soon.

Quint started to fade again.

"No," Aidan shouted, the noise tearing out of his injured throat. He clutched at Quint, trying to force him to stay. If he disappeared, if he got away—but they were both in the void now, and then on hard, dry ground, loose pebbles scattering as they twisted and rolled. The sky arched over them, huge and brilliant with midday sun.

Quint had managed to flip them over, driven by inhuman rage. He spit bloody foam into the dirt next to Aidan's face.

Aidan heard a pebble go flying, then drop and clatter against stone. *A cliff edge.*

Quint shuddered above him. The fit should have taken them back into the Nowhere, but its consequences were local. He couldn't jump. Quint lurched to the side, his hands clawing at Aidan.

Then they fell. Cold air ripped at his clothes and skin.

Back, Aidan thought, desperate for solid ground. It wasn't a plan, but a handhold. *Back up there.*

His panic bore results when he hit rock—not hard enough to kill him. He'd never been so glad to have the wind knocked out of him. Flat and gasping, it took him a moment to realize he was alone.

They'd been entangled, but Quint hadn't come with him.

As soon as he could breathe again, Aidan pushed himself up to peer over the edge, then withdrew. He'd seen enough: Quint's unmoving body, his neck at the wrong angle.

Dead.

Aidan checked again to make sure. There he was, his neck unmistakably broken. The awful sight, both unreal and necessary, became a fixed point in Aidan's vision, blotting out cold, and hunger, and all his injuries.

Quint was dead and he was never going to hurt anyone ever again.

At first, Aidan thought he'd stared so long that his exhausted vision was beginning to waver. But he pinched himself and Quint's corpse continued to shimmer and quiver, disintegrating shred by shred. This was what happened to people who died of the shakes. Their matter fell apart in some way human senses couldn't fully perceive.

Only a dark stain against the rock below remained.

Aidan sat back and wiped a dirty hand over his teary eyes. The past few minutes crystallized in his memory, and his heart slowed its pace. He couldn't suss out whether he was responsible—no, probably not—but he found he couldn't care, either.

Holy shit. He was free.

Tears leaked from his closed eyes, forming tracks along the creases of his smile. He hurt so much, and it was okay. He was okay. He blinked to clear his vision. Under the cloudless sky, a pine forest stretched to the horizon.

Wherever he'd ended up, it was a nice day.

Aidan inhaled a lungful of sweet, cool air, and took himself home to Caleb.

———

THE THIRD TIME Aidan reappeared in the living room, he was alone. Caleb cried out at the sight of him, pale and motionless on the carpet, and flew across the room.

A pulse.

Aidan's eyes flicked open, and his mouth quirked. That seemed to be all he had the energy for, but Caleb didn't need more. Aidan was here and alive and that was enough. Caleb checked for wounds and, not finding any, pulled Aidan into an embrace. He buried his nose in Aidan's hair, which was dusted with dirt and twigs, and didn't ask what had happened. If Quint's corpse wasn't adrift in the void of space, Caleb would be disappointed. He didn't want to ruin the moment just yet.

"I take it Quint isn't on your heels?" his double, inveterate moment-ruiner, asked.

"No," Aidan said. "He's dead."

Thank fuck. They'd never have known peace otherwise. Caleb squeezed Aidan tighter. "I was afraid you—"

"Me too," Aidan said. He rested his forehead against Caleb's shoulder and murmured, "They won't be able to declare him dead for a long time. His body just disappeared."

"Good. No evidence," Caleb's double said. "You'll probably be questioned, but the two of you have enough practice with that. Now let's get out of his house where his blood is staining the carpet. I know you can't jump, and I can't jump, so we'll have to do this the old-fashioned way. Stealing one of Quint's cars is a bad idea. How far can you walk?"

Aidan, who was sitting up only because Caleb was holding him up, waved a hand. "I know a hundred and seventy-eight people who can teleport."

"Oh," Caleb's double said. "That does make this considerably easier."

They spent another night in the Florida safehouse, and Caleb didn't let go the whole time.

Two DAYS LATER, Aidan took pride in landing Other Caleb and himself precisely in the middle of Other Caleb's bedroom. It looked exactly as it had the last time, its bed neatly made and the desk clear except for the paperback novel. Other Caleb set the box of suppressant and the leather-bound book he'd stolen from Quint's house down next to it. "An upgrade."

"Glad you got something out of this," Aidan said. "You've done so much for us already, and I know you had to give up a lot."

"Like I said, better than ending up dead."

"A low bar."

"I'm not entirely useless without it," Other Caleb said.

"Oh, trust me, I know. We owe you."

"You can pay me back by taking care of that fucking hole you blew in the Nowhere before something comes through it."

"*I* was in prison when they made the breach," Aidan said. "But they're on it. I'll make sure of it."

"They'd better be. It was... nice to meet you, sort of."

Aidan couldn't help the face he made at that ringing endorsement. He couldn't blame the man, though. They'd dragged him into this whole affair.

Other Caleb scratched the back of his head, uncharacteristically flustered. "Nothing against you. It's just, you know." He paused for a long time. "I was pissed, when I first saw him in those interviews. I thought he was pretending. Lying. It disgusted me, and not much does."

Aidan had no idea what to say to that.

"And then I realized he wasn't pretending, and that was *worse*," Other Caleb continued. "I've never felt anything like that, and now for the rest of my goddamn life, I'm gonna be stuck wondering if it's because there's only one you."

"It's not," Aidan said, possessed of sudden certainty. "You're not him, he's not you. Don't fall into that trap. You have first-hand experience of the multiverse. The infinite. I'm not worth getting stuck on, I promise."

"You are to him," he said. "And despite everything, it was kind of nice to play a small part in that. Don't fuck it up."

[22]
I KNOW A PLACE

Because Quint had disappeared under a cloud of suspicion, the government seized his assets.

Caleb only followed the news to discern two things: how often suspicion fell on him or Aidan or both of them, and whether anyone had noticed the funds he and Laila had diverted. The unfortunate answer to his first concern was *very often*, but no one could prove anything, and public opinion was more favorable toward Aidan than it had ever been. And as for the second, the amount—more money than Caleb had ever hoped to earn in his life—was so small as to be forgettable, and Laila possessed a skill for financial sleight-of-hand that might as well have been real magic as far as Caleb could tell.

They stayed in the safehouse. It took a week for Caleb to stop thinking *Quint almost killed you* every time he touched Aidan—and he touched Aidan as much as he could. It was a talisman of some kind, or a ritual, and every time he did it, a little more of his numb shock transformed into relief.

Laila stayed with them most of the time, occasionally leaving to take a call or go to a meeting. Aidan didn't inquire about her business, probably because all three of them had side-stepped any conversation topics that veered too close to the serious questions of *last week*, or worse, *next week*. That worked out well for Caleb. He would have lied to preserve the surprise, but he didn't have to.

In the second week, both of them grew restless, cooped up and inactive for too long, and finally Caleb ventured, "What if we went out for a walk?"

Sunlight was pouring through the living room window, glinting off Aidan's dark hair as he turned away from the view of the empty street. "If we're seen here, it puts the safehouse at risk."

"We have to be seen at some point," Caleb said. He'd kept his tablet off the whole time they'd been here, but it was likely full of messages. Authorities had already tracked down his parents, his sister, Miss Tallulah, and many, many friends and exes to ask where he might be. Deb had been on the news saying *don't ask me, he never answers my texts*.

"And," Caleb continued, "I was thinking of somewhere else, anyway."

"Yeah? Where?"

"The old neighborhood," Caleb said. Before Aidan could say anything, he added, "People will see us, but we can handle it."

"Yeah, you're right. I'm eager to get out of here, too."

Aidan embraced him and brought them both to the sidewalk in front of the apartment building where they'd once lived. The brownstone itself was unchanged, but there were different curtains hanging in the windows. The one on the ground floor gave them a glimpse of an impressive collection of potted plants.

Orange and brown leaves dotted the sidewalk. If not for the newer cars parked on the street, it could have been a fall day ten years ago.

Caleb wouldn't have been holding Aidan's hand back then. He tugged on it. "This way."

As they walked, Aidan said, "Where do you think you'll go, after this?"

"Wherever you're going," Caleb said. At last, they could talk about the future. They had a future to talk about now, the whole of it—however many unknown days or weeks or years comprised it—untouched by Oswin Lewis Quint. Caleb wasn't naive enough think the rest of their lives would be free of fear, but they'd closed that particular chapter. Whatever else was out there waiting for them, they'd have each other. He'd never minded getting into trouble, as long as Aidan was there.

Caleb continued, "I hope you're planning to stay somewhere in the city, because I'm kind of attached to it. I've had enough of space, and I still haven't had coffee with Deb. I can't believe she took her complaint to the media."

"You want to live with me?" Aidan asked, ignoring the latter half of what Caleb had said.

"I haven't been doing a very good job expressing my feelings, if you have to ask," Caleb said.

"No, no, I don't doubt that, but... it's hard for me to get an apartment."

"I know," Caleb said. "Me too, now, probably. It doesn't change how I feel. I want us to live together. And I think I know a place."

"You do?"

"Yeah," Caleb said, smiling so hard he had to bite his bottom lip. They'd walked two blocks and were now standing across from a building very much like the one they'd grown up in. He tilted his head toward it. "That one."

———

Aidan didn't understand what he was looking at. A four-story brownstone with a column of bay windows on the left and a rounded arch over its main entrance, but they couldn't *live* there. Even aside from his difficulties renting, there was a sign on the stoop that said "sold."

Oh.

"I wanted the one where we grew up, but it wasn't available," Caleb said. "This one was on the market, though."

"That mean old lady used to live on the ground floor here," Aidan said. Retreating to the past was easier, since the present was overwhelming.

"Mrs. Litman," Caleb said, because of course he remembered her name. "Anyway, I was thinking about how much trouble you always have with landlords, and how nobody will rent to runners, and that's why the Union doesn't have any kind of headquarters or public address where people can find it. And I know some of it's because runners are scared to be found out, or to all gather in one place, but you shouldn't have to be. It's wrong that anyone would keep you from having that. I want that to change. And I thought, well, what if there wasn't a landlord?"

It came out so fast that most of it ran together. Then Caleb finished, "So Laila and I took some of Quint's money and bought a building."

"I'm getting that," Aidan said, and Caleb fished a ring of keys out of his pocket and pressed it into Aidan's hand. "When did you do this?"

"Pretty much from the moment we got into his house. Laila started moving money around while she was waiting for us to come back from interviews, and then it took another couple of weeks to wrap things up. She did all the work. I think she's technically your trustee now. She was really excited about this. Did you know Laila knows a *lot* about finance?"

"That is the least surprising part of this," Aidan said.

"If you don't want it to be owned in trust, we can change that," Caleb said as they walked up the stairs to the entrance. "It's yours."

Aidan shook his head. "Ours."

"I was hoping you'd say that," Caleb said, and kissed him. "There's three apartments on the upper floors, and I was thinking we could use the ground floor and the basement for... communal meeting spaces, maybe?"

"Sounds perfect," Aidan said, sliding the key into the lock. The entryway arched above them. The building wasn't gigantic —far smaller than Quint's mansion—but it felt huge, every unfurnished space bright with potential. They walked through, holding hands and marveling at all of it, until they reached the top floor apartment and Aidan had to catch his breath. "This is... so much. It almost doesn't feel real."

"What would make it feel real?"

Aidan laughed, then caught sight of Caleb—the line between his brows, the uncertain curve of his mouth—and said, with perfect seriousness, "Is there a bed in there?"

"Yeah," Caleb said. "I didn't buy much because I didn't want to make decisions for you, but I knew you didn't own any furniture, so I did put a bed in the top-floor apartment." He paused, embarrassed. "At the time, I wasn't planning... you know."

"It's good that there's a bed," Aidan said, still serious. He unlocked the door and let them both in. Morning sun streamed through the windows onto the bare hardwood floors. Aidan bypassed the kitchen and the living room, heading for the promised bed.

It sat alone in the middle of the room, incongruously already made up with sheets and pillows.

Aidan said, "Because if there wasn't a bed, it would have to be down on the floor or up against the wall."

"I'm happy to offer you either of those options," Caleb said, pushing Aidan's jacket off his shoulders, grabbing the hem of his shirt and stripping it over his head, then setting to work on the fly of his jeans. "But I thought it would be nice if the first time I fucked you was in our bed. In our apartment. That we own."

It was good that someone he'd known his whole life could still surprise him. It promised good things for the future—and right now. Aidan grinned and kissed him, interrupting his work. "You wanna try it, huh?"

"Just like in the rest of my life, I swing both ways."

Aidan huffed. "I'm only laughing because you're obviously so pleased with yourself."

"Oh, you'll be pleased with me, too. That's the whole idea."

Aidan did laugh then. "The bed's good, in that case. Gotta break it in. Take your clothes off already."

Aidan left his jeans and boxers on the floor and perched on the bed. Caleb revealed himself quickly and carelessly, dropping his clothes like he wasn't the most beautiful person in this or any reality. Even after days of being treated to this—every shower, every change of clothes—the thought of Caleb undressing still turned him on. The sight itself overpowered him. He couldn't *not* touch himself. Just a little. Fuck, but that felt good.

"I want you literally all the time," Aidan said. "In any way you will have me."

"Good," Caleb said, and pushed him flat on his back with one hand. "Me too."

"No accounting for taste," Aidan joked.

"You shut up about my boyfriend," Caleb said. He spread Aidan's legs and knelt between them, caressing the sensitive skin of his inner thighs. "You're beautiful."

Aidan shivered as Caleb's fingers dipped lower. He loved getting fingered and fucked, but had rarely allowed his partners to do it. He trusted Caleb.

Caleb paused to pour lube over his hand. When he touched Aidan again, his movements were gentle but confident.

"You've done this before," Aidan said, surprised again.

The look Caleb shot him made him feel sheepish and guilty, and he braced himself for a joke about his alleged sex spreadsheet. Instead, Caleb said, "Yeah, and I'm good at it, too."

"Been holding out on me."

"You're gonna get it," Caleb said, and demonstrated by slowly sliding a finger in. Aidan's entire nervous system lit up with pleasure. He twitched his hips, wanting more.

"I forgot how much I liked this," Aidan said, his voice weak like he'd been screaming. They'd barely started. One finger was nothing.

Caleb obliged him with another, fondling his balls while he did it. He shifted his attention upward, offering a handful of long, slow strokes to Aidan's cock that were nowhere near enough. It was impossibly sexy to watch him work, his brown head bent low and all of his focus trained on the steady motion of his hands like he was ready and willing to do this for hours. Caleb hadn't touched himself yet, and his hard cock bobbed between his thighs, curving upward and dripping, a temptation that Aidan couldn't reach.

Aidan licked his lips. "I want to ride you. Right now."

"Well, when you put it that way," Caleb said, grinning. He took his fingers out, the loss leaving Aidan cool and empty. Caleb flopped down onto the bed, reached for the lube once more, and slicked down his shaft.

Aidan wasted no time in climbing on top of him. Sinking down onto his cock was goddamn glorious. He gasped at the hot, slippery fullness of it, just on the edge of too much, and then levered himself back up and sank down again.

"Fuck," Caleb said, letting his head drop back to the pillow. He lifted it a moment later, unable to look away. He rested his hands on Aidan's hips, then Aidan leaned forward to kiss him, sloppy and hard, and his hands slid up Aidan's chest. "You feel so good. You're so gorgeous. Don't stop."

Caleb's gaze burned right through him, leaving him lightheaded and happy. Fuck, they could do this *every day*. Here. Where they lived.

Still pumping his hips, Aidan seized Caleb's hands. He brought one to his cock and simply held the other. Caleb stroked him, his attention still riveted to the place where their bodies joined, until he closed his eyes. Aidan felt the stutter and release of his orgasm a second later, then Caleb relaxed beneath him, his darkly furred chest rising and falling. Aidan came an instant later, seized with the sweetness of it, heat washing through him and spilling onto Caleb's hand.

After they separated, Aidan tumbled onto his back, the bed soft beneath him. He squeezed Caleb's hand again.

"It's a beautiful place."

It could have been a windowless basement and Aidan would have loved it, because he'd never had a place of his own ever, and Caleb had found one for both of them. And not just any place, but one Aidan would have chosen for himself, if he'd ever thought he had a choice: the neighborhood where they'd grown up, where they'd gotten to know each other and gotten into trouble, the only place in the multiverse where Aidan had roots.

Even without furniture, it was cozy and full of light. With Caleb beside him, it already felt like home.

They moved in right away. It didn't take long, since Aidan had never owned anything and Caleb had sold all his furniture when he'd given up his apartment. It was a few days of indoor camping, but Caleb had never been happier.

The first Sunday morning in their new apartment, Caleb walked into the kitchen after a *very* satisfying lie-in and a long shower and found Laila. He hadn't seen her since Thursday, when he'd texted her to ask where she was and whether she wanted to be there when he showed Aidan the building, and she'd replied that she'd be back in a few days.

She was sitting at the table drinking coffee and scrolling through her phone. Her pink hair was pulled into a bun on top of her head, exposing the black roots near her ears. She didn't have any makeup on.

"Morning," she said. "There's an empty apartment below this one, did you know that?"

"Yeah," he said. "There are two empty apartments, actually."

"No," she said. "There's one."

Aidan walked into the kitchen and stopped beside him, resting a hand on the small of his back. "Uh, good morning, Laila."

"Laila's our downstairs neighbor," Caleb said. "As of right now."

"Also, Kit's gonna call us in a sec, everybody up there wants a tour of this place," Laila said. "I know I'm not officially your stylist anymore, but... maybe put on a shirt?"

"Shit," Aidan said. When he returned, he was fully dressed and might even have attempted to brush his hair.

The doorbell rang. Caleb went to the intercom. "Hello?"

"Hi, it's Anna. I would have just jumped in, but I wasn't sure you were ready for visitors. Can I come up?"

"Look at that," Aidan said, staring at Laila. "Manners."

She gave him an unrepentant shrug and continued drinking her coffee.

When Anna came up, she was carrying a fern in a blue ceramic planter, and she wasn't alone. Deb was with her, a cardboard pastry box in her hand.

"You still owe me coffee," she said, when he blinked at her in surprise. Once he'd finally braved his phone, he'd texted her an apology and their new address, but hadn't expected a visit so soon. "Also, a *long* explanation. But congrats."

She huffed indignantly and pulled him into a one-armed hug.

"It's good to see you, Deb."

"I'm glad you're still alive after that stunt you pulled," Deb retorted. She set the box on the kitchen counter and hugged Aidan. "Don't think you're getting out of this. You're just as much at fault."

"Oh, definitely more," Aidan said.

"As usual," Deb said. She pointed at the box of pastries. "That's a housewarming gift, because I'm a better sibling than either of you." She kissed Aidan on the cheek. "Congratulations. You'd better visit me now that we live in the same city, or I will show you just how good I've gotten at throwing punches."

"Deb," Aidan said, catching her by the hand before she let go of him. "I should apologize to you. I stopped Caleb from having coffee with you a couple weeks ago for the same reason I haven't been in touch these past few years. I was... hiding, more or less. I was worried about endangering people by association. Nothing has really changed on that count—I can't promise I'm not putting you in danger—but I realized I was only hurting myself and the people I cared about."

"Wow," Deb said. "I wasn't expecting to get sincere before noon. Apology accepted. You know I'd rather have you in my life than not." She turned to Caleb. "What's your excuse?"

"Uh," he said, cringing. "I went to space to rescue Aidan, then got a little busy?"

"Uh-huh," Deb said. "I heard all about that from the psychic. You're forgiven, I guess. But why move back to the old neighborhood? Everyone will know where you are."

"That's the idea," Aidan said.

"And I'm hoping fewer reporters will bother you, if we're out in the open," Caleb said.

"You could also try not causing any more huge scandals," Deb suggested, then laughed when they both fell silent. "Oh, I see."

"We're trying something different," Caleb said. "The Union's been really secretive since its founding, but we thought we'd try having a public face. Maybe it'll make it easier for young runners to find us when they need to."

"We?" Deb asked.

"Oh, that was figurative, I'm not—"

"Yeah, he is," Aidan interrupted. "Caleb's been with us since the beginning. He helped me recruit our first members. And he was a runner for weeks, so I figure he's in."

"That's great news," Anna said. "I hope you were serious about making it easier for people to find you, because there are a few more of us coming over."

"There are?" Caleb said. "But we don't really have any... furniture. Or food. Or anything."

Anna waved a hand. "I think we've got it covered."

The Runners' Union showed up in groups of two and three, sometimes carrying a couch or a table, sometimes loaded down with groceries, and soon their apartment was full to the brim with furnishings and food and people.

They did a couple of rounds of hellos and thank-yous at the party, and then Laila found them in the kitchen by the coffee pot, taking a break.

"Thanks for this," Aidan said, gesturing at the building. "Caleb told me you did all the work."

She shrugged. "I live here, too, now. Good luck getting rid of me."

"Can't imagine why we'd want to," Caleb said. "You were brilliant. We like having you around. Let us be grateful."

"I owe you," Laila said, glancing from Caleb to Aidan, then down at her bare feet. She set her coffee on the counter and then clamped her arms around Aidan.

"I didn't think we could do it," she said into his chest. "I thought it was gonna blow up in our faces the whole time, and there was a long period there where I was just waiting to break it to you as gently as possible. I thought I was gonna have to live the rest of my life with him looming over me, and now I *don't*, and that's thanks to you. I know it didn't go the way you planned, and it was pretty awful at the end there, but I'm not sorry about any of it. You always believed and you were *right*. You did it."

He hugged her back. "Not me, us. Nobody works alone. Everything we do around here is a team effort."

"You are so fucking corny all the time," she said, punctuating it with a laugh that was more like a sob. Her voice sank to a reverent whisper. "We lived, Aidan."

"Yeah," he said. Aidan looked like he was on the verge of tears. "We did."

"There hasn't been very much justice in my life."

"Mine either," he said.

She exhaled gustily and then pulled Caleb into the hug. She was soft and smelled like coconut, and she was definitely smearing tears on his shirt. "I'm not supposed to be crying. It's a party."

"You don't have any makeup to mess up, at least," he offered, and she laughed.

"What'll it be like, do you think? Living here where anybody can look us up?" she asked.

Aidan shrugged. "I don't know. More good than bad, I think. That's what I'm hoping. Right now, it feels that way."

"I'm inclined to believe you," Laila said. She let go of them and dabbed at her eyes. "Okay, I'm going back out there. See you later."

"I think you're right, too," Caleb said, leaning up against the counter and sidling close enough to kiss Aidan. "About this being more good than bad."

"I couldn't have envisioned this without you," Aidan said. "That stuff Laila just said about not really believing something was possible until she saw it, I feel that way about all of this. It's amazing. It was only a few weeks ago that I thought I'd be living anonymously in some remote outpost by now. Alone. I'm so, so glad I was wrong about that. I love you."

"I love you, and I'm glad you were wrong about that, too. Wanna go back out there?"

"Yeah," Aidan said, and took his hand and led him into the living room. It was crowded and joyful and loud. Not one person was wearing a mask.

ACKNOWLEDGMENTS

This book was a hard one, partly because this year was a hard one. Here are some people who helped me through.

First, thank you to everyone on the internet and in real life who told me nice things about the first book in this series, or said they were excited for this one. It meant—and still means—a lot to me.

Thank you to Natasha Snow for her beautiful cover design and for always being such a joy to work with.

Thank you to K. R. Collins, who read multiple early drafts of this book and was unflagging in her encouragements. Thank you to my writing buddies Valentine Wheeler and verity, both of whom listened to their fair share of my despair on the topic of this book.

Thank you to Wren Wallis, lawyer and writer and friend, who was willing to answer my ridiculous questions about future laws concerning kidnapping someone into space and confessing to a crime on a live broadcast. Any legal nonsense in this book is my fault, not hers.

Thank you to Olivia Dade, who lives across the ocean but

who wrote alongside me and kept me accountable through Twitter DMs for the final few days of editing this book.

Thank you to Elia Winters, who spent many hours sitting across a café table from me, drinking a London Fog and writing a novel, thus inspiring me to write some words of my own. Our conversations about what we're writing have scandalized or titillated every coffeeshop patron and employee in the area, which makes me feel like a notorious, dissolute rake in a Regency romance—the dream.

Thank you to Ryan Boyd, who edited this book when it was a total mess, whose insights were crucial to making it *less* of a mess, and who was patient and kind and funny the whole time. They were right about everything, which is a priceless quality in an editor, and I am grateful for their work and their friendship.

And, as always, thank you to J, whose wish to remain mysterious and elusive I am contradicting by acknowledging him, but it would be a crime not to record here how much I love him. He listens to a lot of meandering soliloquy for every book I write, and this one was especially torturous. He also answers questions on everything I don't know, which is a vast and varied field. If anything in this book struck you as a cool sci-fi concept, credit goes to my beloved science consultant and would-be cryptid, J. He taught me everything I know about physics (still not much, but that's on me) and everything I know about love (a lot).

ALSO BY FELICIA DAVIN

THE NOWHERE

Edge of Nowhere

Out of Nowhere

THE GARDENER'S HAND

Thornfruit

Nightvine

Shadebloom

ABOUT THE AUTHOR

Felicia Davin is the author of the queer fantasy trilogy *The Gardener's Hand* and the sci-fi romance *Edge of Nowhere*, which was a finalist for Best Bisexual Romance in the 2018 Bisexual Book Awards. Her short fiction has been featured in *Lightspeed*, *Nature*, and *Heiresses of Russ 2016: The Year's Best Lesbian Speculative Fiction*.

She lives in Massachusetts with her partner and their cat. When not writing and reading fiction, she teaches and translates French. She loves linguistics, singing, and baking. She is bisexual, but not ambidextrous.

She writes a weekly email newsletter about words and books called *Word Suitcase* (wordsuitcase.substack.com). You can also find her on Twitter @FeliciaDavin or at feliciadavin.com.